Kids and Cupid
make an unbeatable duo
in three charming novellas
by authors you can't resist!

My Funny Valentine
by
DEBBIE MACOMBER

Mom and Mr. Valentine
by
JUDITH BOWEN

Her Secret Valentine
by
HELEN BROOKS

New York Times bestselling author **Debbie Macomber** always enjoyed telling stories—first to her baby-sitting clients, and then to her own four children. As a full-time wife and mother and an avid romance reader, she dreamed of one day sharing her stories with a wider audience. In the autumn of 1982 she sold her first book, and then began making regular appearances on the *USA Today* bestseller list. Now her heartwarming stories have conquered the *New York Times* bestseller list, and there are over forty-five million copies of her books in print worldwide!

Judith Bowen, a popular writer for Harlequin Superromance, worked as a journalist before turning to fiction after her children were born. Her own childhood was spent in an Alberta logging camp. She's traveled throughout the world and held a number of fascinating jobs—which include working in a fishing lodge, farming on Prince Edward Island and raising sheep in British Columbia's Fraser Valley. She is the winner of several writing awards and has taught a number of writing courses. Judith lives in a historic farming and fishing community in British Columbia with her husband—head of the journalism department at a nearby college—and their three children and assorted pets.

Helen Brooks lives in Northamptonshire, U.K. and is married with three children. As she is a busy housewife and mother, her spare time is at a premium, but her hobbies include reading, swimming, gardening and walking her two energetic, inquisitive and very endearing young dogs. Her long-cherished aspiration to write became a reality when she put pen to paper on reaching the age of forty, and sent the result off to Harlequin Mills & Boon. More than forty novels later, Helen is one of our most popular Harlequin Presents authors and is published in numerous international markets. *A Whirlwind Marriage* will be published in Harlequin Presents in March 2002.

Sealed with a Kiss

DEBBIE MACOMBER

JUDITH BOWEN

HELEN BROOKS

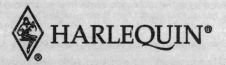

HARLEQUIN®

TORONTO • NEW YORK • LONDON
AMSTERDAM • PARIS • SYDNEY • HAMBURG
STOCKHOLM • ATHENS • TOKYO • MILAN • MADRID
PRAGUE • WARSAW • BUDAPEST • AUCKLAND

ISBN 0-373-83497-7

SEALED WITH A KISS

Copyright © 2002 by Harlequin Books S.A.

The publisher acknowledges the copyright holders of the individual titles as follows:

MY FUNNY VALENTINE
Copyright © 1991 by Debbie Macomber

MOM AND MR. VALENTINE
Copyright © 2002 by J. E. Corser

HER SECRET VALENTINE
Copyright © 2002 by Helen Brooks

This edition published by arrangement with Harlequin Books S.A.

® and TM are trademarks of the publisher. Trademarks indicated with ® are registered in the United States Patent and Trademark Office, the Canadian Trade Marks Office and in other countries.

Visit us at www.eHarlequin.com

Printed in U.S.A.

CONTENTS

MY FUNNY VALENTINE

Debbie Macomber

Chapter One

DIANNE WILLIAMS had the scenario all worked out in her mind. She'd be pushing her grocery cart down the aisle of the local grocery store and gazing over the frozen-food section when a tall, dark, handsome man would casually stroll up to her and with a brilliant smile say, "Those low-cal dinners couldn't possibly be for you."

She'd turn to him and suddenly the air would fill with the sounds of a Rimsky-Korsakov symphony, or bells would chime gently in the distance—Dianne didn't have that part completely worked out yet—and in that instant she would know deep in her heart that this man was the one she was meant to spend the rest of her life with.

All right, Dianne was willing to admit, the scenario was childish and silly, the kind of fantasy only a teenage girl should dream up. But reentering the dating scene after umpteen years of married life created a wealth of problems Dianne didn't want to consider.

Three years earlier, Dianne's husband had left her and the children to find himself. Instead he found a SYT (sweet young thing), promptly divorced

Dianne and moved across the country. It hurt; in fact, it hurt more than anything Dianne had ever known, but she was a survivor, and always had been. Perhaps that was the reason Jack didn't seem to suffer a single pang of guilt about abandoning her to raise Jason and Jill on her own.

Her children, Dianne discovered, were incredibly resilient. Within a year of their father's departure, they were urging Dianne to date. Their father did, they reminded Dianne with annoying frequency. And if it wasn't her children pushing her toward establishing a meaningful relationship, it was her own dear mother.

When it came to locating Mr. Right for her divorced daughter, Martha Janes knew no equal. For several months, Dianne had been subjected to a long parade of single men. Their unmarried status however, seemed their sole attribute.

After dinner with the man who lost his toupee on a low-hanging chandelier, Dianne had insisted enough was enough and she would find her own dates.

This proved to be easier said than done. Dianne hadn't gone out once in six months. Now within the space of a single week, she needed a man. Not just any man, either. One who was tall, dark and handsome. It would be a nice bonus if he were exceptionally wealthy, too, but she didn't have the time to be choosy. The Valentine's dinner at the Port

Blossom Community Center was Saturday night. This Saturday night.

From the moment the notice was posted six weeks earlier, Jason and Jill had insisted she attend. Surely their mother could find a date given that much time! And someone handsome to boot. It seemed a matter of family honor.

Only now the dinner was only days away and Dianne was no closer to achieving her goal.

"I'm home," Jason yelled as he walked into the house. The front door slammed in his wake, hard enough to shake the kitchen windows. He slapped his books on the counter, moved directly to the refrigerator, opened the door and stuck the upper half of his fourteen-year-old body inside.

"Help yourself to a snack," Dianne said, smiling and shaking her head.

Jason reappeared with a chicken leg clenched between his teeth like a pirate's cutlass. One hand was filled with a piece of leftover cherry pie while the other held a platter of cold fried chicken.

"How was school?"

He shrugged, set down the pie and removed the chicken leg from his mouth. "Okay, I guess."

Dianne knew what was coming next. It was the same question he'd asked her every afternoon since the notice for the dinner had been posted.

"Do you have a date yet?" He leaned his hip against the counter as his steady gaze pierced her. Her son's eyes were incredible. They could break through the thickest of resolves, and cut through several layers of deception.

"No date," she answered cheerfully. At least as cheerfully as she could under the circumstances.

"The dinner's this Saturday night."

As if she needed to be reminded. "I know. Stop worrying, I'll find someone."

"Not just anyone," Jason said forcefully, as though he were speaking to someone with impaired hearing. "He's got to make an impression. Someone decent."

"I know, I know."

"Grandma said she could line you up with—"

"No," Dianne interrupted emphatically. "I categorically refuse to go on any more of Grandma's blind dates."

"But you don't have the time to find your own now. It's—"

"I'm working on it," she insisted, though she knew she wasn't working very hard. She *was* trying to find someone to take her to the dinner, only she never dreamed it would be this difficult!

Until the necessity of attending this affair had been forced upon her, Dianne hadn't been aware of how limited her choices were. In the past couple of years, she'd met few single men, apart from the ones her mother had thrown at her. There were a couple of unmarried men where she was employed part-time as a bookkeeper. Neither, however, was one she'd seriously consider dating. They were both too suave, too urbane—too much like Jack. Besides, problems might arise if she were to mingle her social life with her business one. It was simply too risky.

The front door opened and closed again, a little less noisily this time.

"I'm home!" ten-year-old Jill announced from the entryway as she dropped her books on the floor and marched toward the kitchen. She paused on the threshold and planted both hands on her hip as her eyes sought out her brother. "You better not have eaten all the leftover pie. I want some too, you know."

"Don't grow warts worrying about it," Jason said sarcastically. "There's plenty for everyone."

Jill's gaze swiveled from her brother to her mother. The level of severity didn't diminish one bit. Dianne met her daughter's eye and mouthed the words along with her.

"Do you have a date yet?"

Jason answered for Dianne. "No, she doesn't. And she's got five days to come up with a decent guy and all she says is that she's working on it."

"Mom…" Jill's brown eyes filled with concern.

"Children, please."

"Everyone in town's going," Jill claimed as if Dianne wasn't already aware of the fact. "You've got to be there, you've just got to be. I told all my friends you're going."

More pressure! That was the last thing Dianne

needed. Nevertheless, she smiled serenely at her two children and assured them both they didn't have a thing to worry about.

An hour or so later, while she was cooking dinner, she could hear Jason and Jill's voices in the living room. They were huddled together in front of the television, their heads close together. Plotting, it looked like, charting her barren love life. Doubtless deciding who their mother should take to the dinner. Probably the guy with the toupee.

"Is something wrong?" Dianne asked, standing in the doorway. It was unusual for them to watch television this time of day, but more unusual for them to be so chummy. The fact that they'd turned on the TV to drown out their conversation hadn't escaped her.

They broke apart guiltily.

"Wrong?" Jason asked, recovering first. "I was just talking to Jill, is all. Do you need me to do something?"

That offer alone was enough evidence to convict them both. "Jill, would you set the table for me?" she asked, her gaze lingering on her two children for another moment before she returned to the kitchen.

Jason and Jill were up to something. But what, Dianne could only guess. No doubt the plot they were concocting included their grandmother.

Sure enough, while Jill was setting the silverware on the kitchen table, Jason used the phone, stretching the cord as far as it would go and mumbling into the mouthpiece so there was no chance Dianne could hear his conversation.

Dianne's suspicions were confirmed when her mother arrived shortly after dinner. And within minutes, Jason and Jill had deserted the kitchen, saying they had to get at their homework. Also highly suspicious behavior.

"Do you want some tea, Mom?" Dianne felt obliged to ask, dreading the coming conversation. It didn't take Sherlock Holmes to figure out her children had called their grandmother in hopes she'd find a last-minute date for Dianne.

"Don't go to any trouble."

This was her mother's standard reply. "It's no trouble," Dianne replied.

"Then brew the tea."

Because of her evening aerobics class—W.A.R. it was called, for Women After Results—Dianne had changed and was prepared to make a hasty exit at a moment's notice.

While the water was heating, she took a white ceramic teapot from the cupboard. "Before you ask, and I know you will," she said with strained patience, "I haven't got a date for the Valentine's dinner."

Her mother nodded slowly as if Dianne had just announced something of profound importance. Martha was from the old school, and she took her own sweet time getting around to whatever was on her mind, usually preceding it with a long list of questions that hinted at the subject. Dianne loved her mother dearly, but there wasn't anyone on this green earth who could drive her crazier faster.

"You've still got your figure," Martha said, her look serious. "That helps." She stroked her chin a couple of times and nodded. "You've got your father's brown eyes and your hair is nice and thick. You can thank your grandfather for that. He had hair so thick—"

"Ma, did I mention I have an aerobics class tonight?"

Her mother's posture stiffened. "I don't want to be any trouble."

"It's just that I might have to leave before you say what you're obviously planning to say, and I didn't want to miss the reason for your unexpected visit."

Her mother relaxed, but just a little. "Don't worry. I'll say what must be said and then you can leave. Your mother's words are not as important as your exercise class."

An argument bubbled up like fizz from a can of soda, but Dianne successfully managed to swallow it down. Showing any sign of weakness in front of her mother was a major tactical error. Dianne made the tea, then carried the ceramic pot over to the table and sat across from her mother.

"Your skin's still as creamy as—"

"Mom," Dianne said warningly, "there's no

need to tell me all this. I know my coloring is good. I also know I've still got my figure and that my hair is thick and that you approve of my keeping it long. You don't need to sell me on myself.''

"Ah," Martha answered softly, "that's where you're wrong."

Dianne couldn't help it—she rolled her eyes. When Dianne was fifteen her mother would have slapped her hand, but now that she was thirty-three, Martha used more subtle tactics.

Guilt.

"I don't have many years left in me."

"Mom—"

"No, listen. I'm an old woman now and I have the right to say what I want, especially since the good Lord may choose to call me home at any minute."

Stirring a teaspoon of sugar into her tea offered Dianne a moment to compose herself. Bracing her elbows on the table, she raised the cup to her lips. "Just say it."

Her mother nodded, apparently appeased. "You've lost confidence in yourself."

"That's not true."

Martha Janes's smile was meager at best. "Jack left you, and now you think there must be something wrong with you. But, Dianne, what you don't understand is that he would have gone if you were as beautiful as Marilyn Monroe. Jack's leaving had nothing to do with you and everything to do with Jack.''

This conversation was taking a turn Dianne wanted to avoid. Jack was a subject she preferred not to discuss. As far as she could see there wasn't any reason to peel back the scars and examine the wound at this late date. Jack was gone. She'd accepted it, dealt with it, and gone on with her and the children's lives. The fact that her mother was even mentioning her ex-husband had taken Dianne by surprise.

"My goodness," Dianne said, holding out her wrist. "Look at the time—"

"Before you go," her mother said quickly and grabbed her wrist, imprisoning her, "I met a nice young man this afternoon in the butcher shop. Marie Zimmerman told me about him and I went to talk to him myself."

"Mom—"

"Hush and listen. He's divorced, but from what he said it was all his wife's fault. He makes blood sausage and insisted I try some. It was so good it practically melted in my mouth. I never tasted sausage so good. A man who makes sausage like that would be an asset to any family."

Oh, sweet heaven. Her mother already had her married to the guy!

"I told him all about you and he generously offered to take you out."

"Mother, please. I've already said I won't go out on any more blind dates."

"Jerome's a nice man. He's—"

"I don't mean to be rude, but I've really got to leave now, or I'll be late." Hurriedly, Dianne stood, reached for her coat, and called out to her children that she'd be back in an hour.

It wasn't until she was in her car that Dianne realized they'd been expecting her to announce that she had a date for the dinner.

Chapter Two

"DAMN," DIANNE MUTTERED, scrambling through the bottom of her purse for the tenth time. She knew it wasn't going to do the least bit of good, but she felt compelled to continue the search.

"Double damn," she said as she set the bulky leather handbag on the hood of her car. Rain drops spattered all around her, adding to her dismay.

Expelling her breath, she stalked back into the Port Blossom Community Center and stood in front of the desk. "I seem to have locked my keys in my car," she told the receptionist.

"Oh, dear, is there someone you can get in touch with?"

"I'm a member of the auto club so I can call them for help. I also want to call home and say I'll be late. So, if you'll let me use the phone?"

"Oh, sure." The young woman smiled pleasantly, and lifted the phone onto the counter. "We close in fifteen minutes, you know."

A half hour later, Dianne was leaning impatiently against her car in the community center parking lot when a red tow truck pulled in. It circled the area, then eased into the space next to hers.

The driver, whom Dianne couldn't see in the dark, rolled down his window and stuck out his elbow. "Are you the lady who phoned in about locking her keys in the car?"

"No. I'm standing out in the rain wearing a leotard just for the fun of it," she muttered.

He chuckled, turned off the engine and hopped out of the driver's seat. "I take it this has been one of those days."

She nodded, suddenly feeling a stab of guilt at her churlishness. He seemed so friendly.

"Why don't you climb in my truck where it's nice and warm while I take care of this?" He opened the passenger-side door and gestured for her to enter.

She smiled weakly, and as she climbed in, said, "I didn't mean to snap at you just now."

He flashed her an easy grin. "No problem." She found herself taking a second look at him. He was wearing gray-striped coveralls and the front was covered with grease stains. His name, Steve, was embroidered in red across the top of his vest pocket. His hair was neatly styled and appeared to have been recently cut. His eyes were a warm shade of brown and—she searched for the right word—gentle, she decided.

After seeing she was comfortable in his truck, Steve walked around to the driver's side of her compact car and used his flashlight to determine the type of lock she had.

Dianne rolled down the window. "I don't usually do things like this. I've never locked the keys in my car before—I don't know why I did tonight. Stupid."

He returned to the tow truck and opened the passenger door. "No one can be smart all the time," he said cheerfully. "Don't be so hard on yourself." He bent the seat forward a little and reached for a toolbox in the space behind her.

"I've had a lot on my mind lately," she said.

Straightening, he looked at her and nodded sympathetically. He had a nice face too, she noted, easy on the eyes. In fact, he was downright attractive. The coveralls didn't distract from his appeal, but actually suggested a certain ruggedness. He was thoughtful and friendly just when Dianne was beginning to think there wasn't anyone in the world who was. But then, standing in the dark and the rain waiting might make anyone feel friendless, despite the fact that Port Blossom was a rural community with a warm, small-town atmosphere.

Steve returned to her car and began to fiddle with the lock. Unable to sit still, Dianne opened the truck door and climbed out. "It's the dinner that's got me so upset."

"The dinner?" Steve glanced up from his work.

"The Valentine's dinner the community center is sponsoring this Saturday night. My children are forcing me to go. I don't know for sure, but I think they've got money riding on it, because they're making it sound like a matter of national security for me to be there.''

"I see. Why doesn't your husband take you?''

"I'm divorced,'' she said bluntly. "I suppose no one expects it to happen to them. I assumed after twelve years my marriage was as sound as a rock, but it wasn't. Jack's remarried now, living in Boston.'' Dianne didn't know why she was rambling on so, but once she'd opened her mouth, she couldn't seem to stop. It wasn't like her to relate the intimate details of her life to a perfect stranger.

"Aren't you cold?''

"I'm fine, thanks.'' That wasn't entirely true— she was a little chilled—but she was more troubled about not having a date for the stupid Valentine's dinner than freezing to death. Briefly she wondered if Jason, Jill and her mother would accept pneumonia as a reasonable excuse for not attending the dinner.

"You're sure? You look like you're shivering.''

She rubbed her palms together and ignored his question. "That's when my mother suggested Jerome.''

"Jerome?''

"She seems to think I need a little help getting my feet wet.''

Steve glanced up at her again, clearly puzzled.

"In the dating world,'' Dianne explained. "But I've had enough of the dates she's arranged.''

"Disasters?''

"Encounters of the worst kind. On one of them, the guy set his napkin on fire."

Steve laughed outright at that.

"Hey, it wasn't funny, trust me. I was mortified. He panicked and started waving it around in the air until the maître d' arrived with a fire extinguisher and chaos broke loose."

Dianne found herself smiling at the memory of the unhappy episode. "Now that I look back on it, it was rather amusing."

Steve's gaze held hers. "I take it there were other disasters?"

"None that I'd care to repeat."

"So your mother's up to her tricks again?"

Dianne nodded, "Only this time my kids are involved. Mom stumbled across this butcher who specializes in…well, never mind, that's not important. What is important is if I don't come up with a date in the next day or two, I'm going to be stuck going to this stupid dinner with Jerome."

"It shouldn't be so bad," he said. Dianne could hear the grin in his voice.

"How generous of you to say so," she muttered, crossing her arms over her chest. She'd orbited her vehicle twice before she spoke again.

"My kids are even instructing me on exactly the kind of man they want me to date."

"Oh?"

Dianne wasn't completely sure he'd heard her. Her lock snapped free and he opened the door and retrieved her keys, which were in the ignition. He handed them to her, and with a thank-you, Dianne made a move to climb into her car.

"Jason and Jill—they're my kids—want me to go out with a tall dark, handsome—" She stopped abruptly, holding out her arm as if to keep her balance.

Steve looked at her oddly. "Ma'am, are you all right?"

Dianne placed her fingertips to her temple and nodded. "I think so, but then again I'm not sure." She inhaled sharply and motioned toward the streetlight. "Would you mind stepping over there for a minute?"

"Me?" He pointed to himself as though he wasn't sure she meant him.

"Please."

He shrugged and did as she requested.

The idea was fast gaining momentum in her mind. He was certainly tall—at least six foot three, which was a nice complement to her own slender five ten. And he was dark—his hair appeared to be a rich shade of mahogany. As for the handsome part, she'd noticed that right off.

"Is something wrong?" he probed.

"No," Dianne said, grinning shyly—although what she was about to propose was anything but shy. "By the way, how old are you? Thirty? Thirty-one?"

"Thirty-five."

"That's good. Perfect." A couple of years older than she was. Yes, the kids would approve of that.

"Good? Perfect?" He seemed to be questioning her sanity.

"Married?" she asked.

"Nope. I never got around to it, but I came close once." His eyes narrowed suspiciously.

"That's even better. I don't suppose you've got a jealous girlfriend—or a mad lover hanging around looking for an excuse to murder someone?"

"Not lately."

Dianne sighed with relief. "Great."

"Your car door's open," he said, motioning toward it and looking as if he was eager to be on his way. "All I need to do is write down your auto club number."

"Yes, I know." She stood there, arms folded across her chest, studying him in the light. He was even better looking than she'd first thought. "Do you own a decent suit?"

He chuckled as if he found the question amusing. "Yes."

"I mean something really nice, not the one you wore to your high-school graduation."

"It's a really nice suit."

Dianne didn't mean to be insulting, but she had to have all her bases covered. "That's even better," she said. "How would you like to earn an extra thirty bucks Saturday night?"

"I beg your pardon?"

"I'm offering you thirty dollars to escort me to the Valentine dinner here at the center."

Steve stared at her as though he suspected she'd recently escaped from a mental institution.

"Listen, I realize this is a bit unusual," Dianne rushed on, "but you're perfect. Well, not perfect, exactly, but you're exactly the kind of man the kids expect to escort me, and frankly I haven't got time to do a whole lot of recruiting. Mr. Right hasn't showed up, if you know what I mean."

"I think I do."

"I need a date. You fit the bill and you could probably use a little extra cash. I realize it's not much, but thirty dollars sounds fair to me. The dinner starts at seven and should be over by nine. I suspect fifteen dollars an hour is about what you're earning now."

"Ah…"

"I know what you're thinking, but I promise you I'm not crazy. I've got a gold credit card, and they don't issue those to just anyone."

"What about a library card?"

"That, too, but I do have a book overdue. I was planning on taking it back tomorrow." She started searching through her purse to prove she had both cards before she realized he was teasing her.

"Ms.…"

"Dianne Williams," she said stepping forward to offer him her hand. His long, strong fingers wrapped around her hand as his smiling gaze held hers, studying her for perhaps the first time. His eyes softened as he shook her hand. The gesture, though small, reassured Dianne that he was exactly the kind of man she wanted to take her to this silly dinner. Once more she found her mouth rushing to explain.

"I realize this all sounds a bit crazy. I don't blame you for thinking I'm something of a nut case. I'm not, really I'm not. I attend church every Sunday, do volunteer work at the grade school, and help coach a girls' soccer team in the fall."

"Why'd you pick me?"

"Well, that's a bit complicated, but you have nice eyes, and when you suggested I sit in your truck and get out of the rain—actually it was only drizzling—" she paused and inhaled a deep breath "—I realized you had a generous heart, and you just might consider something this…"

"…weird," he finished for her.

Dianne nodded, then looked him directly in the eye. Her defenses were down, and there was nothing left to do but admit the truth.

"I'm desperate. No one but a desperate woman would make this kind of offer."

"Saturday night, you say?"

Just the way her luck was running, he would suddenly remember he had urgent plans for the evening. Something important like dusting his bowling trophies.

"From seven to nine. No later, I promise. If you don't think thirty dollars is enough…"

"Thirty's more than generous."

She sagged with relief. "Does this mean you'll do it?"

Steve shook his head as though to suggest he ought to have it examined for even considering her proposal.

"All right," he said after a moment. "I never could resist a damsel in distress."

Chapter Three

"HELLO, EVERYONE!" Dianne sang out as she breezed in the front door. She paused just inside the living room and watched as her mother and her two children stared openly at her. A sense of quiet astonishment pervaded the room. "Is something wrong?"

"What happened to you?" Jason cried. "You look awful!"

"You look like Little Orphan Annie, dear," her mother claimed, her hand working a crochet hook so fast the yarn zipped through her fingers.

"I phoned to tell you I'd be late," Dianne reminded them.

"But you didn't say anything about nearly drowning. What happened?"

"I locked my keys in the car—I already explained that."

Jill walked over to her mother, took her hand and led her to the hallway mirror. The image that greeted Dianne was only a little short of shocking. Her long thick hair hung in limp sodden curls over her shoulders. Her mascara, supposed to be no-run, had dissolved into black tracks down her cheeks.

She was drenched to the skin and looked like a prize the cat had dragged onto the porch.

"Oh, dear," she whispered. Her stomach muscles tightened as she recalled the odd looks Steve had given her, and his comment that it must be "one of those days." No wonder! She looked like a charity case.

"Why don't you go upstairs and take a nice hot shower?" her mother suggested. "You'll feel worlds better."

Humbled, for more reasons than she cared to admit, Dianne agreed.

As was generally the rule, her mother was right. By the time Dianne reappeared a half hour later, dressed in her thick terry-cloth robe and fuzzy pink slippers, she felt considerably better.

As she brewed herself a cup of tea, she reviewed the events of the evening. Even if Steve had agreed to attend the Valentine's dinner with her out of pity, it didn't matter. What did matter was the fact she had a date. As soon as she told her family, they would be off her back.

"By the way," she said casually as she carried her tea into the living room, "I have a date for Saturday night."

The room went still. Even the television sound seemed to fade into nothingness. Her two children and her mother did a slow turn, their faces revealing their surprise.

"Don't look so shocked," Dianne said with a

light, casual laugh. "I told you before that I was working on it. No one seemed to believe I was capable of finding a date on my own. Well, that simply isn't the case."

"Who?" Martha demanded, her eyes narrowed and disbelieving.

"Oh, ye of little faith," Dianne said feeling only a small twinge of guilt. "His name is Steve Creighton."

"When did you meet him?"

"Ah..." Dianne realized she wasn't prepared for an inquisition. "A few weeks ago. We happened to bump into each other tonight, and he asked if I had a date for the dinner. Naturally I told him I didn't and he suggested we go together. It wasn't any big deal."

"Steve Creighton." Her mother repeated the name slowly, rolling the syllables over her tongue, as if trying to remember where she'd last heard it. Then she shook her head and resumed crocheting.

"You never said anything about this guy before." Jason's gaze was slightly accusing. He sat on the carpet, knees tucked under his chin as he reviewed this unexpected turn of events.

"Of course I didn't. If I had, all three of you would be bugging me about him, just the way you are now."

Martha gave her ball of yarn a hard jerk. "How'd you two meet?"

Dianne wasn't the least bit ready for this line of

questioning. She'd assumed letting her family know she had the necessary escort would have been enough to appease them. Silly of her.

They wanted details. Lots of details, and the only thing Dianne could do was make them up as she went along. She couldn't very well admit she'd only met Steve that night and was so desperate for a date that she'd offered to pay him to escort her to the dinner.

"We met, ah, a few weeks ago in the grocery store," she explained haltingly, averting her gaze. She prayed that would be enough to satisfy their curiosity. But when she paused to sip her tea, the three faces were staring expectantly at her.

"Go on," her mother urged.

"I...I was standing in the frozen-food section and...Steve was there, too, and...he smiled at me and introduced himself."

"What did he say after that?" Jill wanted to know, her young face eager for the particulars. Martha apparently shared her granddaughter's interest. She set her yarn and crochet hook aside, focusing all her attention on Dianne.

"After he introduced himself, he said surely those low-cal dinners couldn't be for me—that I looked perfect just the way I was." The words fell stiffly from her lips like pieces of cardboard. She had to be desperate to divulge her own fantasy to her family like this.

All right, she was desperate.

Jill's shoulders rose with an expressive sigh. "How romantic!"

Jason, however, was frowning. "The guy sounds like a flake to me. A real man doesn't walk up to a woman and say something stupid like that."

"Steve's very nice."

"Maybe, but he doesn't sound like he's got all his oars in the water."

"I think he sounds sweet," Jill countered, rushing to defend her mother by championing Steve. "If Mom likes him, then he's good enough for me."

"There are a lot of fruitcakes out there." Apparently her mother felt obliged to tell her that.

It was all Dianne could do not to remind her dear, sweet mother that she'd arranged several dates for her with men who fell easily into that category.

"I think we should meet him," Jason said, his eyes darkening with concern. "He may turn out to be a serial murderer or something."

"Jason—" Dianne forced a light laugh "—you're being silly. Besides, you're going to meet him Saturday night."

"By then it'll be too late."

"Jason's got a point, dear," Martha Janes said. "I don't think it would do the least bit of harm to introduce your young man to the family before Saturday night."

"I…he's probably busy…. He's working all sorts of weird hours and…"

"What does he do?"

"Ah…" She couldn't think fast enough to come up with a lie and was forced to admit the truth. "He drives a truck."

Her words were followed by a thick silence as her children and mother shared meaningful looks. "I've heard stories about truck drivers," Martha said, pinching her lips tightly together. "None I'd care to repeat in front of the children, mind you, but…stories."

"Mother, you're being—"

"Jason's absolutely right. I insist we meet this Steve. Truck drivers and cowboys simply aren't to be trusted."

Dianne rolled her eyes.

Her mother forgave her by saying, "I don't expect you to know this, Dianne, since you married so young."

"You married Dad when you were sixteen— younger than *I* was when I married," Dianne stated softly, not really wanting to argue, but finding herself trapped.

"Yes, but I've lived longer." She waved her crochet hook at Dianne. "A mother knows these things."

"Grandma's right," Jason said, sounding very adult. "We need to meet this Steve before you go out with him."

Dianne threw her hands up in the air in frustration. "Hey, I thought you kids were the ones so eager for me to be at this dinner!"

"Yes, but we still have standards," Jill said, siding with the others.

"I'll see what I can do," Dianne mumbled.

"Invite him over for dinner Thursday night," her mother suggested. "I'll cook up my stroganoff and bring over a fresh apple pie."

"Ah...he might be busy."

"Then make it Wednesday night," Jason advised in a voice that was hauntingly familiar. It was the same tone Dianne used when she meant business.

With nothing left to do but agree, Dianne said, "Okay. I'll try for Thursday." Oh, Lord, she thought, what had she got herself into?

SHE WAITED until the following afternoon to contact Steve. He'd given her his business card, which she'd tucked into the edging at the bottom of the bulletin board in her kitchen. She wasn't pleased about having to call him. She'd need to offer him more money if he agreed to this dinner. She couldn't very well expect him to come out of the generosity of his heart.

"Port Blossom Towing," a crisp female voice answered.

"Ah...this is Dianne Williams. I'd like to leave a message for Steve Creighton."

"Steve's here." Her words were immediately followed by a soft click and a ringing sound.

"Steve," he answered distractedly.

"Hello." Dianne found herself at a loss for

words. She'd hoped to just leave a message and ask him to return the call at his convenience. To have him there, on the other end of the line, when she wasn't expecting it, left her at a disadvantage.

"Is this Dianne?"

"Yes. How'd you know?"

He chuckled softly, and the sound was pleasant and warm. "It's probably best that I don't answer that. Are you checking up to make sure I don't back out Saturday night? Rest assured, I won't. In fact I stopped off at the community center this morning and picked up tickets for the dinner."

"Oh, you didn't have to do that, but thanks. I'll reimburse you later."

"Just add it to my tab," he said lightly.

Dianne cringed, then took a breath and said, "Actually, I called to talk to you about my children."

"Your children?"

"Yes," she said. "Jason and Jill, and my mother, too, seem to think it would be a good idea if they met you. I assured them they would on Saturday night, but apparently that isn't good enough."

"I see."

"According to Jason, by then it'll be too late, and you might be a serial murderer or something worse. My mother found the fact you drive a truck worrisome."

"Do you want me to change jobs, too? I might have a bit of a problem managing all that before Saturday night."

"Don't worry. Now, about Thursday—that's when they want you to come for dinner. My mother's offered to fix her stroganoff and bake a pie. She uses Granny Smith apples," Dianne added, as though that bit of information would convince him to accept.

"Thursday night?"

"I'll give you an additional ten dollars."

"Ten dollars?" He sounded insulted, so Dianne raised her offer.

"All right, fifteen, but that's as high as I can go. I'm living on a budget, you know." This fiasco was quickly running into a big chunk of cash. The dinner tickets were fifteen each, and she'd need to reimburse Steve for those. Plus, she owed him thirty for escorting her to the silly affair, and now an additional fifteen if he agreed to this dinner with her family.

"For fifteen you've got yourself a deal," he said at last. "Anything else?"

Dianne closed her eyes. This was the worst part. "Yes," she said, swallowing tightly. The lump in her throat had grown to painful proportions. "There's one other thing. I...I want you to know I don't normally look that bad."

"Hey, I told you before—don't be so hard on yourself, you'd had a bad day."

"It's just that I don't want you to think I'm going to embarrass you at this Valentine's dinner. There may be people there you know, and after I made such a big issue over whether you had a suit and everything, well, I thought you might be more comfortable knowing…'' She paused, closed her eyes and then blurted, "I've decided to switch brands of mascara."

His hesitation was only slight. "Thank you for sharing that. I'm sure I'll sleep better now."

Dianne decided to ignore that comment since she'd practically invited it. She didn't know why she should find herself so tongue-tied with this man, but then again, perhaps she did. She'd made a complete idiot of herself. Paying a man to escort her to a dinner wasn't exactly the type of thing she wanted to list on a résumé.

"Oh, and one more thing," Dianne said, determined to put this unpleasantness behind her, "my mother and the kids asked me several questions about…us. How we met and the like. It might be a good idea if we reviewed my answers so our stories match."

"You want to meet for coffee later?"

"Ah…when?"

"Say seven, at the Pancake Haven. Don't worry, I'll buy."

Dianne had to bite back her sarcastic response to his "generous" offer. Instead she murmured, "All right, but I won't have a lot of time."

"I promise not to keep you any longer than necessary."

Chapter Four

"ALL RIGHT," Steve said dubiously, once the waitress had poured them each a cup of coffee. "How'd we meet?"

Dianne told him, lowering her voice when she came to the part about the low-cal frozen dinners. She found it rather humiliating to have to repeat her private fantasy a second time, especially to Steve.

He looked incredulous when she'd finished. "You've got to be kidding."

Dianne took offense at his tone. This was her romantic invention he was ridiculing, and she hadn't even mentioned the part about the Rimsky-Korsakov symphony or the gently chiming bells.

"I didn't have time to think of something better," Dianne explained irritably. "Jason hit me with the question first thing and I wasn't prepared."

"What did Jason say when you told him that story?"

"That you sounded like a flake."

"I don't blame him."

Dianne's shoulders sagged with defeat.

"Don't worry about it," Steve assured her, still frowning. "I'll clear up everything when I meet him

Thursday night.'' He said it in a way that suggested the task would be difficult.

"Good—only don't make me look like any more of a fool than I already do. All right?''

"I'll do my best,'' he said in the same dubious inflection he'd used when they'd first sat down.

Dianne couldn't really blame him. This entire affair was quickly going from bad to worse, and there was no one to fault but her. Who would have dreamed finding a date for the Valentine's dinner would cause such problems?

As they sipped their coffee, Dianne studied the man sitting across from her. She was somewhat surprised to discover that Steve Creighton looked even better the second time around. He was dressed in slacks and an Irish cable-knit sweater the color of winter wheat. His smile was a ready one and his eyes, now that she had a chance to see them in the light, were a deep, rich shade of brown like his hair. The impression he'd given her of a sympathetic, generous man persisted. He must be. No one else would have so readily agreed to this scheme, at least not without a more substantial inducement.

"I'm afraid I might have painted my kids a picture of you that's not quite accurate,'' Dianne admitted. Both her children had been filled with questions about Steve when they'd returned from school that afternoon. Jason had remained skeptical, but Jill, always a romantic—Dianne couldn't imagine where she'd inherited that!—had bombarded Dianne for details.

"I'll do my best to live up to my image," Steve was quick to assure her.

Planting her elbows on the table, Dianne brushed a thick swatch of hair away from her face. "Listen, I'm sorry I ever got you involved in this."

"No backing out now—I've laid out cold cash for the dinner tickets."

Which was a not-so-subtle reminder she owed him for those, Dianne realized. She dug through her bag and brought out her checkbook. "I'll write you a check for the dinner tickets right now while I'm thinking about it."

"I'm not worried." He brushed aside her offer with a wave of his hand.

Nevertheless, Dianne insisted. If she paid him in increments, she wouldn't have to think about how much this fiasco would end up costing her. She had the distinct feeling that by the time the Valentine's dinner was over, she would've spent as much as if she'd taken a Hawaiian vacation.

After adding her signature, with a flair, to the bottom of the check, she kept her eyes lowered and said, "If I upped the ante five dollars do you think you could manage to look...besotted?"

"Besotted?" Steve repeated the word as though he'd never heard it before.

"You know, smitten."

"Smitten?"

Again he made it sound as though she were speaking a foreign language. "Attracted," she tried for the third time, loud enough to attract the waitress's attention. The woman appeared and refilled their near-full cups.

"I'm not purposely being dense—I'm just not sure what you mean."

"Try to look as though you find me attractive," she said, leaning halfway across the table and speaking in a heated whisper.

"I see. So that's what 'besotted' means." He took another drink of his coffee, and Dianne had the feeling he did so in an effort to hide a smile.

"You aren't supposed to find that amusing." She took a gulp of her own drink and nearly scalded her mouth. Under different circumstances she would have grimaced with pain, or at least reached for the water glass. She did none of those things. A woman has her pride.

"Let me see if I understand you correctly," Steve said matter-of-factly. "For an extra five bucks you want me to look 'smitten.'"

"Yes," Dianne answered with as much dignity as she could muster, which at the moment wasn't a great deal.

"I'll do it, of course," Steve said, grinning and making her feel all the more foolish, "only I'm not exactly sure I know how." He straightened, squared his shoulders and momentarily closed his eyes.

"Steve?" Dianne whispered, glancing around,

hoping no one was watching them. It looked as if he were attempting some form of Eastern meditation. She half expected him to start humming. "What are you doing?"

"Thinking about how to look smitten."

"Are you making fun of me?"

"Not in the least. If you're willing to offer me five bucks, then it must be important to you. I want to do it right."

Dianne thought she'd better tell him. "This isn't for me," she said. "It's for my ten-year-old daughter, who happens to have a romantic nature. Jill was so impressed with the story of the way we were supposed to have met that I...I was kind of hoping you'd be willing to...you know." Now that she was forced to spell it out, Dianne wasn't certain of anything. But she knew one thing—suggesting he look smitten with her had been a mistake.

"I'll try."

"I'd appreciate it," she said.

"How's this?" Steve looked toward her, cocked his head at a slight angle, then slowly lowered his eyelids until they were half closed. His mouth curved upward in an off-centered smile while his shoulders heaved in what Dianne suspected was supposed to be a deep sigh of longing. As though in afterthought, he pressed his open hands over his heart while making soft panting sounds.

"Are you doing an imitation of a Saint Bernard?" Dianne snapped, still not sure whether he was making fun of her or seriously trying to do as she suggested. "You look like a...a dog. Maybe Jason's right and you really are a flake."

"I was trying to look besotted," Steve insisted. "I thought that was what you wanted." As if it would improve the image, he cocked his head the other way and repeated the performance.

"You're making fun of me, and I don't appreciate it one bit." Dianne tossed her napkin on the table and stood. "Thursday night, six o'clock, and please don't be late." With that she slipped her purse strap over her shoulder and stalked out of the restaurant.

Steve followed her to her car. "All right, I apologize. I got carried away in there."

Dianne nodded. She'd gone a little overboard herself, but not nearly as much as Steve. Although she'd claimed she wanted him to give the impression of being attracted to her for Jill's sake, that wasn't entirely true. Steve was handsome and kind, and to have him looking at her with his heart in his eyes was a fantasy that was strictly her own.

Admitting as much, even to herself, was something of a shock. The walls around her battered heart had been reinforced by three years of loneliness. For reasons she wasn't entirely sure she could explain, this tow-truck driver made her feel vulnerable.

"I'm willing to try again if you want," he said. "Only..."

"Yes?" Her car was parked in the rear lot where the lighting wasn't nearly as good. Steve's face was hidden in the shadows, and she wasn't sure if he was being sincere or not.

"The problem," he replied slowly, "comes from the fact that we haven't kissed. I don't mean to be forward, you understand. You want me to wear a certain look, but it's a little difficult to manufacture without ever having had any, er, physical closeness."

"I see." Dianne's heart was pounding hard enough to damage her rib cage.

"Are you willing to let me kiss you?"

It was a last resort and she didn't have much choice. But she didn't have anything to lose, either. "All right, if you insist."

Heaving a deep breath, she angled her head to the right, closed her eyes tightly and puckered up. After waiting what seemed an inordinate amount of time, she opened her eyes. "Is something wrong?"

"I can't do it."

Embarrassed in the extreme, Dianne planted her hands on her hips. "What do you mean?"

"You look like you're about to be sacrificed to appease the gods."

"I beg your pardon!" Dianne couldn't believe she was hearing him correctly. Talk about humiliation—she was only doing as he suggested.

"I can't kiss a woman who looks at me like she's about to undergo the most revolting experience of her life."

"You're saying I'm…oh…oh!" Too furious to

speak, Dianne gripped Steve by the elbow and
jerked him over to where his tow truck was parked,
a couple of spaces down from her own car. Hopping
onto the running board, she glared heatedly down
at him. Her higher vantage point made her feel less
vulnerable. Her eyes flashed with fire; his were filled
with mild curiosity.

"Dianne, what are you doing now?"

"I'll have you know I was quite a kisser in my
time."

"I didn't doubt you."

"You just did. Now listen and listen good, because I'm only going to say this once." Waving her
index finger under his nose, she paused and lowered
her hand abruptly. He was right, she hadn't been all
that thrilled to fall into this little experiment. A kiss
was an innocent-enough exchange, she supposed,
but kissing Steve put her on the defensive. And that
troubled her.

"Say it."

Self-conscious now, she shifted her gaze and
stepped off the running board, feeling ridiculous and
stupid.

"What was it you found so important that you
were waving your finger under my nose?" Steve
pressed.

Since she'd made such a fuss, she didn't have any
choice but to finish what she'd begun. "When I was
in high school...the boys used to like to kiss me."

"They still would," Steve said softly, "if you'd give them a little bit of encouragement."

She looked up at him and found it necessary to blink back unexpected tears. A woman doesn't have her own husband walk away from her and not find herself drowning in self-doubts. Jack had gone and left her swimming in a pool of pain. Once she'd been confident and secure; now she was dubious and unsure of herself.

"Here," Steve said, gripping her gently by the shoulders. "Let's try this." Then he gently, sweetly slanted his mouth over hers. Dianne wasn't prepared, in fact she was about to protest when their lips met and the option to refuse was taken from her.

Mindlessly she responded. Her arms went around his middle and her hands splayed across the hard muscles of his back. And suddenly, emotions that had been simmering just below the surface rose like a tempest within her, and her heart went on a rampage all its own.

Steve buried his hands in her hair, his fingers twisting and tangling the thick length, bunching it at the back of her head. His mouth was gentle, yet possessive. She gave a small, shocked moan when his tongue breached the barrier of her lips, but she adjusted quickly to the deepening quality of his kiss.

Slowly, reluctantly, Steve eased his mouth from hers. For a long moment, Dianne didn't open her eyes. When she did, she found Steve staring down at her.

He blinked.

She blinked.

Then, in the space of a heartbeat, he lowered his mouth back to hers.

Unable to stop, Dianne sighed deeply and leaned into his strength, letting him absorb her weight. Her legs felt like mush and her head was spinning with confusion. Her hands crept up and closed around the knitted folds of his collar.

This kiss was long and thorough. It was the sweetest kiss Dianne had ever known—and the most passionate.

When he finally lifted his mouth from hers, he smiled tenderly. For a long moment he didn't say anything. "I don't believe I'll have any problem looking besotted," he whispered.

Chapter Five

"STEVE'S HERE!" Jason called, releasing the living-room curtain. "He's just pulled into the driveway."

Jill's high-pitched voice echoed her brother's. "He brought his truck. It's red and—"

"—wicked," Jason said, paying Steve's choice of vehicles the highest form of teenage compliment.

"What did I tell you," Dianne's mother said, stiffening as she briskly stirred the simmering stroganoff sauce. "He's driving a truck that's red and wicked." Her voice rose hysterically. "The man's probably a spawn of the devil!"

"Mother, 'wicked' means 'wonderful' to Jason."

"I've never heard anything so absurd in my life."

The doorbell chimed just then. Jerking the apron from her slim waist and tossing it aside, Dianne straightened and walked into the wide entryway. Jason, Jill and her mother followed closely, crowding her.

"Mom, please," Dianne pleaded, "give me some room here. Jason. Jill. Back up a little, would you?"

Reluctantly all three moved several paces back, allowing Dianne some space. But the moment her hand went for the doorknob, they crowded forward once more.

"Children, Ma, please!" she whispered frantically. The three were so close to her she could barely breathe.

Reluctantly Jason and Jill shuffled into the living room and sagged into the beanbag cushions near the television set. Martha, however, refused to budge.

The bell chimed a second time, and after glaring at her mother and receiving no response, Dianne opened the door. On the other side of the screen door stood Steve, a huge bouquet of red roses clenched in one hand and a large stuffed bear tucked under his other arm.

Dianne blinked as she calculated the cost of long-stemmed roses, and a stuffed animal. She couldn't even afford carnations. And if he felt it necessary to bring along a stuffed bear, why hadn't he chosen a smaller, less costly one?

"May I come in?" he asked after a lengthy pause.

Her mother elbowed Dianne in the ribs and smiled serenely as she unlatched the lock on the screen door.

"You must be Steve. How lovely to meet you," Martha said as graciously as if she'd always thought the world of truck drivers.

Holding open the outer door for him, Dianne managed to produce a weak smile as Steve entered her home. Jason and Jill had come back into the entryway to stand next to their grandmother, eyeing Dianne's newfound date with open curiosity. For all her son's concern that Steve might turn out to be an ax-murderer, one look at the bright red tow truck and he'd been won over.

"Steve, I'd like you to meet my family," Dianne said, gesturing toward the three.

"So, you're Jason," Steve said, holding out his hand. The two exchanged a hearty handshake. "I'm pleased to meet you, son. Your mother speaks highly of you."

Jason beamed.

Turning his attention to Jill, Steve held out the oversize teddy bear. "This is for you," he said, giving her the stuffed animal. "I wanted something extra special for Dianne's daughter, but this was all I could think of. I hope you aren't disappointed."

"I love teddy bears!" Jill cried, hugging it tight. "Did Mom tell you that?"

"Nope," Steve said, centering his high-voltage smile on the ten-year-old. "I just guessed you'd like them."

"Oh, thank you, thank you." Cuddling the bear, Jill raced up the stairs, giddy with delight. "I'm going to put him on my bed right now."

Steve's gaze followed her daughter, and then his eyes briefly linked with Dianne's. In that split second, she let it be known she wasn't entirely pleased. He frowned slightly, but recovered before presenting the roses to Dianne's mother.

"For me?" Martha cried, and placed her fingertips over her mouth as though shocked by the gesture. "Oh, dear, you shouldn't have! Oh, my heavens, I can't remember the last time a man gave me roses." Reaching for the corner of her apron, she discreetly dabbed her eyes. "This is a rare treat."

"Mother, don't you want to put those in water?" Dianne said pointedly.

"Oh, dear, I suppose I should. It was a thoughtful gesture, Steve. Very thoughtful."

"Jason, go help your grandmother."

Her son looked as though he intended to object, but changed his mind and obediently followed his grandmother into the kitchen.

As soon as they were alone, Dianne turned on Steve. "Don't you think you're laying it on a little thick?" she whispered. She was so furious she was having trouble speaking clearly. "I can't afford all this."

"Don't worry about it."

"I am worried. In fact I'm suffering a good deal of distress. At the rate you're spending my money I'm going to have to go on an installment plan."

"Hush, now, before you attract attention."

The way she was feeling, Dianne felt like doing a whole lot more than that. "I—"

Steve placed his fingers over her lips. "I've learned a very effective way of keeping you quiet— don't force me to use it. Kissing you so soon after my arrival might give the wrong impression."

"You wouldn't dare!"

The way his mouth slanted upward in a slow, powerful smile made her afraid he would. "I was only doing my best to act besotted," he said.

"You didn't need to spend this much doing it. Opening my door, holding out my chair—that's all I wanted. First you roll your eyes like you're going into a coma and pant like a Saint Bernard, then you spend a fortune."

"Dinner's ready," Martha shouted from the kitchen.

Tossing him one last angry glare, Dianne led the way into the big kitchen. Steve moved behind Dianne's chair and held it out for her. "Are you happy now?" he whispered close to her ear as she sat down.

She nodded, thinking it was too little, too late, but she didn't have much of an argument since she'd specifically asked for this.

Soon the five were all seated around the wooden table. Dianne's mother said the blessing, and while she did so, Dianne offered up a fervent prayer of her own. She wanted Steve to make a good impression—but not too good.

After the buttered noodles and the stroganoff had been passed around, along with a lettuce-and-cucumber salad and homemade rolls, Jason embarked on the topic that had apparently been troubling him from the first.

"Mom said you met at the market."

Steve nodded. "She was blocking the aisle and I had to ask her to move her cart so I could get to the Hearty Eater Pot Pies."

Jason straightened in his chair, looking more than a little satisfied. "I thought it might be something like that."

"I beg your pardon?" Steve asked, playing innocent.

Her son cleared his throat, glanced both ways before answering, then lowered his voice. "You should hear Mom's version of the way you two met."

"More noodles?" Dianne said, shoving the bowl forcefully toward her son.

Jill looked confused. "But didn't you smile at Mom and say she's perfect just the way she is?"

Steve took a moment to compose his thoughts while he buttered his third dinner roll. Dianne recognized that he was doing a balancing act between her two children. If he said he'd commented on the low-cal frozen dinners and her figure, then he risked offending Jason, who seemed to think no man in his right mind would say something like that. On the other hand, if he claimed otherwise, he chanced wounding Jill's romantic little heart.

"I'd be interested in knowing myself," Martha added, looking more than pleased that Steve had taken a second helping of her stroganoff. "Dianne's terribly close-mouthed about these things. She didn't even mention you until the other night."

"To be honest," Steve said, sitting back in his chair, "I don't exactly recall what I said to Dianne. I remember being irritated with her for hogging the aisle, but when I asked her to move, she seemed apologetic and was quick to get her cart out of the way."

Jason nodded, appeased.

"But when I got a good look at her, I couldn't help thinking she was probably the most beautiful woman I'd seen in a good long while."

Jill sighed, mollified.

"I don't recall any of that," Dianne said, reaching for another roll. She tore it apart with a vengeance and smeared butter on both halves before she realized she had an untouched roll balanced on the edge of her plate.

"I was thinking after the dishes were done that I'd take Jason out for a ride in the truck," Steve said after a few minutes had passed.

"You'd do that?" Jason nearly leapt from his chair in his eagerness.

"I was planning to all along," Steve explained. "I thought you'd be more interested in seeing how all the gears worked than in any gift I could bring you."

"I am." Jason was so excited he could barely sit still another minute.

"When Jason and I come back, I'll take you out for a spin, Dianne."

She shook her head. "I'm not interested, thanks."

Three pairs of accusing eyes flashed in her direction. It was as if Dianne had committed an act of treason and her family had no choice but to hand her over to the CIA.

"I'm sure my daughter didn't mean that," Martha said, smiling sweetly at Steve. "She's been very tired lately and not quite herself."

Bewildered, Dianne stared at her mother.

"Can we go now?" Jason wanted to know, already standing.

"Sure, if your mother says it's okay," Steve said, with a glance at Dianne. She nodded, and Steve finished the last of his roll and stood.

"I'll have apple pie ready for you when you return," Martha promised, quickly ushering the two out the front door.

As soon as her mother returned to the kitchen, Dianne asked, "What was that all about?"

"What?" her mother demanded, feigning ignorance.

"That I've been very tired and not myself lately?"

"Oh, that," Martha said, clearing the table. "Steve wants to spend a few minutes alone with you. It's only to be expected—so I had to make some excuse for you."

"Yes, but—"

"Your behavior, my dear, was just short of rude. When a gentleman makes it clear he wants to spend a few uninterrupted minutes in your company, you should welcome the opportunity.''

"Mother, I seem to recall your saying Steve was a spawn of the devil, remember?''

"Now that I've met him, I've had a change of heart.''

"What about Jerome, the butcher? I thought you were convinced he was the one for me.''

"I like Steve better. He's a good man, and you'd be a fool to let him slip through your fingers by pretending to be indifferent.''

"I am indifferent.''

With a look of patent disbelief, Martha Janes quickly shook her head. "I saw the way your eyes lit up when Steve walked into the house. You can fool some folks, but you can't pull the wool over your own mother's eyes. You're falling in love with this young man, and frankly, I couldn't be more pleased. I like him.''

Dianne frowned. If her eyes had lit up when Steve arrived, it was because she was trying to figure out a way to repay him for the roses and the teddy bear. What she felt for him wasn't anything romantic. Or was it?

Dear Lord, she couldn't actually be falling for this guy, could she?

The question haunted Dianne as she loaded the dishwasher.

"Steve's real cute,'' Jill announced. Her daughter would find Attila the Hun cute, too, if he brought her a teddy bear, but Dianne resisted the impulse to say so.

"He looks a little bit like Tom Cruise, don't you think?" Jill continued.

"I can't say I've noticed." A small lie. Dianne had noticed a lot more about Steve than she was willing to admit. Although she'd issued a fair number of complaints, he really was being a good sport about all this. Of course, she was paying him, but he'd gone above and beyond the call of duty. Taking Jason out for a spin in the tow truck was one example, although why anyone would be thrilled to drive around in that contraption was beyond Dianne.

"I do believe Steve Creighton will make you a decent husband," her mother stated thoughtfully as she removed the warm apple pie from the oven. "In fact, I was just thinking how nice it would be to have a summer wedding. It's so much easier to ask relatives to travel when the weather's good. June or July would be nice."

"Mother, please! Steve and I barely know each other."

"On the contrary," Steve said, sauntering into the kitchen. He stepped behind Dianne's mother and sniffed appreciatively at the aroma wafting from her apple pie. "I happen to be partial to summer weddings myself."

Chapter Six

"DON'T YOU THINK you're overdoing it a bit?" Dianne demanded as soon as Steve eased the big tow truck out of her driveway. She was strapped into the seat next to him, feeling trapped—not to mention betrayed by her own family. They had insisted Steve take her out for a spin so the two of them could have some time alone. Steve didn't want to be alone with her, but her family didn't know that.

"Maybe I did come on a little strong," Steve agreed, dazzling her with his smile.

It was better for her equilibrium if she didn't glance his way, Dianne decided. Her eyes would innocently meet his and he'd give her one of those heart-stopping, lopsided smiles, and something inside her would melt. If this continued much longer she'd be nothing more than a puddle by the end of the evening.

"The flowers and the stuffed animal I can understand," she said stiffly, willing to grant him that much. "You wanted to make a good impression, and that's fine, but the comment about being partial to summer weddings was going too far. It's just the

kind of thing my mother was hoping to hear from
you.''

''You're right.''

The fact that he was being so agreeable should
have forewarned Dianne something was amiss.
She'd sensed it almost from the first moment she'd
climbed into the truck. He'd closed the door and
almost immediately something pulled wire-taut
within her. The sensation was peculiar, almost wist-
ful—a melancholy pining she'd never felt before.

She squared her shoulders and stared straight
ahead, determined not to fall under his spell the way
her children and her mother so obviously had.

''As it is, I suspect Mom's been faithfully lighting
votive candles every afternoon, asking God to send
me a husband. Mostly she thinks God needs a little
help—that's why she goes around arranging dates
for me.''

''You're right, of course. I should never have
made that comment about summer weddings,''
Steve said, ''but I assumed that's just the sort of
thing a *besotted* man would say.''

Dianne sighed, realizing she didn't have much of
an argument. But he was doing everything within
his power to make her regret that silly request. She
couldn't possibly understand what had led her to
make it; now she was living to regret every syllable.

''Hey, where are you taking me?'' she demanded
when he turned off her street onto a main thorough-
fare.

Steve turned his smile full force on her and twitched his thick eyebrows a couple of times for effect. "For a short drive. It wouldn't look good if we were to return five minutes after we left the house. Your family—"

"—will be waiting at the front door. They expect me back any minute."

"No, they don't."

"And why don't they?" she asked, growing uneasy. This ride wasn't supposed to be anything more than a spin around the block. As it was, she'd had to be coerced into even that.

"Because I told your mother we'd be gone for an hour or more."

"An hour?" Dianne cried, as though he'd just announced he was kidnapping her. "But you can't do that! I mean, what about your time? Surely it's valuable."

"I assumed you'd want to pay me a couple of dollars extra—after all, I'm doing this to give the right kind of impression. It's what—"

"I know, I know," she interrupted. "You're only acting smitten." The truth of the matter was that Dianne was making a fuss over something that was actually causing her heart to pound hard and fast. The whole idea of being alone with Steve appealed to her too much. *That* was the reason she fought it so hard. Every time she was with him she found him more fascinating. Without even trying, he'd managed to cast a spell on her family, and much as she hated to admit it, one on her, too. Steve Creighton was laughter and magic. Instinctively she knew he wasn't another Jack. Not the type of man who would walk away from his family.

Dianne stiffened as the thought crossed her mind. It would be much easier to deal with the hand life had dealt her if she wasn't forced to associate with men as seemingly wonderful as this tow-truck operator. It was easier to view all men as insensitive and thoughtless.

Dianne didn't like the fact that Steve was proving to be otherwise. He was apparently determined to crack the hard shell around her safe, secure world no matter how hard she tried to reinforce it.

"Another thing," she said stiffly, crossing her arms with resolve, but refusing to glance his way. "You've got to stop being so free with my money."

"I never expected you to reimburse me for those gifts," he explained quietly.

"I insist on it."

"My, my, aren't we prickly. I bought the flowers and the toy for Jill of my own accord. I don't expect you to pick up the tab," he repeated.

Dianne didn't know if she should argue with him or not. Although his tone was soft, a thread of steel ran through his words, just enough to let her know nothing she said was going to change his mind.

"That's not all," she said, deciding to drop that argument for a more pressing one. She realized she probably did sound a bit shrewish, but if he wasn't going to be practical about this, *she'd* have to be.

"You mean there's more?" he cried, pretending to be distressed.

"Steve, please," she said and was shocked at how feeble she sounded. She scarcely recognized the voice as her own. "You've got to stop being so...so wonderful," she said finally.

He eased to a stop at a red light and turned to her, draping his arm over the back of the seat. "I don't think I heard you right. Would you remind repeating that?"

"You can't continue being so—" she paused, searching for another word "—charming."

"Charming," he repeated, as though he'd never heard the word before.

"To my children and my mother," she elaborated. "The gifts were one thing. Giving Jason a ride in the tow truck was another, but agreeing with my mother about summer weddings and then playing a game of basketball with Jason were above and beyond the call of duty."

"Personally, I would have thought having your mother measure my chest and arm length so she could knit me a sweater would bother you the most."

"That, too!" she cried.

"Would you mind explaining why this is such a problem?"

"Isn't it obvious? If you keep doing that sort of

thing, they'll expect me to continue dating you after the Valentine's dinner, and, frankly, I can't afford it.''

He chuckled at that as if she was making some kind of joke. Only it wasn't funny. ''I happen to live on a budget—'' she went on.

''I don't think we should concern ourselves with that.''

''Well I am concerned.'' She expelled her breath sharply. ''One date! That's all I can afford and that's all I'm interested in. If you continue to be so...so...''

''Wonderful?'' he supplied.

''Charming,'' she corrected, ''then I'll have a whole lot to answer for when I don't see you again after Saturday.''

''So you want me to limit the charm?''

''Please.''

''I'll do my best,'' he said, and his eyes sparked with laughter, which they seemed to do a good deal of the time. If she hadn't been so flustered, she might have been pleased he found her so amusing.

''Thank you.'' She glanced pointedly at her watch. ''Don't you think we should be heading back to the house?''

''No.''

''No? I realize you told my mother we'd be gone an hour, but that really is too long and—''

''I'm taking you to Jackson Point.''

Dianne's heart reacted instantly, zooming into her

throat and then righting itself. Jackson Point over-looked a narrow water passage between the Kitsap Peninsula and Vashon Island. The view, either at night or during the day, was spectacular, but those who came to appreciate it at night were generally more interested in each other than the glittering lights of the island and Seattle farther beyond.

"I'll take the fact you're not arguing with me as a positive sign," he said.

"I think we should go back to the house," she stated with as much resolve as she could muster. Unfortunately it didn't come out sounding very firm. The last time she'd been to Jackson Point had been a lifetime ago. She'd been a high-school junior and madly in love for the first time. The last time.

"We'll go back to the house in a little while."

"Steve," she cried, fighting the urge to cry, "why are you doing this?"

"Isn't it obvious? I want to kiss you again."

Dianne pushed her hair away from her face with both hands. "I don't think that's such a good idea." Her voice wavered, sounding more like her teenage son than herself.

Before she could think of an argument, Steve pulled off the highway and down the narrow road that led to the popular lookout. She hadn't wanted to think about that kiss they'd shared. It had been a mistake. Dianne knew she'd disappointed Steve—not in the kiss itself, but in her reaction to it. He seemed to be waiting for her to admit how profoundly it had affected her, but she hadn't given him the satisfaction.

Now he wanted revenge.

Her heart continued to hammer when Steve stopped the truck and turned off the engine. The lights sparkled across the water in welcome. The closest lights were from Vashon Island, a sparsely populated place accessible only by ferry. The more distant ones came from West Seattle.

"It's really beautiful," she whispered. Some of the tension eased from her shoulders and she felt herself start to relax.

"Yes," Steve agreed. He moved closer and placed his arm around her shoulder.

Dianne closed her eyes, knowing she was not going to find the power to resist him. He'd been so wonderful with her children and her mother—more than wonderful. Now it seemed to be her turn, and try as she might to avoid it, she found herself falling a willing victim to his special brand of magic.

"You *are* going to let me kiss you, aren't you?" he whispered close to her ear.

She nodded.

His hands were in her hair as he directed his mouth to hers. The kiss was slow and easy, as though he was afraid of frightening her. His mouth was warm and moist over her own, gentle and persuasive. Dianne could feel her bones start to dissolve and knew that if she was going to walk away from this experience unscathed, she needed to think fast. Unfortunately, her thought processes were already overloaded.

When at last they drew apart, he dragged in a deep breath. Dianne sank against the cushion and noted that his eyes were still closed. Taking this moment to gather her composure, she scooted as far away from him as she could, pressing the small of her back against the door handle.

"You're very good," she said, striving to sound unruffled by the experience, and knowing she hadn't succeeded.

He blinked, opened his eyes and frowned. "I'll assume that's a compliment."

"Yes. I think you should." Steve was the kind of man who'd attract attention from women no matter where he went. He wouldn't be interested in a divorcée and a ready-made family, and there wasn't any use in trying to convince herself otherwise. The only reason he'd even agreed to take her to the Valentine's dinner was because she'd offered to pay him. This was strictly a business arrangement.

His finger lightly grazed the side of her face. His eyes were tender as he studied her, but he said nothing.

"It would probably be a good idea if we talked about Saturday night," she said, doing her best to keep her gaze trained away from him. "There's a lot to discuss and...there isn't much time left."

"All right." His wayward grin told her she hadn't fooled him. He knew exactly what she was up to.

"Since the dinner starts at seven, I suggest you arrive at my house at quarter-to."

"Fine."

"I don't think we need to go to the trouble or the expense of a corsage."

"What are you wearing?"

Dianne hadn't given the matter a second's thought. "Since it's a Valentine's dinner, something red, I suppose. I have a striped dress of red and white that will do." It was a couple of years old, but this dinner wasn't exactly the fashion event of the year, and she didn't have the money for something new, anyway.

She looked at her watch, although there wasn't any chance she could read the hands in the darkness.

"Is that a hint you want to get back to the house?"

"Yes," she said.

Her honesty seemed to amuse him. "That's what I thought." Without argument, he started the engine and put the truck into reverse.

The minute they turned onto her street, Jason and Jill came vaulting out the front door. Dianne guessed they'd both been staring out the upstairs window, eagerly awaiting her return.

She was wrong. It was Steve they were eager to see.

"Hey, what took you so long?" Jason demanded as Steve climbed out of the truck.

"Grandma's got the apple pie all dished up. Are

you ready?'' Jill hugged Steve's arm, glancing up anxiously at him.

Dianne watched the unfolding scene with dismay. Steve walked into her house with one arm around Jason and Jill clinging to the other.

It was as if she were invisible. Neither one of her children had said a single word to her!

To his credit, Jason paused at the front door. ''Mom, you coming?''

''Just bringing up the rear,'' she muttered.

Jill shook her head, her young shoulders lifting, then falling, in a deep sigh. ''You'll have to forgive my mother,'' she told Steve confidingly. ''She can be a real slowpoke sometimes.''

Chapter Seven

"OH, MOM," JILL SAID SOFTLY. "You look so beautiful."

Dianne examined her reflection in the full-length mirror once more. At the last moment, she'd been gripped by another bout of insanity. She'd gone out and purchased a new dress.

She couldn't afford it. She couldn't rationalize the expense on top of everything else, but the instant she'd seen the flowered pink creation hanging in the shop window, she'd decided to try it on. That was her first mistake. Correction: that was a mistake in a long list of recent ones where Steve Creighton was concerned.

The dress was probably the most flattering thing she'd ever owned. One look at the price tag had practically caused her to clutch her chest and stagger backward. She hadn't purchased it impulsively. No, she was too smart for that. The fact that she was nearly penniless and it was only the middle of the month didn't help matters. She'd sat down in the coffee shop next door and juggled figures for ten or fifteen minutes before crumpling up the paper and deciding to buy the dress, anyway. It was her birthday, Mother's Day and Christmas gifts to herself all rolled into one.

"I brought along my pearls," Martha announced as she breathlessly bolted into Dianne's bedroom. She was late, which wasn't like Martha, but Dianne hadn't been worried. She knew her mother would be there before she had to leave for the dinner.

Martha stopped abruptly, folding her hands prayerfully and nodding with approval. "Oh, Dianne. You look..."

"Beautiful," Jill finished for her grandmother.

"Beautiful," Martha echoed. "I thought you were going to wear the red dress."

"I just happened to be at the mall and stumbled across this." She didn't mention that she'd specifically made the trip into Tacoma for the express purpose of looking for something new to wear.

"Steve's here," Jason yelled from the bottom of the stairs.

"Here are my pearls," Martha said, reverently handing them to her daughter. The pearls were a family heirloom and worn only on the most special occasions.

"Mom, I don't know..."

"Your first official date with Steve," she insisted as though the event were on a level with God giving Moses the Ten Commandments. Without further ado, Martha formally draped the necklace around her daughter's neck. "I insist. Your father insists."

"Mom?" Dianne asked, turning around to search

her mother's face. "Have you been talking to Dad again?" Dianne's father had been gone for more than ten years. However, for several years following his demise, Martha Janes claimed they carried on regular conversations.

"Not exactly, but I know your father would have insisted, had he been here. Now off with you. It's rude to keep a date waiting."

Before leaving her bedroom, Dianne briefly closed her eyes. She was nervous. Which was silly, she told herself. This wasn't a *real* date, since she was paying Steve for the honor of escorting her. She'd reminded herself of that the entire time she was dressing. The only reason they were even attending this Valentine's dinner was because she'd asked him. Not only asked, but offered to pay for everything.

Jill rushed out of the bedroom door and down the stairs. "She's coming and she looks beautiful."

"Your mother always looks beautiful," Dianne heard Steve say matter-of-factly as she descended the first steps. Her eyes were on him, standing in the entryway dressed in a dark gray suit, looking tall and debonair.

He glanced up and his gaze found hers. She was gratified to note his eyes rounded briefly.

"I was wrong, she's extra beautiful tonight," he whispered, but if he was speaking to her children, he wasn't looking at them. In fact his eyes were riveted on her, which only served to make Dianne more uneasy.

They stood staring at each other like star-crossed lovers until Jill tugged at Steve's arm. "Aren't you going to give my mom the corsage?"

"Oh, yes, here," he said, looking as though he'd completely forgotten he was holding an octagon-shaped plastic box.

Dianne frowned. They'd agreed earlier he wasn't supposed to do this. She was already over her budget, and flowers were a low-priority item, as far as Dianne was concerned.

"It's one for the wrist," he explained, opening the box for her. "I thought you said the dress was red, so I'm afraid this might not go with it very well." Three white rosebuds were fashioned between a froth of red-and-white silk ribbons. Although her dress was several shades of pink, there was a spattering of red in the center of the flowers that matched the color in the ribbon perfectly. It was as if Steve had seen the dress and chosen the flowers to complement it. "It's..."

"Beautiful," Jill supplied once more, smugly pleased with herself.

"Are you ready to go?" Steve asked.

Jason stepped forward with her wool coat as though he couldn't wait to be rid of her. Steve took the coat from her son's hands and helped Dianne into it, while her son and daughter stood back looking as proud as peacocks for having arranged the entire affair.

Before she left the house, Dianne gave her children their instructions and kissed them each on the cheek. Jason wasn't much in favor of letting his mother kiss him, but he tolerated it.

Martha continued to stand at the top of the stairs, dabbing her eyes with a soft tissue and looking down as if the four of them together were the most romantic sight she'd ever witnessed. Dianne sincerely prayed that Steve didn't notice.

"I won't be late," Dianne said as Steve opened the front door.

"Don't worry about it," Jason said pointedly. "There isn't any need to rush home."

"Have a wonderful time," Jill called after them.

The first thing Dianne noticed once they were out the door was that Steve's tow truck was missing from her driveway. She looked around, half expecting to find the red monstrosity parked on the street.

With his hand cupping her elbow, he led her instead to a luxury car. "What's this?" she asked, thinking he might have rented it. If he had, she wanted it understood this minute that she had no intention of paying the fee.

"My car."

"Your car?" she asked. He opened the door for her and Dianne slid onto the supple white leather. Tow-truck operators apparently made better money than she'd assumed. If she'd known that, she would have offered him twenty dollars for this evening instead of thirty.

Steve walked around the front of the sedan and got into the driver's seat. They chatted on the short ride to the community center, with Dianne making small talk in an effort to cover her nervousness.

The parking lot was nearly full, but Steve found a spot on the side lot next to the sprawling brick building.

"You ready?" he asked.

She nodded. Over the years, Dianne had attended a dozen of these affairs. There was no reason to feel nervous. Her friends and neighbors would be there. Naturally there'd be questions about her and Steve, but this time she was prepared.

Steve came around the car, opened her door and handed her out. She noticed that he was frowning.

"Is something wrong?" she asked anxiously.

"You look pale."

She was about to explain it was probably nerves when he said, "Not to worry, I have a cure for that." Before she realized his intention, he leaned forward and brushed his mouth over hers.

He was right. The instant his lips touched hers, hot color exploded in her cheeks. She felt herself swaying toward him, and Steve caught her gently by the shoulders.

"That was a mistake," he whispered once they'd eased apart. "Now the only thing I'm hungry for is you. Forget the dinner."

"I...think we should go inside now," she said, glancing around the parking lot, praying no one had witnessed the kiss.

Light and laughter spilled out from the wide double doors of the Port Blossom Community Center. The soft strains of a romantic ballad beckoned them inside.

Steve took her coat and hung it on the rack in the entryway. She waited for him, feeling more jittery than ever. When he'd finished, Steve placed his arm about her waist and led her into the main room.

"Steve Creighton!" They had scarcely stepped into the room when Steve was greeted by a robust man with a salt-and-pepper beard. Glancing curiously at Dianne, the stranger slapped Steve on the back and said, "It's about time you attended one of our functions."

Steve introduced Dianne to the man, whose name was Sam Horton. The name was vaguely familiar to her, but she couldn't quite place it.

Apparently reading her mind, Steve said, "Sam's the president of the Chamber of Commerce."

"Ah, yes," Dianne said softly, impressed to meet one of the community's more distinguished members.

"My wife, Renée," Sam said, absently glancing around, "is somewhere in this mass of humanity." Then he turned back to Steve. "Have you two found a table yet? We'd consider it a pleasure to have you join us."

"Dianne?" Steve looked to her.

"That would be very nice, thank you." Wait until her mother heard this. She and Steve dining with the Chamber of Commerce president! Dianne couldn't help smiling. No doubt her mother would attribute this piece of good luck to the pearls. Sam left to find his wife, eager to introduce her to Dianne.

"Dianne Williams! It's so good to see you." The voice belonged to Betty Martin, who had crossed the room, dragging her husband, Ralph, along with her. Dianne knew Betty from the PTA. They'd worked together on the spring carnival the year before. Actually, Dianne had done the majority of the work while Betty had done the delegating. The experience had been enough to convince Dianne not to volunteer for this year's event.

Dianne introduced Steve to Betty and Ralph. Dianne felt a small sense of triumph to note the way Betty eyed Steve. This man was worth every single penny of the thirty dollars he was costing her!

The two couples chatted for a few moments, then Steve excused himself. Dianne watched him as he walked through the room, observing how the gazes of several women followed him. He did make a compelling sight, especially in his well-cut suit.

"How long have you known Steve Creighton?" Betty asked the instant Steve was out of earshot, moving closer to Dianne as though she was about to hear some well-seasoned gossip.

"A few weeks now." It was clear Betty was hoping Dianne would elaborate, but Dianne had no intention of doing so.

"Dianne." Shirley Simpson, another PTA friend, moved to her side. "Is that Steve Creighton you're with?"

"Yes." She'd had no idea Steve was so well known.

"I swear he's the cutest man in town. One look at him and my toes start to curl."

When she'd approached Steve with this proposal, Dianne hadn't a clue she would become the envy of her friends. She really *had* got a bargain.

"Are you sitting with anyone yet?" Shirley asked. Betty bristled as though offended she hadn't thought to ask first.

"Ah, yes. Sam Horton has already invited us, but thanks."

"Sam Horton," Betty repeated and she and Shirley shared a significant look. "My, my, you are traveling in elevated circles these days. Well, more power to you. And good luck with Steve Creighton. I've been saying for ages that it was time someone bagged him. I hope it's you."

"Thanks," Dianne said, feeling more than a little confused by this unexpected turn of events. Everyone knew Steve, right down to her PTA friends. It didn't make a lot of sense.

Steve returned a moment later, carrying two slender flutes of champagne. "I'd like you to meet some friends of mine,'' he said, leading her across the room to where several couples were standing. The wide circle opened up to include them. Dianne immediately recognized the mayor and a couple of others.

Dianne threw Steve a puzzled look. He certainly was a social animal, but the people he knew... Still, why should she be surprised? A tow-truck operator would have plenty of opportunity to meet community leaders. And Steve was such a likable man, who apparently made friends easily.

A four-piece band began playing forties' swing, and after the introductions, Dianne found her toe tapping to the sound.

"Next year we should make this a dinner-dance," Steve suggested, smiling down on Dianne. He casually put his hand on her shoulder as if he'd been doing that for months.

"Great idea," Port Blossom's mayor said, nodding. "You might bring that up at the March committee meeting."

Dianne frowned, not certain she understood. It was several minutes later before she had a chance to ask Steve about the comment.

"I'm on the board of directors for the community center," he explained briefly.

"You are?" Dianne took another sip of her champagne. Some of the details were beginning to get muddled in her mind, and she wasn't sure if it had anything to do with the champagne.

"Does that surprise you?"

"Yes. I thought you had to be, you know, a business owner or something to be on the board of directors."

Now it was Steve's turn to frown. "I am."

"You are?" Dianne asked. Her hand tightened around the long stem of her glass. "What business?"

"Port Blossom Towing."

That did it. Dianne drank what remained of her champagne in a single gulp. "You mean to say you *own* the company?"

"Yes. Don't tell me you didn't know."

She glared up at him, her eyes narrowed and distrusting. "I didn't know."

Chapter Eight

STEVE CREIGHTON had made a fool of her.

Dianne was so infuriated she couldn't wait to be alone with him so she could give him a piece of her mind. Loudly.

"What's that got to do with anything?" Steve asked.

Dianne continued to glare at him, unable to form any words yet. It wasn't just that he owned the towing company or even that he was a member of the board of directors for the community center. It was the way he'd deceived her.

"You should have told me you owned the company!" she hissed.

"I gave you my business card," he said, shrugging.

"You gave me your business card," she mimicked in a furious whisper. "The least you could have done was mention the fact. I feel like an idiot."

Steve was wearing a perplexed frown, as if he found her response completely unreasonable. "To be honest, I assumed you knew. I wasn't purposely keeping it from you."

That wasn't the only thing disturbing her, but the second concern was even more troubling than the first. "While I'm on the subject, what are you? Some sort of...love god?"

"What?"

"From the moment we arrived all the women I know, and even some I don't, have been crowding around me asking all sorts of leading questions. One friend claims you make her toes curl and another...never mind."

Steve looked exceptionally pleased. "I make her toes curl?"

How like a man to fall for flattery! "That's not the point."

"Then what is?"

"Everyone thinks you and I are an item."

"So? I thought that was what you wanted."

Dianne thought she was going to scream. "Kindly look at this from my point of view. I'm in one hell of a mess because of you!" He frowned as she elaborated. "What am I supposed to tell everyone, including my mother and children, once tonight is over?" Why, oh why hadn't she thought of this sooner?

"About what?"

"About you and me," she said slowly, softly, using short words so he'd understand. "I didn't even want to attend this dinner. I've lied to my own family and, worse, I'm actually paying a man to escort me. This is probably the lowest point of my life, and all you can do is stand there wearing a silly grin.''

Steve chuckled and his mouth twitched as though he were struggling to restrain his amusement. ''This silly grin you find so offensive is my besotted look. I've been practicing it in front of a mirror most of the week.''

Dianne covered her face with her hands. ''Now...now I discover that I'm even more of a fool than I realized. You're this upstanding businessman and, worse, a...a playboy.''

''I'm not a playboy,'' he corrected.

''Maybe not—I wouldn't know about that part, but I do know that's the reputation you've got. There isn't a woman at this dinner who doesn't envy me.''

The whole thing had taken such an unbearable turn, it was all Dianne could do not to break down and weep. All she'd wanted was someone presentable to escort her to this dinner so she could satisfy her children. She lived a quiet, uncomplicated life, and suddenly she was the most gossip-worthy member of tonight's affair.

Sam Horton stepped to the microphone in front of the hall and announced that dinner was about to be served, so would everyone please go to their tables.

''Don't look so discontented,'' Steve whispered in her ear. He was standing behind her, and his hands rested gently on her shoulders. ''The woman who's supposed to be the envy of every other one here shouldn't be frowning. Try smiling."

"I don't think I can," she muttered, fearing she might break down and cry. Having Steve casually hold her this way wasn't helping. She found his touch reassuring and comforting when she didn't want either, at least not from him. She was confused enough. Her head was telling her one thing and her heart another.

"Trust me, Dianne, you're blowing this whole thing out of proportion. I didn't mean to deceive you. Let's enjoy the evening."

"I feel like such a fool." Several people walked past them on their way to the tables, pausing to smile and nod. Dianne did her best to respond appropriately.

"You're not a fool." He slipped his arm around her slim waist and led her toward the table where Sam and his wife, as well as two other couples Dianne didn't know, were waiting.

Dianne smiled at the others while Steve held out her chair. A gentleman to the very end, she thought wryly. He opened doors and held out chairs for her, and the whole time she was making an idiot of herself in front of an entire community.

As soon as everyone was seated, he introduced Dianne to the two remaining couples—Larry and Louise Lester, who owned a local restaurant; and Dale and Maryanne Atwater. Dale was head of the town's most prominent accounting firm.

The salads were delivered by young men in crisp white jackets. The Lesters and the Atwaters were making small talk, discussing the weather and other bland subjects. Caught in her own churning thoughts, Dianne ate her salad and tuned them out. When she was least expecting it, she heard her name. She glanced up to find six pairs of eyes studying her. She hadn't a clue why.

She lowered the fork to her salad plate and glanced at Steve, praying he'd know what was happening.

"The two of you make such a handsome couple," Renée Horton said. Her words were casual, but her look wasn't. Everything about her said she was intensely curious about Steve and Dianne.

"Thank you." Steve answered, then turned to Dianne and gave her what she'd referred to earlier as a silly grin and what he'd said was his besotted look.

"How did you two happen to meet?" Maryanne Atwater asked nonchalantly.

"Ah…" Dianne's mind spun, lost in a haze of half-truths and misconceptions. She didn't know if she dared repeat the story about meeting in the local grocery, but she couldn't think fast enough to come up with anything else. She thought she was prepared, but the moment she was in the spotlight, all her resolve deserted her.

"We both happened to be in the market at the same time," Steve explained smoothly. The story had been repeated so many times it was beginning to sound like the truth.

"I was blocking Steve's way in the frozen-food section," she said, picking up his version of the story. She felt embarrassed seeing the three other couples listening so intently to the fabrication.

"I asked Dianne to kindly move her cart, and she stopped to apologize for being so thoughtless. Before I knew it, we'd struck up a conversation."

"I was there!" Louise Lester threw her hands wildly into the air, her blue eyes shining. "That was the two of you? I saw the whole thing!" She dabbed the corners of her mouth with her napkin and checked to be sure she had everyone's attention before continuing. "I swear it was the most romantic thing I've ever seen."

"It certainly was," Steve added smiling over at Dianne, who restrained herself from kicking him in the shin, although it was exactly what he deserved.

"Steve's cart inadvertently bumped into Dianne's," Louise continued, grinning broadly at Steve.

"Inadvertently, Steve?" Sam Horton teased, chuckling loud enough to attract attention. Crazy though it was, it seemed that everyone in the entire community center had stopped eating in order to hear Louise tell her story.

"At any rate," Louise went on, "the two of them stopped to chat, and I swear it was like watching something out of a romantic comedy. Naturally

Dianne apologized—she hadn't realized she was blocking the aisle. Then Steve started sorting through the items in her cart, teasing her. We all know how Steve enjoys kidding around.''

The others shook their heads, their affection for their friend obvious.

"She was buying all these diet dinners," Steve supplied, ignoring Dianne's glare. "I told her she couldn't possibly be buying those for herself."

The three women at the table sighed audibly. It was all Dianne could do not to slide off her chair and slip under the table.

"That's not the best part," Louise said, beaming with pride at the attention she was garnering. A dreamy look stole over her features. "They must have stood and talked for ages. I'd finished my shopping and just happened to stroll past them several minutes later, and they were still there. It was when I was standing in the checkout line that I noticed them coming down the aisle side by side, each pushing a grocery cart. It was so cute, I half expected someone to start playing a violin."

"How sweet," Renée Horton whispered.

"I thought so myself and mentioned it to Larry once I arrived home. Remember, honey?"

Larry nodded obligingly. "Louise must have told me that story two or three times that night," her husband reported.

"I just didn't realize that was you, Steve. Just imagine, out of all the people to run into the grocery and I just happen to stumble upon you and Dianne the first time you met. Life is so ironic, isn't it?''

"Oh, yes, life is very ironic," Dianne answered softly. Steve shared a subtle smile with her, and she couldn't hold one back herself.

"It was one of the most beautiful things I've ever seen," Louise finished.

"CAN YOU BELIEVE that Louise Lester?" Steve said later. They were sitting in his luxury sedan waiting for their turn to pull out of the crowded parking lot.

"No," Dianne said simply. She'd managed to make it through the rest of the dinner, but it had demanded every ounce of poise and self-control she possessed. From the moment they'd walked in the front door until the time Steve helped her put on her wool coat at the end of the evening, they'd been the center of attention. And the main topic of conversation.

Like a bumblebee visiting a flower garden, Louise Lester had breezed from one dinner table to the next spreading the story of how Dianne and Steve had met and how she'd been there to witness every detail.

"I've never been so..." Dianne couldn't think of a word that quite described how she'd felt. "This may well have been the worst evening of my life." She slumped against the back of the seat and covered her eyes.

"I thought you had a good time."

"How could I?" she cried, dropping her hand long enough to glare at him. "The first thing I get hit with is that you're some rich playboy."

"Come on, Dianne. Just because I happen to own a business doesn't mean I'm rolling in money."

"Port Blossom Towing is one of the fastest-growing enterprises in Kitsap County," she said, repeating what Sam Horton had been happy to tell her. "What I don't understand is why my mother hasn't ever heard of you. She's been on the lookout for eligible men for months. It's something of a miracle she didn't—" Dianne stopped abruptly, pinching her lips together.

"What?" Steve pressed.

"My mother was looking, all right, but she was realistic enough to stay within my own social realm. You're a major-league player. The only men my mother knows are in the minors—butchers, teachers, everyday sort of guys."

Now that she thought about it, however, her mother had seemed to recognize Steve's name when Dianne had first mentioned it. She probably *had* heard of him, but couldn't remember from where.

"Major-league player? That's a ridiculous analogy."

"It isn't. And to think I approached you, offering you money to take me to this dinner." She stiffened, as humiliation washed over her again, then gradually she relaxed. "One thing I want to know—why you didn't already have a date." The dinner had been only five days away, and surely the most eligible bachelor in town, a man who could have his choice of women, would have had a date!

"Simple. I didn't have a sweetheart."

"I bet you got a good laugh over my offering to pay you to escort me." Not to mention the fact she'd made such a fuss over his owning a proper suit.

"As a matter of fact, I was flattered."

"No doubt."

"Are you still upset about that?"

"You could say that, yes." *Upset* was putting it mildly.

Since Dianne's house was only a couple of miles from the community center, she reached for her purse and checkbook. She waited until he pulled into the driveway and stopped, before writing out a check and handing it to him.

"What's this?" Steve asked.

"What I owe you. Since I didn't know the exact cost of Jill's stuffed animal, I made an educated guess. The cost of the roses varies from shop to shop so I took an average price."

"I don't think you should pay me until the evening is over," he said, opening his car door.

As far as Dianne was concerned it had been over the minute she'd learned who he was. When he came around to her side of the car and opened her door, she said, "Just what are you planning now?" He led her by the hand to the front of the garage, which was illuminated by a floodlight. They stood facing each other, his hands braced on her shoulders.

She frowned, gazing up at him. "I'm fully intending to give you your money's worth," he replied.

"I beg your pardon?"

"Jason, Jill and your mother."

"What about them?"

"They're peering out the front window waiting for me to kiss you, and I'm not about to disappoint any of them."

"Oh, no, you don't," she objected. But the moment his eyes held hers, all her anger drained away. Then, slowly, as though he recognized the change in her, he lowered his head. Dianne knew he was going to kiss her, and at the same instant she knew she wasn't going to do anything to stop him....

Chapter Nine

"YOU HAVE THE CHECK?" Dianne asked once her head was clear enough for her to think again. It was a struggle to pull herself free from the magic Steve wove so easily around her heart.

Steve pulled the check she'd written from his suit pocket. Then, without ceremony, he tore it in two. "I never intended to accept a penny."

"You have to! We agreed—"

"I want to see you again," he announced, gripping her shoulders firmly and looking intently at her.

Dianne was struck dumb. If he had announced he was an alien, visiting from the planet Mars, he couldn't have surprised her more. Not knowing what to say, she eyed him speculatively. "You're kidding, aren't you?"

A smile flitted across his lips as though he'd anticipated her reaction. The left side of his mouth canted slightly higher in that lazy, off-center grin of his. "I've never been more serious in my life."

Now that the shock had worn off, it took Dianne all of one second to decide. "Naturally, I'm flattered—but no."

"No?" Steve was clearly taken aback, and it took him a second or two to compose himself. "Why not?"

"You mean after tonight you need to ask?"

"Apparently so," he said, stepping away from her a little. He paused and shoved his fingers through his hair with enough force to make Dianne flinch. "I can't believe you," he muttered. "The first time we kissed I realized we had something special. I thought you felt it, too."

Dianne couldn't deny it, but she wasn't about to admit it, either. She lowered her gaze, refusing to meet the hungry intensity of his eyes.

When she didn't respond, Steve continued, "I have no intention of letting you out of my life. In case you haven't figured it out yet, and obviously you haven't, I'm crazy about you, Dianne."

Unexpected tears clouded her vision as her gaze briefly shot up to his. She rubbed the heels of her hands against her eyes and sniffled. This wasn't supposed to be happening. She wanted the break with him to be clean and final. No discussion. No tears.

Steve was handsome and ambitious, intelligent and charming. If anyone deserved an SYT it was this oh-so-eligible bachelor. She'd been married, and her life was complicated by two children and a manipulating mother.

"Say something," he demanded. "Don't just stand there looking at me with tears in your eyes."

"Th-these aren't tears. They're..." Dianne couldn't finish as fresh tears scalded her eyes.

"Tomorrow afternoon," he offered, his voice gentling, "I'll stop by the house, and you and the kids and I can all go to a movie. You can bring your mother along, too, if you want."

Dianne managed to swallow a sob. She held out her hand, scolding him with her index finger. "That's the lowest, meanest thing you've ever suggested."

His brow folded into a frown. "Taking you and the kids to a movie?"

"Y-yes. You're using my own children against me and that's—"

"Low and mean," he finished, scowling more fiercely. "All right, if you don't want to involve Jason and Jill, then just the two of us will go."

"I already said no."

"Why?"

Her shoulders trembled slightly as she smeared the moisture across her cheek. "I'm divorced." She said it as if it had been a well-kept secret and no one but her mother and children were aware of it.

"So?" He was still scowling.

"I have children."

"I know that, too. You're not making a lot of sense, Dianne."

"It's not that—exactly. You can date any woman you want."

"I want to date you."

"No!" She was trembling from the inside out. She tried to compose herself, but it was hopeless with Steve standing so close, looking as though he was going to reach for her and kiss her again.

When she was reasonably sure she wouldn't crumble under the force of her fascination with him, she looked him in the eye. "I'm flattered, really I am, but it wouldn't work."

"You don't know that."

"But I do, I do. We're not even in the same league, you and I, and this whole thing has got completely out of hand." She stood a little straighter as though the extra inch in height would help. "The deal was I pay you to escort me to the Valentine's dinner, but then I had to go complicate matters by suggesting you look smitten with me and you did such a good job of it that you've convinced yourself you're attracted to me and you aren't, you couldn't be."

"Because you're divorced and have two children," he repeated incredulously.

"You're forgetting about my manipulating mother."

Steve clenched his fists at his sides. "I haven't forgotten her. In fact, I'm grateful to her."

Dianne narrowed her eyes. "Now I know you can't be serious."

"Your mother's a real kick, and your kids are great, and in case you're completely blind, I think you're pretty wonderful yourself."

Dianne's finger fumbled with the pearls at her neck, twisting the strand between her fingers. The man who stood before her was every woman's dream, but she didn't know what was right anymore. She knew only one thing. After the way he'd humiliated her this evening, after the way he'd let her actually pay him to take her to this dinner, make a total fool of herself, there was no chance she could continue to see him.

"I don't think so," she said stiffly. "Goodbye, Steve."

"You really mean it, don't you?"

She was already halfway to the front door. "Yes."

"All right. Fine," he said, slicing the air with his hands. "If this is the way you want it, then fine, just fine." With that he stormed off to his car.

DIANNE KNEW that her family would give her all kinds of flack. The minute she walked in the door, Jason and Jill barraged her with questions about the dinner. Dianne was as vague as possible and walked up the stairs to her room, pleading exhaustion. There must have been something in her eyes that convinced her mother and children to leave her alone, because no one disturbed her again that night.

She awoke early the next morning, feeling more than a little out of sorts. Jason was already up, eating a huge bowl of cornflakes at the kitchen table.

"Well," he said, when Dianne walked into the kitchen, "when are you going to see Steve again?"

"Ah, I don't know." She put on a pot of coffee, doing her best to shove every thought of her dinner companion from her mind. And not succeeding.

"He wants to go out on another date with you, doesn't he?"

"Ah, I'm not sure."

"You're not sure?" Jason demanded. "How come? I saw you two get mushy last night. I like Steve, he's fun."

"Yes, I know," she said, standing in front of the coffee machine while the liquid dripped into the glass pot. Her back was to her son. "Let's give it some time. See how things work out," she mumbled.

To Dianne's relief, her son seemed to accept that and he didn't question her further. That wasn't the case, however, later that same day, with her mother.

"So talk to your mother," Martha insisted, working her crochet hook as she sat in the living room with Dianne. "All day you've been quiet."

"No, I haven't." Dianne didn't know why she denied it. Her mother was right, she had been introspective.

"The phone isn't ringing. The phone should be ringing."

"Why's that?"

"Steve. He met your mother, he met your children, he took you out to dinner..."

"You make it sound like we should be discussing wedding plans." Dianne had intended to be flippant, but the look her mother gave her suggested she shouldn't joke over something so sacred.

"When are you seeing him again?" Her mother tugged on her ball of yarn when Dianne didn't immediately respond, as if that might bring forth a response.

"We're both going to be busy for the next few days."

"Busy? You're going to let busy stand in the way of love?"

Dianne ignored the question. It was easier that way. Her mother plied her with questions on and off again for the rest of the day, but after repeated attempts to get something more out of her daughter and not succeeding, Martha reluctantly let the matter drop.

THREE DAYS after the Valentine's dinner, Dianne was shopping after work at a grocery store on the other side of town—she avoiding going anywhere near the one around which she and Steve had fabricated their story—when she ran into Betty Martin.

"Dianne," Betty called, racing down the aisle after her. Darn, thought Dianne. The last person she wanted to chitchat with was Betty, who was certain to be filled with questions about her and Steve.

She was.

"I've been meaning to phone you all week,"

Betty said, her smile so sweet Dianne felt as if she'd stepped into a vat of honey.

"Hello, Betty." She made a pretense of scanning the grocery shelf until she realized she was standing in front of the disposable-diaper section. She jerked away as though she'd been burned.

Betty's gaze followed Dianne's. "You know, you're not too old to have more children," she said. "What are you? Thirty-three, thirty-four?"

"Around that."

"If Steve wanted children you could—"

"I have no intention of marrying Steve Creighton," Dianne answered testily. "We're nothing more than friends."

Betty arched her eyebrows. "My dear girl, that's not what I've heard. Why, all of Port Blossom is buzzing with talk about you two. Steve's been such an elusive bachelor. He dates often, or so I've heard, but from what everyone is saying, and I do mean everyone, you've got him hooked. Why, the way he was looking at you Saturday night was enough to bring tears to my eyes. I don't know what you did to that man, but he's yours for the asking."

"I'm sure you're mistaken." Dianne couldn't very well announce she'd paid Steve to look besotted. He'd done such a good job of it that he'd convinced himself and everyone else he was head over heels in love with her.

Betty grinned. "I don't think so."

As quickly as she could, Dianne made her excuses, paid for her groceries and hurried home. Home, she soon discovered wasn't exactly a haven. Jason and Jill were waiting for her, and it wasn't because they were eager to carry in the grocery sacks.

"It's been three days," Jill said. "Shouldn't you have heard from Steve by now?"

"If he doesn't phone you, then you should call him," Jason insisted. "Girls do that sort of thing all the time now, no matter what Grandma says."

"I…" Dianne looked for an escape. Of course there wasn't one.

"Here's his card," Jason said, taking it from the corner of the bulletin board. "Call him."

Dianne stared at the raised red lettering. Port Blossom Towing, it said, with the phone number in large numbers below. In the corner, in smaller, less-pronounced lettering was Steve's name, followed with one simple word: owner.

Dianne's heart plummeted and she closed her eyes. He'd really meant it when he'd said he had never intentionally misled her. He assumed she knew, and with good reason. The business card he'd given her spelled it out, only she hadn't noticed.

"Mom." Jason's voice fragmented her introspection.

She opened her eyes to see her son and daughter staring up at her, their young eyes, so like her own, intent and worried.

"What are you going to do?" Jill wanted to know.

"W.A.R."

"Aerobics?" Jason said. "What for?"

"I need it," Dianne answered. And she did. Dianne had discovered long ago that when something was weighing on her, heavy-duty exercise helped considerably. It cleared her mind. She didn't enjoy it exactly; pain rarely thrilled her. But the aerobic classes at the community center had seen her through more than one emotional trauma. If she hurried, she could be there for the last session of the afternoon.

"Kids, put those groceries away for me, will you?" she said, heading for the stairs, ripping the sweater over her head as she raced. The buttons to her blouse were too time-consuming, so she peeled that over her head the moment she entered the bedroom, closing the door with her foot.

Within five minutes flat she'd changed into her leotard, kissed the kids and was out the door. She had a small attack of guilt when she pulled out of the driveway and glanced back to see both her children standing on the porch looking decidedly woebegone.

The warm-up exercises had already begun when Dianne joined the class. For the next hour she leapt, kicked, bent and stretched, doing her best to keep up with everyone else. By the end of the session, she was exhausted—and no closer to deciding whether or not to phone Steve.

With a towel draped around her neck, she walked out to her car. Her cardiovascular system might have been fine, but nothing else about her was. She searched through her purse for her keys and then her coat pocket.

Nothing.

Dread filled her. Cupping the sides of her face with her hands, she peered inside the car. There, innocently poking out of the ignition, were her keys.

Chapter Ten

"JASON," DIANNE SAID, closing her eyes in thanks that it was her son who had answered the phone and not Jill. Her daughter would have plied her with questions and more advice than "Dear Abby."

"Hi, Mom. I thought you were at aerobics."

"I am, and may be here a whole lot longer if you can't help me out." Without a pause, she continued, "I need you to go upstairs, look in my underwear drawer and bring me the extra set of keys to my car."

"They're in your underwear drawer?"

"Yes." It was the desperate plan of a desperate woman. She didn't dare contact the auto club this time for fear they'd send Port Blossom Towing to the rescue in the form of one Steve Creighton.

"You don't honestly expect me to sort through your, uh, stuff, do you?"

"Jason, listen to me, I've locked my keys in my car, and I don't have any other choice."

"You locked your keys in the car? Again? What's with you lately, Mom?"

"Do we need to go through all this now?" she demanded. Jason wasn't saying anything she hadn't already said to herself a hundred times over the past few minutes. She was so agitated it was a struggle not to break down and weep.

"I'll have Jill get the keys for me," Jason agreed, with a sigh that told her it demanded a good deal of effort, not to mention fortitude, for him to comply with this request.

"Great. Thanks." Dianne breathed out in relief. "Okay. Now the next thing you need to do is get your bicycle out of the garage and ride it down to the community center."

"You mean you want me to *bring* you the keys?"

"Yes."

"But it's raining!"

"It's only drizzling." True, but as a general rule Dianne didn't like her son riding his bike in the winter.

"But it's getting dark," Jason protested next.

That was something that did concern Dianne. "Okay, you're right. In that case, the best thing to do is call Grandma and ask her to stop off and get the keys from you and then have her bring them to me."

"You want me to call Grandma?"

"Jason, are you hard of hearing? Yes, I want you to call Grandma, and if you can't reach her, phone me back here at the community center. I'll be waiting by the phone." She read off the number for him. "And listen, if my car keys aren't in my underwear drawer, have Grandma bring me a wire clothes hanger, okay?"

He hesitated. "All right," he said after another burdened sigh. "Are you sure you're all right, Mom?"

"Of course I'm sure." But she was going to remember his attitude the next time he needed her to go on a Boy Scout camp-out with him.

Jason seemed to take an eternity to do as she'd asked. Since the front desk was now busy with the after-work crowd, Dianne didn't want to trouble the staff for the phone a second time to find out what was keeping her son.

Forty minutes after Dianne's aerobic class was over, she was still pacing the foyer of the community center, stopping every now and again to glance outside. Then, on one such glance she saw a big red tow truck turn into the parking lot.

She didn't need to be psychic to know that the man driving the truck was Steve.

Mumbling a curse under her breath, Dianne walked out into the parking lot to confront him.

Steve was standing alongside her car when she approached. She noticed that he wasn't wearing the gray-striped coveralls he'd worn the first time they'd met. Now he was dressed in slacks and a sweater, as though he'd come from the office.

"What are you doing here?" The best defense was a good offense, or so her high-school basketball coach had advised her about a hundred years ago.

"Jason called me," he said, without looking at her.

"The turncoat," Dianne muttered.

"He said something about refusing to search through your underwear and his grandmother couldn't be reached. And that all this has something to do with you going off to war."

Although Steve was speaking in an even voice, it was clear he found this situation comical.

"W.A.R. is my aerobics class," Dianne explained stiffly. "You don't need to look so concerned—I haven't volunteered for the French Foreign Legion."

"I'm glad to hear it." He walked around to the passenger-side door of the tow truck and brought out the instrument he'd used to open her door the first time. "So," he said leaning against the side of her compact. "How have you been?"

"Fine."

"You don't look so good, but then I suppose that's because you're a divorced woman with two children and a manipulating mother."

Naturally he'd taunt her with that. "How kind of you to say so," she returned with an equal dose of sarcasm.

"So how's Jerome?"

"Jerome?"

"The butcher your mother wanted to set you up with," he answered gruffly. "I figured by now the two of you would have gone out once, maybe a couple of times." His words had a biting edge.

"I'm not seeing Jerome." The thought of having to eat blood sausage was enough to turn her stomach.

"I'm surprised," he returned. "I'd have thought you'd leap at the opportunity to date someone other than me."

"If I wasn't interested in him before, what makes you think I'd go out with him now? And why aren't you opening my door? That's what you're here for, isn't it?"

He ignored her question. "Frankly, Dianne, we can't go on meeting like this."

"Funny, very funny." She crossed her arms defiantly.

"Actually I really came here to talk some sense into you," he said after a moment.

"According to my mother you won't have any chance of succeeding. I'm hopeless."

"I don't believe that. Otherwise I wouldn't be here." He walked over to her and gently placed his hands on her shoulders. "Maybe, Dianne, you've been fine these past couple of days, but frankly I've been a wreck."

"You have?" As Dianne looked at him she thought she'd drown in his eyes. And when he smiled, it was all she could do not to cry.

"I've never met a more stubborn woman in my life."

She blushed. "I'm awful, I know."

His gaze became more intent as he asked, "How about if we go someplace and talk?"

"I...think that would be all right." At the moment there was little she could refuse him. Until he'd arrived she'd had no idea what to do about the situation between them. Now the answer was becoming clear....

"You might want to call Jason and Jill and tell them."

"Oh, right, I should." How could she have forgotten her own children? She began heading for the building.

Steve stopped her. He was grinning from ear to ear. "Don't worry, I already took care of that. While I was at it, I phoned your mother, too. She's on her way to your house now. She'll make the kids' dinner." He paused, then said, "I figured if I was fortunate enough I might be able to talk you into having dinner with me. I understand Walker's has an excellent seafood salad."

If he was fortunate enough he might be able to talk her into having dinner with him? Dianne felt like weeping. Steve Creighton was the sweetest, kindest, handsomest man she'd ever met, and *he* was looking at *her* as if he was the one who should be counting his blessings.

Steve promptly opened her car door. "I'm going to buy you a magnetic key attachment for keeping a spare key under your bumper so this doesn't happen again."

"You are?"

"Yes, otherwise I'm going to worry about you."

No one had ever worried about her, except her immediate family. Whatever situation arose, she handled it. Broken water pipes, lost checks, a leaky roof—nothing had ever defeated her. Not even Jack had been able to break her spirit, but one kind smile from Steve Creighton and she was a puddle of emotions. She blinked back tears and made a mess of thanking him, rushing her words so that they tumbled over each other.

"Dianne?"

She stopped and bit her lower lip. "Yes?"

"Either we go to the restaurant now and talk, or I'm going to kiss you right here in this parking lot."

Despite everything, she was able to smile. "It wouldn't be the first time."

"No, but I doubt I'd be content with one kiss."

She lowered her lashes, thinking she probably wouldn't be, either. "I'll meet you at Walker's."

He followed her across town, which took less than five minutes, and pulled into the empty parking slot next to hers. Once inside the restaurant, they were seated immediately at a table next to a window overlooking Sinclair Inlet.

Dianne had just picked up her menu when Steve said, "I'd like to tell you a story."

"Okay," she said, puzzled. She put aside the menu. Deciding what to eat took second place to listening to Steve.

"It's about a woman who first attracted the attention of a particular man at the community center about two months ago."

Dianne picked up her water and took a sip, her eyes meeting his above the glass, her heart thumping loudly in her ears. "Yes…"

"This certain lady was oblivious to certain facts."

"Such as?" Dianne prompted.

"First of all, she didn't seem to have a clue how attractive she was or how much this guy admired her. He did everything but stand on his head to attract her attention, but nothing worked."

"What exactly did he try?"

"Working out the same hours as she did, pumping iron—and looking exceptionally good in his T-shirt and shorts."

"Why didn't this man say something to…this woman?"

Steve chuckled. "Well, you see, he was accustomed to women giving him plenty of attention. So this particular one dented his pride by ignoring him, then she made him downright angry. Finally it occurred to him that she wasn't *purposely* ignoring him—she simply wasn't aware of him."

"It seems to me this man is rather arrogant."

"I couldn't agree with you more."

"You couldn't?" Dianne was surprised.

"That was when he decided there were plenty of other fish in the sea and he didn't need a pretty divorcée with two children—he'd asked around about her and so knew a few details like that."

Dianne smoothed the pink linen napkin across her lap. "What happened next?"

"He was sitting in his office one evening. The day had been busy and one of his men had phoned in sick, so he'd been out on the road all afternoon.

He was feeling more than ready to go home and take a hot shower. Just about then the phone rang. One of the night crew answered it and it was the auto club. Apparently some lady had locked her keys in her car at the community center and needed someone to come rescue her.''

"So you, I mean, this man volunteered?''

"That he did, never dreaming she'd practically throw herself in his arms. And not because he'd unlocked her car, either, but because she was desperate for someone to take her to the Valentine's dinner.''

"That part about her falling into your arms is a slight exaggeration,'' Dianne felt obliged to tell him.

"Maybe so, but it was the first time a woman had ever offered to pay him to take her out. Which was the most ironic part of this entire tale. For weeks he'd been trying to gain this woman's attention, practically killing himself to impress her with the amount of weight he was lifting. It seemed every woman in town was impressed except the one who mattered.''

"Did you ever stop to think that was the very reason he found her so attractive? If she ignored him, then he must have considered her something of a challenge.''

"Yes, he thought about that a lot. But only after he met her and kissed her he realized that his instincts had been right from the first. He was going to fall in love with this woman.''

"He was?" Dianne's voice was little more than a hoarse whisper.

"That's the second part of the story."

"The second part?" Dianne was growing confused.

"The happily-ever-after part."

Dianne used her napkin to wipe away the tears, which had suddenly welled up in her eyes again. "He can't possibly know that."

Steve smiled then, that wonderful carefree, vagabond smile of his, the smile that never failed to lift her heart. "Wrong. He's known that for a good long while. All he needs to do now is convince her."

Sniffing, Dianne said, "I have the strangest sensation that this woman has real trouble recognizing a prince when she sees one. For a good portion of her life, she was satisfied with keeping a frog happy."

"And now?"

"And now she's...I'm ready to discover what happily-ever-after is all about."

MOM AND
MR. VALENTINE

Judith Bowen

CHAPTER ONE

"GOD BLESS MOMMY and Daddy-in-heaven and Poppa and Nana and Grandma and also Grandpa Dan and Coach Milfort and Boxer and Trev and Mr. Valentine and, please God, make Mr. Valentine help coach the Ravens 'cause we need him bad...."

Lisa smiled and smoothed back the cowlick on her son's damp forehead. He was screwing up his face, eyes tightly closed, in his fervent plea to the Almighty. His little eight-year-old hands—fingernails none too clean, she noted, despite the bath—were clasped over his chest.

Lisa wondered how he got any sleep at night. He was wearing his favorite Vancouver Canucks PJ's with the duvet pulled up to his chin. Every other inch of the bed had an item of hockey equipment jammed onto it, including the new goalie equipment he'd received for Christmas—pads, gloves, even his helmet next to his pillow. She hoped it was just a stage he was going through.

Boxer, the unfortunately named dog of the same breed—an SPCA rescue—lay quietly in her basket by the door. Lisa suspected that the one small clear space at the end of the bed, near Tim's legs, was reserved for Boxer, and the second Lisa left the bedroom, that was exactly where the dog would be.

"Who's Mr. Valentine, honey?" Lisa asked as she bent to drop a good-night kiss on her son's cheek.

His blue eyes were huge. "*You* know Mr. Valentine, Mom. You've seen him on TV. He's really Patrick McCarthy. *You* know *him*, Mom, he's the best player on the Canucks! Wham! Bam!" Her son made some knock-'em, sock-'em gestures under the covers.

"Oh, yes." Lisa grimaced and smoothed his duvet over his chest. "*That* Mr. Valentine. Now, you go straight to sleep. Big field trip tomorrow, remember?"

Her son reached up and squeezed her around her neck.

"'Night, Mom," he whispered, with the crooked grin she knew so well. So like his father, sometimes, it broke her heart.

Ah, *that* Mr. Valentine. She'd seen him on television many times. Patrick McCarthy was a big, tough winger on Tim's favorite NHL hockey team. He was what they called an "enforcer," a physical player whose job it was to "protect" the star scorers. Tim and his buddy, Trevor, never missed a game on television.

Lisa gathered up an armful of laundry and left Tim's room, quietly closing the door behind her. The Mr. Valentine part? She'd seen the advertising.

It was something to do with the Canucks raising money for a good cause. Children's Hospital, she thought. "Mr. Valentine" was a hockey player designated each February to be some lucky lady's Valentine date, the result of a draw, tickets twenty bucks apiece. She'd seen McCarthy's face on billboards and posters promoting the event. *Lucky?* She supposed some women were attracted to the type. Sporty women. The same women, maybe, who loved WWF wrestling.

Not her.

Lisa frowned as she stuffed clothes into the washer. *Hero worship, that's all it is.* Tim would grow out of it. She did her best to be both mom and dad to her son, but sometimes it was hard to know if she was succeeding.

Since they'd moved to White Rock in October, Tim had lived, breathed and slept hockey—witness his room. He'd begged her to sign him up for the local Atom team and after he'd made goalie, she'd heard of nothing else. He'd asked Santa for goalie pads for Christmas, and he was saving up his allowance so he and Trevor could go to a real hockey game at GM Place someday. When he wasn't on skates or in school, he and his friends, a motley crew of boys and girls ranging from Tim's age to young teenagers, played road hockey nearly every afternoon in the parking lot of their condo development, to the chagrin of some of the neighbors.

Thank heaven his schoolwork wasn't suffering.

Not that they had much homework in Grade Two. She'd met with Mrs. Shepherd just last week, and the motherly, gray-haired woman had said that Tim was doing well for someone who'd transferred partway through the school year. His reading skills were sound, she'd said, he had plenty of friends and he seemed to have been blessed with a robust imagination. Lisa worried briefly—was that school code for *tells lies?*

Imagination! He had plenty of that, all right, as long as it involved hockey.

"GOT YOUR RAIN JACKET, just in case?" Lisa glanced out the kitchen window as she deposited her plate and cutlery in the dishwasher. It looked like rain. Of course, at the end of January, almost every day looked like rain here on the West Coast.

"In my backpack," Tim replied, without raising his eyes from his bowl of Froot Loops. "The Enforcer might help coach our team, Mom!"

"Your phone money?" Lisa always made sure her son had two dollars in quarters for phone calls. So far, she hadn't sprung for the extra expense of a cell phone but realized more and more how handy it would be to have one, especially when she had to make unexpected changes in the arrangements for Tim's care. What she would've done without Dan Kristofferson next door, she didn't know. Dan was Tim's best friend's grandfather, and her son called him Grandpa Dan, just as Trevor did.

"Yeah," he said, looking up at her. "Did you hear me, Mom? The Enforcer—" here Tim put down his spoon and eagerly punched the air, with several bam! boom! sounds to go along with it "—might help coach our team, Mom. Isn't that great?"

"Yes, that's great, honey," Lisa murmured, frowning despite herself. Mrs. Shepherd's reference to her son's robust imagination was a little too accurate. It was beginning to worry Lisa. Now he'd invented the scenario of a professional hockey player coming out to White Rock to help coach his Atom team! "Finish up, honey. I want to leave in about five minutes."

She made Tim's bed quickly and checked her appearance in the mirrored closet door one more time, brushing her hand over the trim lines of her navy skirt. Lint? Didn't see any. Her freshly ironed white cotton blouse and navy sweater looked professional. Yesterday she'd worn a red turtleneck and vest with the same skirt. She didn't have a huge wardrobe; everything she bought, almost always on sale, had to mix and match.

"Okay?" Lisa grabbed her purse, car keys and plain beige trenchcoat. Sometimes she yearned to put on something that wasn't sensible at all. Something flamboyant. Fun. Impractical. Expensive.

Something that wasn't navy or beige.

Tim knelt, both arms around Boxer, indulging in his usual prolonged goodbye, while Boxer whined and "kissed" his cheek enthusiastically, her stubby back end wagging fiercely. What a dog. You couldn't help being totally charmed by the irrepressible boxer personality—and at the same time feel totally exasperated by the exact same personality. Eagerness, enthusiasm, endless affection, nicely balanced with plenty of slobber and unlimited energy.

Not to mention absolutely no aptitude for learning even the simplest command, like "sit!" Lisa knew she had to take action. Check out doggie school, perhaps. Someone at work had told her that consistency was the key, ten-minute sessions repeated several times a day, but where did she have those minutes except on weekends?

After dropping Tim off, Lisa had a fifteen-minute trip to South Langley, where her employer was located. She enjoyed the drive. Green fields in the dead of winter, ducks and geese, and those wonderful long-necked, black-beaked swans, drifting like powder puffs in the water-filled ditches or grazing in fields. The trumpeters overwintered here, before going south in the summer, and many Canada geese stayed year-round.

This little corner of British Columbia was beginning to feel like home. Moving to their beautiful, affordable condominium in White Rock from Toronto last fall was their last move, she vowed. What could be better? Only four blocks from the sea. A mild damp winter, which was an agreeable change from snow. Close to shopping and on a bus route.

Two bedrooms, a huge patio, even a laundry room. Her in-laws, bless them, had helped her with a down payment and now it was up to her. A new life.

She was determined to make it happen. The job she'd landed with the South Langley construction firm, Shitako Homes, was a good start. It made the hard slog of the past few years worthwhile. She'd been a single mother, widowed at twenty-one with a new baby, living on insurance money at first and then with her in-laws. She'd gone to school part-time to get her certified general accountancy qualifications, and she'd worked part-time taking care of plants every spring and summer at a nursery, saving every penny.... It hadn't been easy.

But all that had changed. She wasn't even lonely anymore, she'd decided. Now she had a dog with no discernible manners to train, a son who needed her to go with him to practices and games, and extra tax-preparation work, which meant welcome extra dollars. With all of that, Lisa was too busy to worry about meeting someone to share her life.

Lydia Lane, her friend in Toronto who'd been a real support through the hell of the past seven years, thought she should be dating. Lydia said all work and no play made for a very dull girl and Dave had been gone a lot of years and it was high time. Perhaps so, but that was easy for Lydia to say, a single woman with no dependents and a great job.

Dull? If that was true, dull was just fine with Lisa Hudson. Dating was...well, risky. And time-consuming. She didn't know anyone in Vancouver or White Rock, beyond the people at work and Dan Kristofferson next door and he had to be about a hundred and ten! Well, seventy at least. Hardly the sort who was in a position to introduce her to suitable younger men.

Had she remembered to put a note in Tim's backpack asking Dan to take him to his seven o'clock hockey practice? She was planning to stay late today.

Grandpa Dan—everyone called him that—was her lifesaver. He was a retired train engineer, a widower, who lived right next door and baby-sat regularly for his son and daughter-in-law, both of whom worked, so he was generally available to pick up his grandson, Trevor, and Tim after school. Not only that, he didn't mind taking her son to practices and even games if Lisa couldn't make it. Lisa paid him for the after-school care, plus the meals he fed her son. The arrangement was ideal.

She called Dan from work, suspecting she had, in fact, forgotten to put a note in Tim's pack. No answer, which worried her a little. Finally, on the third call, she left a message and asked him to leave *her* a message if he couldn't make it. He was probably out getting groceries or taking back a video.

She checked her answering machine at four o'clock and there was no message from Dan. That was a relief. It must've worked out or Tim would have called her himself from either school or the condo. He had a key—as did Grandpa Dan, who also walked Boxer most days around noon—and strict instructions to inform her of any change in their agreed-upon plans or general daily routine. Tim had always been good about that.

When she got home at eight-thirty, he was there, watching television. All the doors to the condo were locked, in accordance with their family rules.

"Have a good practice, hon?" she asked after she'd changed into jeans and a T-shirt and was rummaging through the fridge for some of yesterday's casserole. She was hungry, and Tim would have eaten at Dan's place. If Lydia could see her now— with her carefully organized and regulated life, right down to the casseroles she prepared on the weekend and froze, labelled Monday, Tuesday and Thursday. Wednesday they had fresh chicken or fish and on Friday they often splurged on takeout.

"Yep, and guess what, Mom?" Tim's eyes were shining. "We're gonna have The Enforcer coaching our team! I guess that's gonna scare the Vipers all to heck." The Vipers, another Atom team from nearby Newton, were the nemesis of Tim and Trevor's team.

"The Enforcer?" She caught her son's eye and smiled slightly, inviting him to come clean. It was one thing to be swept up in this childish hero worship. It was quite another to be telling her—and probably other people, like Mrs. Shepherd—that you knew this Canucks player personally, that he was going to be coaching your pip-squeak hockey team, for heaven's sake!

Tim's face grew serious. ''Well, he says I should call him Patrick 'cause that's his name, but me 'n' Trev like calling him The Enforcer 'cause that's what he is!'' At these words, Tim amused himself with his usual feinting and dodging and air-punching, all the way back to the television in the living room. He flung himself onto the carpet and was immediately joined by Boxer, who grabbed the heel of one of his socks and started growling and pulling frantically, like some demented terrier. Tim giggled and kicked his feet and Boxer barked madly.

Oh, what would the neighbors say? Lisa threw an aggrieved look at the ceiling and put a plate of left-over casserole into the microwave. She set the timer for thirty minutes.

One thing was certain. This garbage about the hockey player had gone too far. Lisa wasn't sure what she should do—confront the boy directly? She wished she had someone to ask. Maybe she'd talk to Dan; he'd raised a family. Trevor might be as caught up in this as Tim was. Should she deflate her son's fantasy by insisting he introduce her to the new ''coach''? That seemed cruel.

That night, after Tim had gone to bed, surrounded as usual by all his sports paraphernalia, Lisa went through his backpack, as she did about once a week. There was his partly eaten lunch from that day, along with the note she'd written to Dan, which, obviously, he hadn't passed on. Good thing she'd phoned. There was a half-eaten apple and a rather poisonous-looking banana from a day or two before that. Yech.

She found a few wrinkled papers that had come from the school—forms for immunization permission, a flyer about a fund-raiser to be held in February and a receipt for a donation Lisa had made to a school library project before Christmas. She sighed. Generally, Tim was good about giving her the various notes and papers sent home from school. The hockey obsession had made him distracted and careless.

One last note, folded several times and soiled with food and juice stains wasn't one she recalled writing. Double yech. Lisa unfolded it gingerly.

From Dan? How long had this been in there? Lisa read hurriedly:

Called away to a family emergency in Ontario. Good buddy taking over for me here while I'm gone. No problem. He'll do school pick-up, walk Boxer, take boys to practice. Left you a message, but wanted to pass this along, too. Just in case. Yours, Dan K.

Just in case! A perfect stranger had been picking up her son from school, walking her dog and taking Tim to practice! For how long?

Lisa fumbled with her sneakers, finally stepping down the backs in her anxiety. This wasn't the first time Tim had accidentally deleted messages. She wrenched open the door and locked it carefully behind her before hurrying to her neighbor's place. The condos were linked by a covered outdoor walkway. She hammered on 15A. The outside spotlight came on and the door swung open. A tall, broad-shouldered man with a faintly familiar face stood silhouetted against the light from inside. He wore a T-shirt, athletic shorts and had a blue brace wrapped around his left knee.

"Yes?" He frowned. "Can I help you?"

Lisa gasped and grabbed for the support of the low cedar railing. *Omigod!* Patrick McCarthy—*The Enforcer!*—was staying at Grandpa Dan's!

CHAPTER TWO

SO, THIS WAS THE KID'S MOTHER. The one who made Tim those nice lunches, told him bedtime stories and trained her dog by leaving messages like "sit!" and "good girl!" on her telephone answering machine.

Two days ago, when he'd sauntered next door to pick up Boxer for a short walk in the neighborhood park, as per Dan's instructions, he happened to hear the phone ring twice and then a woman's voice instructing, "Boxer, come! Boxer, sit! *Good girl!*" repeated three times. Or something like that. Patrick had been so astonished, he hadn't caught the whole message.

The dog had looked nervously at him, then stared at the machine and sat, got up, turned around, sat again, whined, jumped up on his chest, then lay down and rolled over before rushing to the window to bark at a cat across the street.

The voice had been nice and sexy. Mellow, appealing. Too bad the reality didn't measure up. This woman had shoulder-length bedraggled-looking curly dark hair, a pale frightened face, no makeup, and she was dressed for taking out the garbage—sneakers, shapeless T-shirt and faded jeans.

"You must be Tim's mother." He congratulated himself on being a master of the self-evident. He moved to one side of the open doorway. "Come in. I'm Patrick McCarthy. Nice to meet you."

He held out his hand and after a second's hesitation, she shot her own hand out for a lightning-quick clasp, before dropping his as though he had some kind of social disease that was readily transmitted by palm-to-palm contact. Both her hands disappeared behind her back.

"No, I can't. Tim's asleep." She darted an agitated glance toward the door to her condo. "I—uh, I just got Dan's note and I had no idea he'd gone away. I wanted to see what was—"

"What was going on?" he interrupted pleasantly. "Well, as you can see, I'm house-sitting for Dan while my knee heals...." He watched as her eyes, an interesting mixture of green and blue, moved briefly to his injured left knee. "That should be a couple weeks. If you came over to thank me for taking the boys to practice, walking your dog, picking up the kids at school—hey, no problem. My pleasure."

"I—I didn't come over for that," she stammered, her eyes huge. She took a big breath. Patrick felt real irritation. What the hell was she so nervous about? "Well, I mean, I *did,* of *course* I did. But I wanted to, first of all, apologize for not getting in touch with you before this. I only found Dan's note in the bottom of Tim's school bag five minutes ago. I have no idea how long it's been there."

"Probably four or five days."

"Four or five *days!*"

"Yeah, Dan left Monday morning and I came out Monday afternoon. So, everything's okay?" It wasn't really a question. Patrick was bored with the whole exchange. Sure, he'd been curious to know what Tim's mother looked like, but now he knew. A typical suburban type. Overprotective. He wanted to get back to the Celtics-Lakers game he'd been watching.

She stared at him for a full five seconds, during which it crossed his mind that maybe she was more interesting than he'd thought. She had nice eyes. Very nice. That unusual greenish blue, with long dark lashes. Then she burst out, "Well, no, it isn't okay, actually. When will Dan be back? I—I'll make other arrangements, Mr. McCarthy. You're a busy man. I'm sure you have better things to do than take my son to practice and pick him up from school."

"Dan said maybe a week, two weeks, max. His brother broke his hip and Dan's helping him out. You'd better come in for a few minutes and we can talk about this." Patrick sent a quick glance over his shoulder. The crowd was going wild and he was missing all the action. Couldn't play hockey anymore, couldn't even catch a damn basketball game on television!

"No, Tim's—"

"Yeah, I know, Tim's asleep. But, hell, he's what? Seven? Eight? And we're thirty steps away? It's not like you're going grocery shopping or out to a bar or anything."

A bar! What do you take me for? She didn't say it but he could hear her thinking it, loud and clear.

She came in, leaving her sneakers in Dan's ceramic-tiled foyer. That was when he realized she'd actually stepped down the backs in her hurry to get over here. And she wasn't wearing any socks. Now *that* was an amazingly sexy thing, Patrick had always thought. He wondered if other men did. Bare feet. Painted toenails.

Forget sexy. For some reason, Mrs. Hudson was one riled-up mama.

"Forgive me, but I don't think you can really appreciate a parent's concern about a young boy," she said stiffly, turning to him again as they reached the small living room. He supposed Dan's place was pretty much the same layout as hers. "Maybe I'm overcautious, but that's just how it is. We live in a dangerous world. I'd never forgive myself if anything happened to Tim, not after—" She bit her lip, hard.

Patrick gave her a curious look, then limped over to the side table and picked up the remote. He switched off the game with a sigh of regret.

I'll bite, he decided. "Not after what?"

"Never mind. Listen, if you'll give me a day to get organized, I promise you I'll find someone else to pick up Tim and—"

"But why?" He just didn't get this woman. "Tim and Trev are best buddies. They go to school together, they play hockey together, they watch TV together, half the time they eat together. I like kids, and I don't have a criminal record. I swear, it's not a problem for me, so why is it for you?"

She looked anguished and all of a sudden Patrick wished he hadn't been so hard on her. Hell, if she wanted someone else to pick up Tim, that was okay by him.

"Tim's going to be furious with me," she whispered, turning toward the window and blinking rapidly. "Just *furious*." Patrick realized he hadn't bothered to pull the curtains yet and it was totally dark, midwinter, the end of January. It was strange, the sensation that anyone passing by could stop and look in on them.

"Why's that?" he asked gently.

She swung to face him. He'd been right; there were a few tears in those stormy eyes, so at odds with her pale complexion. "I know who you are. You're a famous hockey player—"

"Hardly famous, Mrs. Hudson," Patrick said dryly. Tempting as it might be to believe that, Patrick knew exactly where he fit into the hockey world. And *famous* wasn't it.

"Famous or not, my son has pointed you out many times on television. We've seen the Mr. Valentine ads." She pressed her lips together briefly, then continued. "You're famous to him. He idolizes you, haven't you noticed? He thinks hockey players are gods, all hockey players, and he thinks you're the absolute best there is."

Patrick tried not to grin. Damn, it felt good to know he was Number One in somebody's world, even an eight-year-old kid's. "Hero worship. Common enough. Is that a problem?"

She met his eyes straight on. "It is. I have done my best to teach him that violence has no place in our lives. He calls you The Enforcer. You—you know what that means."

Patrick gazed out the window for a few seconds. All he could see was his own reflection, his and hers. His jaw hardened. "What do *you* think it means—by the way, what's your name?"

"Lisa. Lisa Hudson."

"Maybe we should start over," he said, holding out his hand again, in an ironic gesture. "I'm Patrick. I play hockey for a living."

She smiled and shook it a little more warmly. That was a relief, however slight. But he could have saved his breath, because she picked up right where she'd left off.

"They call you The Enforcer because you get paid to knock people around. Hurt people."

"Hey, wait a minute." This was getting crazy. "It's a game."

"Maybe it's a game to you, but I'm a mother and I have to concern myself with the influences in my son's life. You make your living by violence. I'm sorry to have to say this—" he could tell she wasn't a bit sorry "—but you are not a good role model for my son."

He laughed. He couldn't help it. "Me? Do I look violent? Look at me." He waved his hand toward his bad leg. "Gimped up with a knee injury, maybe facing surgery again, maybe not. Can't play the rest of the season, no more Mr. Valentine, facing the boot at thirty-five. No prospects, no options, no kids, no wife, no family—"

She looked surprised. "What happened to the Mr. Valentine thing?"

Patrick smiled. "They wanted someone else. I've done it several times in the past five or six years, but apparently I don't have the right image anymore."

Her eyebrows crooked a question. *Why not?*

"Too mean, too tough and now—" he raised his left knee ruefully "—too busted up. Hell, instead of kicking me around even more, Mrs. Hudson, you should be feeling sorry for me."

He could see she wanted to laugh. *Really* wanted to laugh but wouldn't let herself. Humor warred with prim disapproval. He could practically hear her thinking, *what goes around comes around.*

"I've got to get back." She glanced nervously at the door, which he'd left slightly ajar. Didn't want her to think he was trying to trap her in his lair and—well, who knew what bad, violent men like him might have in mind? Nor, having had his share of experience with puck bunnies, did he want *her* getting any ideas. *As if.*

He accompanied her to the door. "You want me to pick Tim up tomorrow after school?" He added hastily, "Just until you make other arrangements, of course."

She slipped her feet into her sneakers, properly this time, and straightened. "If you wouldn't mind, that would be terrific. I'm not sure how easy it'll be to round up someone else on such short notice...."

"I promise I won't talk him into considering wrestling or hockey or even a race-car driving career, cross my heart," Patrick said, doing just that with one thumb. "And I won't even mention bronc-busting."

"Okay. I appreciate that." Had she really believed he would?

Patrick shook his head after she'd left, staring at the closed door. She hadn't mentioned the dog-walking. And he hadn't mentioned that ridiculous business about her trying to train her dog from work via the answering machine. It wasn't the sort of thing he could ignore.

Maybe next time. When—if—he got to know her a little better. Now that he'd agreed to help out the kids' team, he'd be seeing her occasionally, he supposed. Patrick didn't know whether he was looking forward to that or not.

He hobbled back to the living room and picked up the remote. Damn, the Lakers were down six.

CHAPTER THREE

"WAY TO GO, TIM!" Lisa shouted, four risers up from the player's box. "Good save!"

In addition to their regular Tuesday afternoon practice—the one Lisa could never get to—and Thursday evening practice, Tim and Trevor's team, the White Rock Ravens, had scrimmages at seven o'clock every second Friday night. Her son had just made a great save, even though it was only in a practice game.

Of course, Lisa reminded herself, they were all seven- and eight-year-olds. Some had difficulty just staying upright on the ice for more than five minutes. Quite a few of them couldn't skate backward yet.

As the boys lined up for the face-off, she eyed the tall, jeans-clad figure skating lazily around the perimeter of the rink. As Tim had said, Patrick McCarthy was lending a hand, taking Grandpa Dan's place while he was away.

"Patrick McCarthy?!" the woman next to her said when Coach Milfort made the announcement, her face shocked. "*The* Vancouver Canucks' *Patrick* McCarthy?"

Lisa nodded.

"The *Enforcer?*"

Lisa nodded again. Well, yes. That was the sad part, wasn't it? He was hardly a role model for all these little boys, never mind her own son.

The players, predictably enough, were awestruck and Coach Milfort, a good-natured dumpling of a man in a green windbreaker, long red scarf and brand-new Eddie Bauer skates, had a hard time settling them down.

Lisa liked to leave work a little early on Fridays, if possible, so she could get home around half-past three, when Tim was delivered from school, courtesy of Grandpa Dan or, in this case, Patrick McCarthy. She generally made a point of working through her lunch hour several times a week so she didn't feel guilty leaving two hours before the office closed on Fridays.

Not that her boss, Mr. Shitako, minded. "Family Is Number One" was Mr. Shitako's motto. He was the smiling, unflappable patriarch of a large, extended Japanese family, many of whom worked in the family construction company. He always urged Lisa to take whatever time she needed to tend to Tim's needs. Lisa had the feeling he didn't exactly approve of a mother with a career, although he was far too polite to say so. In today's world, a job outside the home was a necessity for many mothers, even those who weren't single moms.

Today it had been especially critical that she be

there when Tim got home. If she could have managed to pick him up herself she'd have done it, but her work was fifteen minutes to the east of White Rock, while the school—and their condo—was on the west side of town, near Boundary Bay.

So far, she hadn't found anyone who could take over after-school pick-up until Dan got back. She dreaded asking any of Tim's classmates' parents to help out; she still had only a nodding acquaintance with most of them. Plus, there was the added complication of the Tuesday afternoon practice. The Atom team came from all over White Rock, not necessarily just from Tim's school. She knew a few of these parents slightly better, but still hadn't approached one of them about picking Tim up.

Coward, she told herself.

The Enforcer. She couldn't believe the bad luck. Fortunately, it was a temporary situation. The worst thing of all—she'd been ready to blame her own son for lying. Lisa was sorry she'd suspected Tim. Sure, he had an active imagination, and she was glad he did, but this time he'd been telling the truth.

The hockey player had gotten a raw deal from his own team when they'd dropped him as Mr. Valentine. On top of being injured, too, she'd mused earlier that afternoon, pulling into her parking spot at the back of the condo. She was still thinking about him as she unlocked the hatchback so she could carry in the groceries she'd bought on the way home.

Dan's house-sitter had been on her mind more than she'd want to admit. Despite his professional role as a bully and a bruiser, Patrick McCarthy had a certain kind of male appeal that was obvious even to her, with no one in her life since Dave died. You couldn't count the one disastrous physical encounter she'd had three years ago with the insurance salesman she'd dated.

She and Dave had had a deeply satisfying physical relationship, but she'd been young then, young and healthy and brimming with appetites of all kinds. She'd been just over twenty-one when Dave was killed, married less than two years. With a three-month-old infant, a sketchy education and a future that was suddenly uncertain.

The hard work, the worry, the sleepless nights... she hadn't thought about a relationship of any kind for a long, long time. Until Ray Brogan had come into her life. And gone out of it again in fairly short order. He'd probably been as appalled as she was by their failed sexual encounter. She'd burst into tears the moment he'd unbuttoned her blouse and had continued blubbering until he finally ran out the door, like a man pursued. She'd never heard from him again and no wonder. Poor man. She could smile about it now, but at the time she'd been horrified by her own behavior.

Sitting in the stands, watching the boys skate around, Lisa thought back to what had happened this afternoon.

She'd set the first armful of groceries on the kitchen counter and let the ecstatic Boxer accompany her back to the car. Luckily, Boxer was good about one thing: she generally came when she was called. The animal had a lot of shortcomings but Lisa was glad that wasn't one of them. Actually, since she'd begun "talking" to the dog throughout the day via her answering machine, giving her short training sessions, Lisa thought Boxer was improving. Sometimes she actually sat on the "sit!" command. Mind you, she often lay down or chased her stump of a tail, too, but she *did* sit occasionally. That was progress.

"Mom!"

Tim came running from behind the concrete abutment that hid Grandpa Dan's parking spot. Lisa hugged him hard. The powerful sense of love and gratitude she always associated with her son flooded her heart. "Baby!"

"Oh, Mom," he scowled, extricating himself from her grasp. She'd forgotten; he was starting to hate it when she called him pet names.

She pushed back his cowlick, an automatic gesture, and smiled at him. "Want to help me unload the groceries?"

"Sure. Can Trev help, too?"

Trev. That meant someone else might be joining them. "Of course, he can if he wants to," she replied lightly. As she half expected, Patrick McCarthy and Trevor emerged from behind the abutment

in response to Tim's yelled invitation. They must
have driven in about the same time she did.

"Hey, guess who *this* is?" Tim asked, his voice
full of excitement. Lisa didn't know if he was talking to her or to McCarthy.

"Hello," she said politely. The hockey player
was dressed casually in faded jeans, leather hiking
boots and a fisherman's sweater. He wore reflective
sunglasses.

He acknowledged her with a nod, his hands
jammed in his back pockets. She noticed that her
face looked silly reflected in his lenses—squashed
and worried-looking.

"Hey, do you guys know each other?" Tim demanded suspiciously, then he went into full action.
"Bam! Slam! Ta-da! This-is-*MY MOM*."

Patrick pushed his sunglasses high on his forehead and grinned at her. "Sorry about that, Mom."
He winked. "Can't seem to get the guys to quit with
the video-game sound effects."

"I thought those were hockey-game sound effects," she shot back.

"Whatever. Want a hand with those?"

Lisa was disarmed by the simple offer and before
she knew it, they were in her apartment and the boys
were arguing over what kind of pizza to order. They
had to eat early to make the Friday scrimmage.

"Hold it, guys!" Patrick had said after he'd
placed the rest of her groceries on the kitchen
counter. "How about both kinds? One Hawaiian

and one pepperoni, large. Okay?'' He swung around to get her approval. She nodded uncertainly. Boxer was sniffing Patrick's knee.

"And then you can eat over at our place. Dan's place,'' he corrected. "We might as well go to practice together, right?'' Again, he looked to her for approval.

"Hey, wait a minute,'' Lisa protested. What was she getting into? "I'll order the pizza, like I always do on Fridays, and—''

"Nope. We've already decided, we're having pizza next door,'' Patrick said firmly. "My treat. Trev? You coming now?'' He moved toward the entrance.

"I wanna watch something with Tim. I'll be over after,'' Trevor said. The two boys were already settled on the floor in front of the television, with Boxer squeezed between them. Large, white, no doubt man-eating sharks moved slowly through the blue-green water on the screen.

"Okay with you?''

Lisa got the impression that it really didn't matter what she said. "Well, it's very kind of you to order the pizza, but I'll take them to practice,'' she said stiffly, surprised at how readily he agreed.

"No sense taking two cars, right?'' Patrick had said, smiling, when he'd arrived with the boys on her doorstep at quarter past six. She hadn't joined them for pizza, after all, deciding she'd rather keep some distance.

"*Me* drive?" Lisa squeaked. That, it appeared, was the plan.

"Mom, he's gonna coach us!" Tim said, sounding exasperated that his mother was so dense. "He *has* to come with us."

"Besides, this way I can keep my bad leg straight."

It would have been churlish to argue. Somehow, they'd all squeezed into her little Honda, the hockey sticks and bags stuffed into the hatchback cargo space, the boys in the back seat, and the front area seeming a whole lot smaller with a very large Vancouver Canucks forward crammed into the passenger seat, his left leg extended.

On the way she'd learned two things: he'd already had surgery on his knee twice, although not recently, and he didn't want to talk about it.

Fine. She'd only been trying to make conversation.

"Mom! You missed the turn."

Well, okay, that had been a little embarrassing, but Lisa had recovered smoothly, finding a parking spot at the rear of the rink, near the back entrance so the boys wouldn't have to haul their equipment too far to the dressing rooms.

Lisa always helped Tim in the dressing room, but this time he stopped her at the door. "It's okay, Mom. Patrick can help me and Trev."

"Oh! All right." But she'd been hurt that he suddenly wanted Patrick McCarthy to tighten his skates, not her. A guy thing? But it wasn't as though all the parents in the boys' dressing room were dads. A few hockey moms brought their sons regularly, as she did.

Including the woman sitting to her left in the stands now. "Patrick McCarthy, huh? He was Mr. Valentine last year, did you know?" she asked Lisa. "And the year before that, too."

Lisa shrugged. "Oh?" She didn't really want to discuss this. Then, thinking she'd been a little short, she added, "I'm not as up on all this hockey stuff as Tim is."

"Oh, yes." The woman gazed admiringly after McCarthy, who had made another loop around the arena, this time at what seemed to be breathtaking speed, at least compared to Coach Milfort. He was talking to the boys, who'd lined up at center ice and were paying attention in a way they never paid attention to poor Ernie Milfort. "He's even better-looking in person than on TV, don't you think?"

Lisa glanced at Patrick again. She supposed he was fairly good-looking. Maybe even handsome. Many women apparently thought so. She couldn't get past the violence thing herself.

The woman beside her nudged Lisa and winked. "He can park his skates under my bed any time!"

Lisa stared at her, shocked. But the other woman was already on her feet, cheering her son, who was the team's top scorer. Ten goals in eight games. Lisa never knew if that was because her boy was really good or if it was just that the goalies at this level were so bad. She felt disloyal—Tim was a goalie, one of three on the team—but Lisa wasn't fooling herself, as she suspected a lot of these parents were, that their little Wayne or Mario would make the NHL one day, become their ticket to vicarious fame and fortune. If Tim wanted to be a farmer or a plumber or even a dot-com guy, that was just fine with her.

A pro hockey player? Anything but!

PATRICK FINSIHED WASHING up the dishes and hung the tea towel neatly on the rack inside the lower cupboard door. It was a good system—rinse throughout the day, stack in the sink, then wash up once.

This playing house, even if it wasn't his own house, was kind of fun. A nice change from being on the road five or six nights out of seven from October to June. His own apartment, a two-bedroom rental on Vancouver's False Creek, was more like a hotel room than a home. Beer and eggs in the fridge, furniture straight from a department-store floor display and nothing, not even a mattress, in the sparc bedroom. Visitors? Never got any—at least not any who required their own beds—so he'd never bothered furnishing it. He'd always felt it was pointless to invest energy or money in a home. You never knew when you'd be traded. Play a game on Friday night for one team and on Saturday for your new team.

The place seemed quiet with the boys gone. Evie Kristofferson, Trevor's mother, had come to the arena to pick up her son, so Patrick had asked her to drop him off at the condo on their way home. Trev had passed the message on to Tim and, he hoped, Lisa.

That woman bugged him. Wouldn't accept the coffee he'd offered to buy her at the rink, quibbled over paying for half the pizza he'd ordered, yet hadn't joined them to eat it. He rarely got the feeling that a woman thoroughly disliked him from the moment she met him, but he couldn't help thinking Tim's mother was that kind of woman.

Too bad. He popped the tab on a can of beer he pulled out of the fridge. Tim was a great little guy. Hockey, hockey, hockey. He'd lived for it at that age, too. And he was still living for it, even though the writing was on the wall for a smart guy to read: you're too old, McCarthy. Too old, too slow, too busted-up.

Retirement. The word made his stomach freeze up and his skin crawl. Retirement was for old guys, like Dan. He was thirty-five. But hockey was a young man's game. Not many players, even if they weren't injured, played past thirty-five or thirty-six. He had a lot of good years left—doing what? What skills did he have except a little bit of jackknife carpentry, a decent golf game, a crushing body check and a knack for getting a cold stiff glove on an opponent's face and shoving it around before he got his own face "washed"?

Sure, he had plenty of dough, most of it invested, unlike many of his colleagues, and his contract didn't run out for another year. They had to pay him even if they didn't play him. But the time had come to consider some alternatives.

First things first. Get this knee working the way it should. Do this favor for Dan, who'd been like a second father to him all his life, ever since he'd boarded with the Kristofferson family, a skinny, scared sixteen-year-old, his first time away from home. He'd been an Ontario Hockey League junior, on his way to the NHL, dreaming of being the next Wayne Gretzky.

Next…get things straightened out with the princess next door. She couldn't even train her own dog. Couldn't even *name* it—who ever heard of a boxer called Boxer?

For her son's sake, he had to make peace.

Tim—and Trevor—looked up to him so much it was painful. He couldn't let the boy down. Hero worship was common enough in kids of that age, but at seven or eight, you definitely deserved to have your dreams come true.

He remembered himself at that age, going to sleep every night with a signed Guy LaFleur hockey card his grandfather had given him under his pillow.

If he'd actually *met* one of his hockey heroes at that age…

Fourteen years later, when he'd played his first game against Gretzky, the thrill was still huge.

Patrick glanced at his watch. Ten o'clock. The sprout should be in bed and asleep by now. Good time to have a few quiet words with the mother.

CHAPTER FOUR

THE RAIN WAS COMING DOWN like crazy and her porch roof had a leak in it. He knocked and waited, one arm over his head, then glanced up and got an eyeful. He swore. The chain rattled and the door opened a crack.

"Yes? Oh, it's you! Just a minute." To his amazement, she shut the door again. He heard Boxer snuffling at the base of the door and whining.

A minute later she was back and this time she opened the door wide. The dog was all over him, sniffing his butt and licking his knee over the brace he wore. He'd noticed earlier that the mutt had a fondness for neoprene.

Lisa Hudson was staring at him, eyes wide. She looked a little frightened. Hell, she probably wasn't used to opening her door at this time of night. Not to anyone. She had on a tatty pink robe, cinched tightly around her waist, and slippers on her feet. The flip-flop kind. Her hair was loose and glossy, well-brushed.

"Sorry." He held his hands wide. "Look, I can come back tomorrow. I don't want to disturb you—"

"Oh, you're not disturbing me, Mr. McCarthy. I just watched *Antiques Roadshow* and I was thinking about going to bed soon."

Bed. The word hung in the air between them. Patrick frowned. Why? This woman didn't do a thing for him—annoyed him, if anything—so why was he suddenly wondering what she had on under that shapeless pink sack?

She closed the door and he let his hands fall to his sides. She seemed flustered, putting the chain lock on, then taking it off again. She must have realized it didn't make any sense to lock him in with her.

Okay—take a real good look while she's busy, he told himself. Get over it. She'd obviously rushed off and put on the robe before she let him in the door. *A modest woman*. He saw white lace peeping below the hem, from a nightgown. Probably long-sleeved, high-necked and padlocked, he decided. Federal-issue flannel, no question.

She finally turned away from the door and led him down the short hallway toward her living room.

"Tim's asleep?"

"Oh, yes! He goes to bed at nine on weekends and he's always out like a light. He's an active boy." She smiled uncertainly. She was wondering why he was here. He was beginning to wonder the same thing.

"Good," Patrick heard himself saying. "That's good." He glanced around the apartment, congratulating himself on his conversational skills. The place looked different than it had this afternoon. Warm, inviting, cosy, a shaded lamp on by the sofa, the television sound muted. He could see Peter Mansbridge, the CBC news anchor, yakking silently away.

"Did you want to see me about something?" She looked worried. "Sit down. Would you like some coffee? Tea?"

"No, thanks. I won't stay long. I just, well, I had a few questions I wanted to ask you."

"About Tim?"

"Tim, among other things."

"Please sit down. A glass of water? Herbal tea?"

"Never touch the stuff." Patrick noticed a mug on the end table beside the sofa, beside an open magazine. "I'll have whatever you're having, Mrs. Hudson."

She flushed a little. It became her. "Please call me Lisa," she said.

"Okay." He nodded stiffly. "If you'll call me Patrick."

"Not The Enforcer?" She raised a brow.

Patrick felt as though someone had dumped a load of ice water on him, not just the trickle that had landed in his eye on her porch. "No, not that. If you don't mind."

She hurried off to the small kitchen and he looked around for a place to sit. Scowling, he decided on the armchair across from the sofa. So *that* was it—

the tough guy thing. It wasn't just the hockey-is-a-violent-game business.

Boxer came and sat in front of him. "Lie down," he ordered softly. The dog collapsed onto the floor, looking up eagerly. "Good girl." He patted her shoulder. "Now, hide," he said quietly. She put both paws over her eyes. Patrick found it pretty comical.

Tim's mother brought a tray into the room and quickly set it down on the coffee table. "What in the world is she doing?"

As if on cue—which was not the case—the dog took one paw off one eye, gazed up at her mistress, then covered her eye again. Lisa burst out laughing. Patrick felt tremendously pleased with himself. He'd taught Boxer that trick the first two times he'd had her out for a walk in the park.

"Hide-and-seek. It's her best trick," he said.

"I didn't know she knew how to do that," Lisa said, real animation in her voice. *Quite a change from the way she regarded The Enforcer.* "We got her from the SPCA, you know. Maybe Tim told you?" She glanced at him and he shook his head. He took the cup she handed him. Something murky, steaming.

"Yes. She was already named and everything. Nobody seems to have trained her, so I've been trying to teach her a bit lately." She laughed pleasurably, which did rather interesting things to Patrick's heart rate, he noted—to his surprise.

"Actually, I'd decided she was totally hopeless, but she's improving a lot lately. I've been—" She bit her lip and bent her head, hair swinging over her cheek so he couldn't see her expression. He'd bet dollars to doughnuts she'd been about to confess her answering-machine dog-training method. "Would you like one?" She held out a plate of cookies.

"Thanks." Oatmeal with raisins and walnuts, plain and nutritious. "What is this, by the way?" He raised his cup.

"Ovaltine."

Ovaltine? He took a sip. Hot, sweet and...weird.

"So. What did you want to talk to me about?" She sat on the sofa, straight up, her knees together, her back stiff, and reached for her mug.

"I've been wondering why you dislike me so much."

She started and quickly set her cup down again. Telltale color crept up from the limp collar of her robe to her throat as she stared at him. "*Dislike* you? Wherever did you get that idea?"

"Don't get me wrong, it's not that *I* care all that much personally, you understand." Somewhere, deep down, he dredged up a careless laugh. "I mean, women don't have to find me appealing. But since Trev and Tim are such good friends and with me helping their team right now, it could make things awkward. You know, if you're always on my case about something. Who buys the pizza, who ties his skates...." He took another sip of the kiddie drink, then dared to meet her gaze. "Don't you agree?"

"I suppose you mean because he worships the ground you walk on." She sounded hurt, bitter even.

He nodded again. "Something like that. Hell, it's just kid stuff, but I don't think Tim should feel he has to take sides. Maybe I happen to be his sports hero right now but, hey, you're his mom." Patrick smiled. Encouragingly, he hoped. "In a couple of weeks, I'm gone and everything here is back to normal."

Lisa Hudson studied her own hands for a moment, then folded them in her lap. She took a deep breath. "You know, don't you, that—that Tim's father isn't with us?" She was sitting even straighter than before, her drink neglected on the end table beside her.

"Tim's never said anything about his father." Patrick wondered why she'd put it that way—*isn't with us*. "I, er, gathered he wasn't in the picture...."

"He's dead," she said. "He was murdered."

Patrick stared at her.

"Yes, he was murdered." She closed her eyes and the sight of her hands, small and white, tightly clasped in her lap, tore at Patrick's heart. "Tim was three months old. We were visiting Dave's brother and his wife in Montreal, showing them the new baby. Dave had always suspected his brother was mixed up with criminal elements, drugs, maybe even organized crime of some kind. Anyway, on Sunday morning, Dave went out to get the newspaper on the steps and—''

Her mouth quivered. Patrick wanted to take her in his arms. He couldn't believe what a lout he was, saying something that must have brought all this back to her. ''Never mind, you don't have to tell me this—''

''I *want* to tell you,'' she interrupted fiercely, opening her eyes. ''So you'll understand.''

Understand?

''Dave bent over to pick up the newspaper. A car drove by and three shots were fired. Someone shot my husband. He—'' She swallowed. ''He was killed instantly. It was an accident. The bullets were meant for his brother. Whoever did it was never caught,'' she finished on a whisper, her voice catching. Her hands twisted the end of the cloth belt around her waist and she stood quickly and walked to the window, erect, graceful. Dignified. The curtains were drawn but she stared at them as though she could see right through the fabric.

''I don't know what to say,'' Patrick murmured. ''I can't tell you how sorry I am about that.'' He shut up then. Time to leave. He didn't want to hear any more details. He'd like to know what the story had to do with him, with hockey, but he wasn't pursuing the topic. Not now.

Poor kid. Poor woman.

Over seven years ago, and it looked like they'd

had a rough time of it since. None of the furniture in the room was new, although everything was well taken care of, polished and dusted. The robe, the old T-shirt she'd been wearing when he'd first met her—obviously she didn't waste a cent on herself. How could she afford to have Tim in hockey? It wasn't a cheap sport, and goalie equipment was the most expensive on the team.

He stood and set his mug down. "I'd better go."

She didn't turn and Patrick realized, to his horror, that her shoulders were shaking slightly. Against his will, he took a step toward her. He couldn't stand it if she was crying. "Lisa?"

She didn't answer and he took another step, reaching out to put a hand on her shoulder. She cringed and he felt a twinge of anger again. *Was she afraid of him?*

"Lisa? I'm sorry."

"It's not your fault." She turned to him, wiping at her face with her sleeve. Her cheeks were wet, her eyes brimming with tears. Good going, McCarthy! *What the hell had he said that brought this on?*

"Oh, God, Lisa," he said and pulled her into his arms. "I'm so sorry." He wrapped his arms around her and drew her gently toward him. She didn't resist. He felt her lay her cheek briefly against his shoulder, felt her shoulders slump as she leaned on him. Something snapped in his brain. He held her tighter and lowered his head, daring to breathe in the scent of her hair, her skin, daring to touch her with his lips. She smelled clean, sweet...

What was he doing?

"P-please forgive me," she mumbled. He felt her back tense and her palms press against his chest as she moved away. He let her go instantly.

She looked embarrassed. "Oh, my goodness. I feel so silly. I mean—" She blew her nose with a tissue she retrieved from one pocket. "I don't usually cry. Not about this. It's not as if I'm still, you know—grieving or anything. I just—" She tried to laugh and failed miserably.

"Never mind." Patrick fought the urge to take her in his arms again, dry her tears, kiss her cheek softly, tell her he'd take care of her. Tell her she could lean on him, no matter what....

What the hell had hit him? *He wasn't even interested in this woman!* "It's my fault. I'm afraid something I said must have reminded you—"

"Don't you see?" Her eyes were animated, over-bright with tears. "What happened to my husband—it's why I'm so horrified by violence of any kind." She shuddered. "I know Tim loves hockey now, but I really, really hope that changes before the boys start checking, slamming into each other...I couldn't bear it." She covered her face briefly with her hands, then put them in her pockets again. Her nose was red.

"Hey, that's not for a long time yet," he said,

trying to jolly her out of her violence-in-sport tirade. "Not until they get to Bantam level at least...."

Her eyes held his. The passion he saw there astounded him. "It disturbs me terribly to see players hit each other, even have actual *fights,* and watch my son cheer. Especially you! You're part of that world. You represent a horrible kind of violence and you live right next door!"

Patrick held up his hand. "I understand. Really. But you've got to realize it's not as bad as it looks. We're trained athletes. We're conditioned to take that kind of punishment. There's no way one player would ever really injure another player, except by accident. We respect each other too much. Most of it's sham and show." He gave a quick shrug. "Entertainment."

"But don't you see? That's just it. The crowd screams for blood. They want people smashed into the boards, taken down—"

"That's how you see me?" It dawned on Patrick that she'd put him in the same category as the Mafia hit men who'd gunned down her husband.

She nodded. "They call you The Enforcer, in the newspaper and everywhere. That says it all, doesn't it? I see how Tim adores you, admires you, and I feel like such a failure as a parent. I wish his father was alive. I keep thinking I must be doing something wrong."

"Don't blame yourself. Boys are physical." Patrick shrugged again. "Boxing, wrestling, monster trucks, you name it. It's hardwired into the chromosomes—"

"I can't help feeling the way I do," she burst in. "Especially considering how his father died. I wish my son admired another kind of man. A kinder, gentler kind of man. A *real* hockey player."

Boxer whined and Patrick reached down to run his hand along her back, glad of the interruption. She had no idea how those last words of hers had hurt him and he had no intention of ever letting her know.

He summoned a smile from somewhere. "I can see I'm not going to convince you. Go ahead, make other arrangements to pick Tim up from school. Do whatever you feel you have to so you can protect him from men like me," he said, adding with sarcasm, "I hope you don't object that I'm helping coach the team."

She threw him an anguished look. "Of course not!"

He knew it wasn't fair. Her emotion was genuine. But it irritated him that she couldn't figure out that the Patrick McCarthy she saw on television—"The Enforcer"—was not the man standing in front of her now.

"I'd better go," he muttered.

She led the way down the hall. *Couldn't wait to get rid of him.*

"Don't misunderstand. I do appreciate everything you've done for Tim," she said politely as she unlocked the door to let him out. "He's so thrilled he got to meet you." The rain was still pouring down outside and a trickle of water gushed through the roof in the spot that had dumped on him earlier.

"You need to get that fixed," he said, glancing up.

"I know," she said, looking in the same direction. She bit her lip, which put two ideas into Patrick's head. One, he wondered if she was worried about the expense....

"I could patch that for you," he offered, knowing she'd refuse.

"Oh, no!" she said, her eyes wide. "I couldn't ask you to do that."

"You're not asking. I'm offering. For free."

He smiled. And there was the second thing he wanted to know. Just how *soft* those pink lips were.

"Oh!"

He put his arms around her and pulled her toward him for the second time that evening. "I find you're wrong about a lot of things, Mrs. Hudson. Maybe, considering what kind of guy you think I really am, you were expecting this...."

He leaned forward a few inches and covered her mouth with his. He was right—incredibly kissable. Warm, luscious, yielding...

To his amazement, after the first few seconds, she was kissing him back. He deepened the kiss, pulling her tightly against him, pressing her hips against his—his libido rocketing wildly as he suddenly pictured her without that tatty robe, without that pad-locked flannel nightgown.

Whoa. He hadn't exactly planned *this*.

"Oh, my goodness!" she said as he released her, clasping her hands to her cheeks. "What are you *doing?*"

"You might ask yourself that, my dear," he said, putting his forefinger on her soft, wet mouth. Her deliciously astonished soft, wet mouth. He nearly gave in to the overwhelming desire to kiss her again just to see if she'd kiss him back. "Good night, Mrs. Hudson," he said instead, with his best wicked grin. "Sweet dreams."

Then he stepped outside, closing the door behind him before she had a chance to slam it shut. He paused long enough to get a drenching from the leak and to hear her immediately scrabble at the door, fastening the locks.

He laughed delightedly, wondering what had possessed him. He was crazy! Any gains he might have made with her this evening, he'd turned around and totally destroyed. Acted like the lout she'd expected, from the sounds of it.

Hit man! She equated him with some Mafia thug.

He shook his head. No sweet dreams for him. He knew he was going to have a restless night, and it wasn't because his knee was killing him.

CHAPTER FIVE

LISA TRIED TO SLEEP IN on weekends, not always successfully. On Saturdays, Tim usually got up early, poured himself a bowl of cereal and milk and ate it watching cartoons on television, with the ever-agreeable Boxer. Now that he was a little older, he usually remembered to keep the volume down. Sometimes he'd join his friends for a game of road hockey after breakfast, but never without telling her.

The morning after Patrick's visit, she woke up early with one thought on her mind: he'd kissed her. She'd had a hard time falling asleep with that thought ricocheting in her mind. *Why* had he done that? Lisa couldn't think of any reason at all, except that he'd wanted to prove something. And what would that be? That he was rude, inconsiderate, arrogant? The very image of the God's-gift-to-women star athlete she thought he was?

Even more confusing: she'd kissed him back! Not a lot, but a little. That really horrified her. Of course, there'd been the surprise factor. And she hadn't been kissed in a long, long time; she couldn't remember how long, certainly not since she'd moved to British Columbia. But, heavens, you didn't respond to a man who kisses you just because he grabbed you unexpectedly! Wouldn't most women scream and kick? Slam the door in his face?

Of course, she'd had a sleeping child to consider. But, frankly, the thought of waking or not waking Tim had not crossed her mind. No, she'd kissed Patrick McCarthy. That was all there was to it.

She should have objected. She should have slapped him or something, although that did seem kind of old-fashioned, not to mention rather over-the-top, in view of the offence. Instead she'd kissed him back, just like all the other blond, beautiful sports groupies he probably amused himself with most days—and nights—of the week.

Except she wasn't blond. Or beautiful. And she'd been wearing that horrid old housecoat she'd received as a hand-me-down from Dave's sister, Janet, four years ago. She was throwing that old thing out. The least she could do for herself was buy a new one. She and Tim didn't have a lot of spare money but there was no longer any need for the kind of penny-pinching she'd had to do in the past.

Lisa got out of bed and turned back the duvet to air. She went to the window. Still rain, but there were bright patches in the sky to the west. The weekend forecast was for sun.

Today was shopping with Tim before lunch, then spending the afternoon in the kitchen, preparing the week's casseroles and baking. Saturday evening

Lisa and Tim often went to a movie or out to a fast-food restaurant of Tim's choice. Sometimes Trevor came with them, if his parents were working and his big sister wasn't home. Trevor's parents both worked shifts, his mom in a bakery in Langley and his father at the Peace Arch Hospital, where he was on the cleaning staff. His sister was nineteen, worked at a department store, and was naturally more interested in her social life than she was in baby-sitting her little brother.

Lisa had just dressed—her usual jeans and T-shirt—and brushed her teeth when there was a knock at her bedroom door. She hurried over to open it. "Yes, honey? Something wrong?"

Tim was still in his pajamas and had serious pillow hair. He looked agitated and was hopping from one foot to the other. "Nothing. I just need to use the bathroom. Mom, you gotta come to the phone. Patrick wants to talk to you!"

"Okay, sir!" She made a mock salute and stepped aside as Tim raced toward the main bathroom down the hall.

What did Patrick McCarthy want so early? Except, possibly, to apologize. Somehow, she didn't think it was that....

Lisa took a deep breath before picking up the receiver, which her son had left lying on the arm of the sofa. "Hello?" That was fine—brisk and businesslike.

"Good morning." He paused and Lisa was glad

he hadn't come to the door himself. His voice was even deeper and sexier on the phone than it was in person. She was sure her face was bright red. "Sleep well?" he asked.

"*Very* well, thank you." She glanced at the wall clock visible in the kitchen. Nearly ten o'clock! She must have fallen back asleep after she'd first awakened from her restless night.

"That's good. The, uh, rain bothered me," he said and she was quite sure it was a lie. Conscience, maybe? Then she remembered his injured knee.... "Listen," he went on, "I wanted to ask you about something before I mentioned it to Tim, although Trevor may have told him already."

"What's that?"

"Trevor's dad and I are going out to set a crab trap in Boundary Bay this afternoon if the weather clears, and we're taking Trevor along. He wants Tim to come."

"In a *boat?*"

He paused, then said, "Yeah. That's the idea. It's Pete's boat."

"Are you, you know—experienced?" Lisa felt her face flush hotly. She was embarrassed to be quizzing him like this.

"Very experienced, both of us," he answered calmly. If he was annoyed by her questions, he didn't let on. "Life jackets, spare oars, bilge pump, marine radio, flares on board, the works. Don't worry, Tim will be fine."

"I'm sure he'll be fine. But you know I'll worry," she said softly into the receiver. She had heard Tim come out of the bathroom.

"Yeah, you're a mother," he said and she could hear the humor in his voice. "You're allowed. So, will you let Tim come with us?"

"Yes," Lisa said. She knew Tim would be in seventh heaven about going out on Trevor's dad's boat with his best buddy and his hockey idol. How could she stop him? And did she want to? No, of course she didn't. Tim wasn't a baby, as he was only too quick to remind her when she forgot. With no father in his life, all-male outings like this were seldom and precious. "When should he be ready?"

"I'll pick him up around noon, if that's okay. Slack tide's just after one o'clock. It's best to set the traps on the incoming tide, so we want to get out there just as it turns."

"What about lunch? Shall I send some lunch with him?"

"We'll stop at McDonald's on the way."

He'd thought of everything. "All right. I'll have him ready. And, Patrick—" She held the phone so tightly she heard her knuckles crack.

"Yes?"

"Thanks for this."

There was a pause and then, "Hey, don't mention it."

She felt better when she hung up. There'd been no apology for the kiss on the doorstep and she'd managed not to mention it, either. That was as it should be. Just a foolish impulse that he probably regretted in the hard light of morning. Most men weren't good at apologizing. And he'd doubtless thought she'd be thrilled to bits by the attention. Why apologize for a good thing?

Lisa smiled to herself as she set about making coffee. That wasn't fair. He seemed a reasonable man—so far. Maybe inviting Tim to go out crabbing with him and Pete Kristofferson was his way of making amends.

LISA SPENT THE AFTERNOON baking two batches of oatmeal and coconut cookies and one batch of chocolate chip, which she put in the freezer. She made a tuna casserole, a pan of lasagna and some chicken soup, which she also froze. The chicken she usually took off the bones and made into chicken pot pies, with—she cheated—premade pastry cases and then she froze those as well. Tim's favorite after-school snack was one of her homemade chicken pot pies warmed up in the microwave. Considering how many he went through in a week, she was beginning to think it was Trevor's favorite, too. Or Boxer's.

Today she decided to make a large chicken pot pie with real pastry for their supper. Frozen burritoes would have to do for snacks this week. In the rush of their departure, she'd forgotten to ask Patrick when they expected to be back, but it didn't matter. The pie would keep warm if they were late.

Tim had been at the window every two minutes, checking for Patrick's arrival, and the instant Patrick knocked, Tim was out the door, with a yell to her and a wave of his hand. No goodbye kiss.

From the open door, one hand on Boxer's collar, she'd watched them leave. Tall strong man with slight limp, in jeans and expensive Goretex jacket, smiling down at kid in bargain-basement jeans, rain jacket and rubber boots, talking a mile a minute. Patrick's dark eyes had searched hers when she'd opened the door to see them off, and her stomach had done a little wiggle for a second or two, but that was that. Between the phone conversation and this brief meeting, she felt she'd dispensed with the issue of the aggravating kiss the previous evening. If he didn't mention it, she certainly wasn't going to.

Lisa kept an eye on the weather as she worked in the kitchen and was relieved to see the sky clear completely by two o'clock. She took Boxer to Crescent Beach, where dogs were allowed off-leash from October to April. Boxer loved to run, although she hated to go in the water and didn't chase sticks at all. Lisa peered out over Boundary Bay, toward Point Roberts, wondering which boat, if any, belonged to Trevor's dad. Clouds had begun to build in the west and by four o'clock, when she got back to the condo, it was raining lightly.

There was nothing on television so she tried to read, all the while watching the sky outside, feeling her tension mount. *Her little boy, her only child— her baby!—was out there in a storm at sea....* She tried to tell herself she was being silly; Patrick had talked about incoming tides and slack tides and flares and bilge pumps. That *sounded* like someone who knew what he was doing.

Wind whipped the leafless branches of the big weeping willow outside her condo window. By six o'clock, she couldn't stand it anymore and decided to call Evie to see if she'd heard anything.

"Oh, Lisa, don't worry." Evie Kristofferson was a big woman with a boisterous laugh. "They're probably in by now, but they have to take care of the boat and all that. Tell you what, if they're not home in another couple of hours, we'll both call the Coast Guard, okay? Listen, I'm glad you phoned because I need a favor...."

Evie's car was going into the garage on Wednesday and she wondered if Lisa could give her a lift to work in Langley, since it wasn't far out of her way.

Lisa agreed and hung up, only a little comforted. *The Coast Guard!* Good heavens, suddenly she began to picture a rescue at sea. She told herself she was overreacting and went to check on the pie in the oven. It would have to come out soon.

Boxer whined, then began to bark, her excited, boy-I'm-glad-to-see-you bark, and whirled around in a circle a few times. Lisa turned the oven on low and took off her apron.

They were back!

PATRICK DIDN'T THINK he'd ever experienced a more heartfelt homecoming. The sight of Lisa Hudson's brilliant eyes, her smile, the way she wrapped her son in her arms and kissed him all over his tousled head and kept laughing, even though the boy protested strongly, made him want to step up and say, "Hey, my turn."

And he wouldn't try to get away, either, as Tim was doing. He'd kiss her back. How had he ever thought her plain and ordinary, even for a minute? Even in that old T-shirt, with her hair disheveled...

Tim finally escaped from her embrace and her smile cooled ever so slightly when she turned to him. Oh, yeah, he forgot—the big, bad hockey guy was standing in her foyer. "How was it?"

"Decent. We didn't catch our limit but—"

"Hey, Mom! We got four crabs to keep for ourselves and Patrick put them in a bucket and they're really scratchin' around in there, you should see 'em! They've got big googly eyes and when you put your hand in, they try and pinch you like this—" Tim made some pinching motions in the air and Boxer whined with excitement. There was nothing that didn't delight that dog, Patrick had decided.

"Tim, honey, you're interrupting—"

"That's okay," Patrick said. "He had an exciting day."

"No," she said, shaking her head. "He needs to remember his manners." Her eyes held his and she swallowed. "I—I saw a storm blow up out on the bay. Were you caught in that?"

"Storm?" He took a step backward, toward the still-open door. Might as well get that bucket of crabs. "Heck, it was just a little blow."

"Yeah." The boy broke in again. "There were big waves, Mom, and we went up and down and up and down and Trevor got sick and barfed up his french fries right over the side of the boat!"

"Sick?" Her look of alarm would have been funny if she hadn't been so serious. He wished Tim hadn't mentioned the swells. It *had* been a little rough out there on the return trip.

"But I didn't, Mom! I told Trevor he was a baby, but Patrick said he gets sick sometimes, too, and—" He raced off with the dog, swooping and diving, his arms out to the sides. Airplane or boat? Patrick wondered if he'd ever had that much energy.

She tilted her head. "You do?"

"Yeah," he said. "Sometimes. I thought it wouldn't hurt for him to know that anybody can get seasick."

"Even a big, tough hockey player like you," she added, eyes twinkling. Damn, she was teasing him.

"I'll just go get those crabs for you."

"Oh, we don't need any crabs." She made a face. "I wouldn't know what to do with them. You keep them. You've been so generous with Tim already, taking him out this afternoon and everything."

"Anytime. It was my pleasure," Patrick said. He meant it. He'd had a lot of fun with the two boys, teaching them to put bait on a hook, throw over a line while they waited to pull the traps. Neither boy had caught anything, but that wasn't the point. Sure, you fished to catch a fish, but most of the fun was just throwing your hook over and hoping.

"What's for dinner, Mom?" Tim said as he raced through the foyer again, still swooping and diving.

"What does it smell like? Your favorite," she said, smiling. She had that soft, feminine look in her eye, a look he rarely saw on a woman anymore. Certainly not on the puck bunnies who littered a pro hockey player's life, at home and away. Patrick knew the look was for her son but he allowed himself to pretend, just for a second, that it included him, too.

"Chicken pot pie!" Tim yelled and disappeared again, Boxer on his heels.

"Smells great in here."

"Would you like to join us for supper?" she asked quickly, then colored. "It's pretty simple but you're welcome to stay." Her eyes searched his and he felt the same little…something that he'd felt before he'd grabbed her and kissed her last night. "Unless you've got other plans."

"Hell, that's a tough one," he said, thinking of his near-empty fridge. "Man, let's see…" He pretended to deliberate. "What'll it be, sitting with a real family over some homemade chicken pot pie or driving down to Tim Horton's and having a bowl of chili...."

She smiled again. "So? Which is it?"

"I'll join you. On one condition," he warned, holding up his hand. Then he corrected himself, admiring his own quick thinking. "*Two* conditions."

"Which are?"

"One, I contribute the crabs and a bottle of wine. I insist."

She laughed. "Okay. As long as you cook them yourself."

"Done."

"And?"

"This one's going to be tough for you, Lisa," he said, lowering his voice just in case Tim was around the corner.

"Oh?" Her eyes widened. "Why's that?"

"Because you're proud and independent. You like to do things for other people but you hate to let anybody do things for you. Like take your kid fishing. Like fix that leak over your porch for free."

She was silent, her jaw firmly set. He'd hit the nail on the head, no question. "Condition number two?" she asked, frowning.

"You'll have to come next door for dinner sometime this week and I'll cook. Show you that I'm good at more than smashing a guy into the boards."

"With Tim?" she asked quickly.

"Well, of course with Tim," he said. Damn, he hadn't factored her son into this at all. He was thinking of her. Just her and him. Some wine. Some candlelight. His terrific rib steak dinner. Or maybe his equally terrific frozen chicken cordon bleu entrée from Costco. With salad, of course. He made a great Caesar salad. "Hell, Boxer, too, if you want. We can settle it now. How about Friday?"

CHAPTER SIX

WAS HE SMOOTH or was he *smooth?*

She'd agreed to dinner at his place on Friday before she could think of a good reason to refuse. It wasn't as though she had anything else planned. Tim's hockey scrimmages were alternate Fridays, and this Friday was free.

Smooth? Of course. He'd had lots of practice.

Still, she didn't regret her impulsive invitation. Lisa set the table for three and prepared the salad while Patrick, seeming very large in her small kitchen, had done whatever he'd had to do to the crabs. She didn't watch. They were huge, healthy Dungeness crabs—delicious. Even Tim had tried a morsel from a claw and hadn't complained, although he'd refused more. He was happy with his chicken pie.

After dinner, Lisa did the dishes and cleared up the kitchen while Patrick played some game with the dog that started out as "roll over" and turned into Tim and Boxer trying to move Patrick as he lay stretched out on the floor. Boxer growled and pulled at one of Patrick's socks while Tim tugged at a leg. At somewhere around two hundred pounds of muscle and bone, she'd guess, Patrick didn't have to do much more than lie there with his eyes closed, grinning.

Watching the three of them on the living room carpet brought back vivid memories of the joy she'd felt when she and her two brothers had finally managed to triumph over their father in one of their tug-of-war games. Fathers taught their children important physical truths—how much force was too much, what hurt and what didn't. How to play fair and with honor. No pulling hair or pinching, for instance. When to persevere, when to give up. When to switch strategy, as she recalled the times her two brothers had combined forces with her.

Their father had made sure it worked out that way, just as Patrick did now with her son. From the kitchen, she saw him place his palms on the floor and gradually shift his weight backward, making it appear as though Boxer and Tim were finally succeeding.

"Look, Mom! Look, me 'n' Boxer are doing it!" Tim's red, happy face said it all.

She reached into the cupboard for a teapot. Tim was missing all that guy stuff in his life. Her brothers lived in Ontario and Dave's only brother was in jail, so there weren't even any uncles around.

Tim was going to really miss Patrick when he went back to Vancouver. Somehow, Grandpa Dan, much as Tim loved him, didn't quite fill the same bill, certainly not on the physical level.

When Patrick finally got up to accept the cup of tea that Lisa offered, he leaned forward to speak to her softly. "See? What did I tell you?"

His bold "told-you-so" expression made her laugh. She decided she'd been a little unfair. Sure, he made his living playing a violent, bone-crunching sport, but that obviously didn't mean he was a violent man. The time he took with Tim, with Boxer, demonstrated that. In fact, he was a very patient man...who loved to roughhouse, just as Tim and Boxer did.

She might have been wrong about *him,* but nothing had changed her opinion about the sport he played or his role in it. She still wished Tim would abandon his interest in hockey for a gentler sport— swimming, say, or baseball.

Tim crashed early, exhausted after his busy day, and Patrick left almost immediately. At the door, she thanked him again for taking her son fishing.

"That was a wonderful meal, Lisa," he said, his expression more serious than she thought the occasion warranted. His words warmed her. "You're a terrific cook. I don't get a lot of home-cooked meals. And thanks for something else...."

"What's that?" Her cheeks were warm from his praise of the meal, simple and down-to-earth as it was.

"I had such a good time over here, I actually forgot what day it is."

"Oh?"

"Saturday night. That means hockey. Doesn't Tim usually watch?"

"Oh, yes! On CBC." The Canadian Broadcasting Corporation had been televising hockey games on Saturdays since the fifties.

He touched his left knee. "If I'd been home alone, I would've caught the Canucks game and—" He shrugged and Lisa heard real pain in his voice. "Believe me, there's nothing worse than watching your team play when you can't be there to help them out."

Home alone. Somehow Lisa didn't think of Patrick McCarthy as *ever* being home alone. She'd thought of him at glamorous clubs, with beautiful women on his arm, ordering room service in lavish hotel rooms, giving autographs, talking to reporters.

But maybe a hockey star could be just as alone, just as lonely, as a single mom in a new town with a son she adored but few friends and too little money.

Maybe star athletes sometimes watched television alone and went to bed early. By themselves.

She'd never thought of that before.

SUNDAY AFTERNOON, Tim's team lost 8-2 to the dreaded Newton Vipers. The other two Raven goalies let in two shots apiece, but four of the goals from the opposing team went in while Tim was in net. Each shout of the crowd—well, hardly a crowd, more a knot of jubilant parents from the other side—sent a shudder through Lisa. Poor Tim!

When he came out of the dressing room half an hour after the game, he was red-eyed and his face was blotchy. He'd been crying.

She felt horrible for him and her feelings of pity turned to fury when Tim reported that Patrick hadn't been very sympathetic.

"He told me to button up and dry my eyes," Tim said in a wobbly voice as they drove home. "He said I played a good game." Lisa could tell he was proud of that, even though he obviously still believed he was responsible for losing the game. "He said to save crying for when you didn't give it your best. And I gave it my best, Mom!" Tim looked at her desperately, his eyes welling up again. "I did, 'cept my head hurts—"

"Oh, honey! Have you got a headache? Maybe you're getting a cold." Lisa wanted to stop the car and take her son in her arms.

Told him to button up and dry his eyes! How— how unfeeling!

Now Tim was probably getting sick and he'd have to miss school and she'd have to call in and miss work, and all because Patrick took Tim out in the boat and they'd been caught in a rainstorm the day before....

"Yeah," Tim said stoically, and sniffed, glancing her way. She could see he was torn between wanting to get as much sympathy as he could from her, his

mother, and still act like a tough team player as
Patrick, his coach and hero, would expect.

"I said I thought we'd win 'cause we've got him
coaching us now, but he says coaches don't win
games, players do. Hey, there's Jason!" he said as
they drove into the parking area. Tim often played
road hockey with Jason Everett, a boy of about
twelve and leader of a gang of older kids who
played road hockey in the complex. Jason had been
considerably more attentive to Tim and Trevor since
Patrick had arrived.

"What about your headache?" Lisa called as Tim
leaped out of the vehicle and raced toward Jason
and a few other boys, some of whom, Lisa was relieved to see, were closer to her son's age.

When she went out half an hour later to check on
him, Trevor had joined the gang, along with…Patrick.
He grinned and waved his stick in the air. The usual
six or seven kids had grown to a jubilant twenty or
so, including several girls, all chasing a dingy
tennis ball around the parking lot. They'd have
something to tell their friends at school tomorrow, that
was for sure.

Kids. She shook her head and went back inside,
smiling. And men. Some of them never grew up, did
they?

LISA DIDN'T SEE much of her neighbor through the
rest of the week. Tuesday, as usual, he picked up
Tim from school, along with Trevor, and took them

both to afternoon practice, but she didn't see him when they returned. On Wednesday he came to the door briefly, looking a little grim.

"You okay?" she asked, wondering if she *should* ask and surprised at how pleased she was to see him. He wore his usual jeans and windbreaker and had come over to borrow a screwdriver because he wanted to fix something in Dan's condo and couldn't find Dan's tools.

"I'm fine," he said.

"How's the knee?" She glanced briefly at his left knee. "Is it bothering you?" She'd noticed that he was limping more than usual.

"No, it's not bothering me, dammit. Where's the screwdriver? In here?" He frowned at the little locked shed on her deck.

"I'll get it." She retrieved the screwdriver from the cupboard over her washer. It was the all-in-one kind that seemed to do the job.

"You don't have a Phillips screwdriver?" He looked incredulously at the tool she held out.

"Everything's in there." She wasn't sure what a Phillips screwdriver was. "You just open the handle and take out the one you want and—"

"I know how they work, Lisa," he muttered, adding, "or don't work. Well, thanks." He smiled, or tried to—Lisa could see that something was definitely on his mind. "I'll get this back to you right away."

"No hurry. If we're not home, just put it in the

box.'' She indicated the exterior brass-plated mailbox she'd installed—which had been the last time she'd used the screwdriver, come to think of it—because Boxer insisted on chewing up any mail that came in through the slot.

He started to leave and Lisa impulsively stepped forward. "Patrick…"

"Yes?" He turned, frowning.

"It's your knee, isn't it?"

"Yeah," he admitted grimly. "I saw the doctor this morning. It's not healing the way it should and…"

"You don't want to talk about it."

He nodded and gave her a sheepish grin. "Yeah, I don't want to talk about it."

On Thursday, Tim met her at the condo door when she arrived, groceries in her arms. "Mom, we have to go out and get the present."

"What present?" She set the bags on the kitchen counter. "Who for?"

"Trevor. It's his birthday on Friday and it's a sleepover and everything."

"*Birthday* party?" This was the first Tim had mentioned it, and she didn't recall seeing any invitation. Probably in the bottom of his backpack, where Dan's note had languished for four or five days last week. Maybe she should call Evie, see what this was all about.

"Yeah, Trev's turning eight," Tim explained, "just like me and we're gonna go to Surrey with a bunch of other kids and play laser tag. Pow! Bam! Yow-wee!'' He started blasting his way through the apartment, with Boxer's full support.

Friday? She nearly dropped the eggs as she started to put them in the fridge. *Patrick's dinner invitation.*

Well, of course, the birthday party would have to take priority. Trevor was Tim's best friend; Patrick would understand. They'd eat early and then leave an hour or so before practice so Tim could pick out a present for his friend. On the way, she could knock at Patrick's door and tell him dinner was off.

He didn't understand at all.

''Sure,'' he said, nodding when she told him Tim would be going to the birthday sleepover. ''No problem. Dinner for two coming right up.''

''Two?'' She clutched her purse tighter to her side.

''Bring Boxer if you want.'' His smile unnerved her.

''Oh, there's no need to go to all that trouble just for me, Patrick. Really.'' They were on their way to London Drugs to try and find something suitable for an eight-year-old. She had a feeling Tim was going to get her into a real toy store before the evening was over, though.

''You promised, remember?'' The glint in his eye, the challenge, was unmistakable. ''We made a deal.'' The pain she'd glimpsed the day before was gone, and he was back to his usual sexy, relaxed self. "Don't tell me you've got something else on." He rolled his eyes dramatically and placed his hand on his chest, over the white T-shirt he was wearing, which revealed the muscle definition of his very fit athlete's body. Part of it, anyway. "I hope not, because you'd break my heart."

"Patrick!"

"Seriously, I've got the menu planned, most of the shopping done, the place cleaned up—"

"Oh, I couldn't," she said weakly, wishing she did have something else to do. Would a trip to the library count?

"Sure you can. Why not?" He winked and made a wolfish face. "Live a little. Take a walk on the wild side with a big, bad hockey player—oh, is that my phone I hear ringing? See you tomorrow around six. Bye!" With that, he ducked back inside the condo and shut the door.

Laughing, she was sure. *Live a little.* And he did have a point—why not?

CHAPTER SEVEN

WHAT TO WEAR? A dress was too formal. Skirt—maybe. Pants—she was a skirt or jeans person. She didn't have any dressy slacks and jeans were out.

Besides, she kept reminding herself, this wasn't a *date*. This was a simple dinner with one of her neighbors in the same condo complex. And he was merely returning a favor.

She felt like a teenager, digging in her closet late Thursday night and rejecting one outfit after another. Finally, she sat on her bed and put her head in her hands. Skirts, blouses, sweaters. She was so sick of beige and navy! She wanted a—a really hot tangerine number, with a slit up the side and a back that went down to—

Live a little.

At the Willowbrook Mall in Langley, on her lunch break, she found a robin's egg blue sweater with some angora in it, the fiber and the cut—scoop-necked and sleeveless—giving it a little more zip than any she owned. Okay, it wasn't outrageous but it was very suitable and it was on sale. She bought black slacks, too, a modern, slim-fitting cut and a fabric that she decided made her look more sophisticated. Even a little taller. With a short unlined linen jacket she had, she could wear the outfit to business meetings, as well. Double duty.

She eyed the neckline critically in the three-way mirror. Slightly more revealing than she might have liked, but then she was used to T-shirts, crewnecks and buttoned blouses.

Besides—revealing? Hardly, by today's standards. What was she thinking? Just because it wasn't beige? Her friend Lydia back in Toronto would have termed the outfit "casual chic" and that was exactly what Lisa wanted. Despite herself, she wanted Patrick to see her in something besides faded denim and shapeless T-shirts. It was a craving—a deep, feminine craving—and she couldn't rationalize it away. She hadn't felt this kind of compulsion, this kind of desire to dress up in almost a decade.

With the little starfish earrings Tim had made for her in the community center art class last year, she'd be perfect.

Well, at least okay.

"Ah! I SEE you brought Boxer," Patrick said, opening the door wide. Ten past six. Lisa, he'd guessed, was one of those habitually on-time types. "Good! I was hoping you'd bring a friend."

Lisa laughed. "She's been alone all day. I thought you wouldn't mind for an hour or two."

"Not at all." He felt ridiculously pleased that

he'd made her laugh. She looked fantastic. In black pants and a blue top that made her eyes glow like sapphires. "What's this?"

"Oh, just something I brought for dessert," she said, stepping inside and wiping her shoes carefully on the mat.

"You made it?" Why the hell had she brought the dog? Protection?

"No, I stopped at the bakery driving back from Trevor's," she said with a nervous smile. Even her hair was different—softer and curlier.

"Shall I take your jacket?"

"No, I'll keep it on for now. Thanks." She grabbed the lapels and tugged them more firmly over her breasts. Very nice breasts, too. The blue sweater thing, as he'd noticed right away, just skimmed the beginning swell of—

"Nice earrings." He led the way to the living room.

"Oh!" She fingered one in a self-conscious gesture. "You like them? Tim made them last year in his art class. Wow, it looks great in here!"

Patrick had to admit he'd outdone himself. He'd vacuumed and dusted and cleaned up the week's accumulation of newspapers, and when that didn't make the place look quite the way he wanted it, he'd gone out and bought a huge floral arrangement, which sat grandly on Dan's scarred coffee table, dominating the small room.

"What heavenly flowers!" she said, and dipped her head to smell the blossoms.

"Great, aren't they?" Patrick said, wishing he'd remembered to put on some music before the doorbell rang. Nothing romantic, of course. He didn't want her to think he really was a big, bad hockey player—even if he was. The type who noticed a woman's breasts right away—even if he did. "*What* are they, that's the question?"

She laughed again, a sound he found extraordinarily pleasing. "Lilies, here—" she touched two blooms and then a third "—and roses, look at them, apricot and white and yellow. Some eucalyptus and fritillaria and baby's breath and, gosh, I don't know what all." She glanced at him. "This must've cost a fortune!"

"What can I get you to drink? Wine? Beer? Soda?" He'd been a little shocked at the price of the arrangement himself, but how often did he buy flowers?

"A glass of wine would be nice. Thank you."

"White? Red?"

"White, please."

Patrick went to the kitchen and pulled a bottle of champagne from the refrigerator, then chucked some ice cubes into the elderly wine bucket he'd discovered in a lower cupboard. Champagne qualified as white, in his books. Most of his at-home entertaining was done strictly with seduction in mind, and he'd bought two bottles of bubbly before he'd realized that tonight was different.

As he popped the cork, she appeared at the small counter that separated Dan's kitchen from the dining area. The dog yelped as the cork hit the cupboard and bounced on the floor.

"Oh, Boxer!" She leaned down to pat the animal's head. "Champagne? Are we celebrating something?"

He poured the straw-colored fizzing liquid into two wineglasses—Dan didn't seem to stock any champagne glasses—and tried to think of an acceptable response. He handed her a glass and raised his in a toast. "To Trevor. The birthday boy. How old is he today? Eight?"

"Yes." Lisa took a sip and blinked her eyes. "Oh, it went up my nose!"

"Have another sip," he advised. Boxer had parked herself beside him and was looking fondly at his left knee. "Music?" He indicated Dan's sound system with one hand. "I've got a few things I still need to do."

Lisa disappeared around the corner of the living room, and a few minutes later he heard the low strains of some instrumental thing. Middle of the road. He set the table in record time. Plates, cutlery, napkins—

"When it comes to music, Dan doesn't have a lot to choose from, does he?"

He was giving the glasses a quick wipe when she

came back into view. "Not if you don't count Stan Rogers and The Canadian Brass," he admitted. "Or European men's choirs. It can get a little wearing."

She smiled. "Would you like help with anything?"

"No, this is completely my event." He walked into the tiny kitchen and reached for the salad bowl on the counter. "You just sit there and look decorative and offer advice from time to time. If you feel you must."

"Okay." She giggled, taking another sip of champagne, and sat on one of the three tall stools Dan had on the dining-room side of the counter. "What's on the menu? Or is it a secret?"

He could catch a glimpse down the front of her top as she leaned forward—not much, just enough to make the prospect of standing on his side of the counter to make the salad a very pleasant one. "No secret. I hope you like seafood."

"After the crabs, you have to ask?"

"Good. Shrimp cocktail, for starters." And that was because he could buy top-quality shrimp, already shelled, and he could buy decent cocktail sauce in a jar.

"Sounds lovely." Her eyes were twinkling and Patrick realized he'd do anything to keep her looking that way—happy and relaxed. Mellow. It was a nice change from being serious all the time.

"And then, madam—" He bowed and Boxer barked madly. Damn dog. "We have grilled steak with Bernaise sauce and steamed asparagus, baked potato and a spectacular salad that is my specialty.''

"Your specialty?"

"Yes. Caesar salad McCarthy." He raised both hands, hamming it up a bit. "Completely from scratch. Even the dressing.''

"Oh, my. I'm impressed."

"You ought to be. More wine?" He picked up the bottle.

"I shouldn't,'' she said and held out her glass.

"You don't have to drive home.'' *You don't have to go home at all if you don't want to, Mrs. Hudson.*

"So, tell me something about yourself.'' Patrick got the romaine from the crisper. "I don't even know what you do when you go to work every day."

"You don't?" She seemed surprised. "I'm an accountant. I work for a construction company in South Langley.''

"An accountant? Now, *I'm* impressed."

"I enjoy the work. And it was something I thought I could earn a living at after—well, after Dave died." She studied her wineglass and ran the pad of her thumb over the condensation.

"And what kind of work did Dave do?'' he asked gently. Seven years or not, it wasn't as though her husband—and the circumstances of his death—were ever far from this woman's mind.

"Hardware. Family business." She looked a bit sad, reflective.

"I see." Nothing dangerous or violent about that—not like hockey, Patrick thought, annoyed at his cynical reaction. He started tearing up the romaine. "I hope he left you and Tim lots of money."

"A bit of insurance money, that was all. Dave's parents helped me get through my accountancy qualifications. Now, enough about me." She set her glass down firmly. "What about you?"

"Me?"

"Yes." She smiled up at him and Patrick smiled back, feeling rather stunned. His nerves had been on full alert since she'd arrived. God, to think he'd ever considered her plain. She was one of the most beautiful women he'd ever met. "You."

"Well, let's see, I was raised near Winnipeg, typical small prairie town, played hockey since I was Tim's age, played in the Ontario Hockey League as a junior, went to university in Maine on a hockey scholarship, got drafted by the Dallas Stars, traded to a few other teams, finally ended up with the Canucks."

"No brothers? Sisters? Parents?"

"My mother and father live in Florida. I bought them a house in Tarpon Springs and my dad retired early. He was a farmer. My sister lives in Winnipeg, three kids. That's about it." He turned to the stove. The asparagus was in a steamer, ready to be fired up, and the baked potatoes were in the oven.

"Did you always want to be an enforcer-type player?"

"No." He looked coolly at her. *Remember your dreams....* "As a matter of fact, my goal was to be the top goal-scorer in the NHL. Isn't every kid's? My coaches had other ideas. It was a hard lesson for a boy with a head full of dreams." He shrugged. He'd put the hurt behind him; he'd had to. Hockey was a business first, they'd been only too quick to remind him....

"So, what about this Mr. Valentine thing? Are you disappointed they didn't want you this year?"

"Hardly," he said with a laugh. *Relieved* was more like it.

"How many times have you done it?"

"Three times." He glanced at her. He was actually rather pleased at being grilled. Showed she'd been thinking about him. "Why?"

"Oh, I just wondered what it was like, you know, to go out with people you don't even know, just because they won a contest."

"Hell, it's okay. They're always thrilled to win, of course. They pick what to do on the date, that's part of the deal. One year the winner wanted to go on a harbor cruise. Dinner, dancing. Real hockey fanatics, most of them."

"I guess. I suppose they're attracted to the type."

"The type?" He frowned. This woman was full of misconceptions. He didn't have time to set her straight about all of them before he left.

"You know—star athletes. Celebrities." She

played with the stem of her glass. "You ever sleep with any of them?"

He stared at her. "Now what kind of question is that?"

She was beet-red. "Oh, I'm sorry—"

"No, you were curious. It fits your image of arrogant, aggressive hockey players, right? Well, I'd like to satisfy your curiosity, but it's not the kind of question a gentleman answers."

"Patrick—" She looked appalled. "I didn't mean it that way! I don't know why I said anything so stupid."

"Forgiven, my dear." He handed her two water glasses. "Hey, mind putting these on the table? And then I think we can eat."

So, Mrs. Hudson had more on her mind than a decent meal....

Patrick told himself that, tempting as it was, he wasn't going to take advantage. She tried hard, but she was basically a naive, vulnerable woman, nothing like the women who usually drifted in and out of his life. Maybe that was what he found so appealing about her. But seducing Mrs. Hudson would be no challenge at all, and he always hated waking up in the morning wondering why he'd done what he'd done the night before.

He held her chair and she sat down, then he went back to the fridge to bring out the shrimp cocktails, already prepared and in their little iced bowls. He sat across from her and lifted his glass. "Let's not talk about hockey. *Bon appetit.*"

The shrimp cocktail was excellent, if he said so himself, thanks to modern food technology and distribution. "What about you—any plans for Valentine's Day? Big date, I guess?"

"Oh, no!" She colored again. "It's a kids' day, really, isn't it? They're much fairer about it now than they were when I went to school."

"In what way?" So, she had no plans. Too bad there was a Canucks home game then, the Valentine's game. He had to be there. They'd be announcing the winner of this year's contest, who'd be dating Juri Selinek, one of the team's European players, a handsome blond giant.

"The teachers say that if you're going to give out valentines at school, you have to include everyone in the class."

He nodded, wondering if he should've put on the heat under the asparagus already. All the cookbooks said it only took a few minutes to cook, but he wasn't sure he trusted that advice. Somehow, steam didn't seem as, well, definite as boiling water....

"You don't mind about the Mr. Valentine business?"

He shook his head. "What's that?" He hadn't been paying attention.

"You don't mind being bumped from the Mr. Valentine slot because of your knee injury?"

"Hell. Photo ops, talk shows, open lines, all the

publicity they can squeeze out of it. It's not my thing. Of course, I'd do it again if I was asked but I'd much rather be right here, house-sitting for Dan and having dinner with his neighbor—''

"Really?'' She seemed inordinately pleased.

"Really.''

The meal went very well, in Patrick's estimation. He managed to grill the steaks without setting the place on fire, using Dan's oven broiler when he would've preferred a barbecue. Lisa liked her steak medium-rare, which was to her credit. Most women preferred well-done, he'd found, and he considered that out-and-out steak abuse. The asparagus was overcooked since he'd gone with his instincts instead of the book's advice, but Lisa didn't complain. The baked potatoes—well, what could you do to baked potatoes? And the Bernaise sauce was excellent; everything from Sal's Catering in Granville Island was excellent. He'd had the sauce couriered from Vancouver, but she didn't need to know that.

Her box contained two small marzipan tarts, which they consumed, then he suggested retiring to the living room with coffee. Patrick set the dishwasher on four-hour delay. He hoped she wasn't going to race back to her place.

"When does Dan return? Have you heard from him?'' She'd perched on a chair across from the sofa where he sat, fondling Boxer's ears.

"This week sometime, as far as I know. He called the day before yesterday, said his brother's doing well.'' Patrick got up to change the CD and wondered if he should put on one of his own discs. Diana Krall? No. Maybe k.d. lang.

"So you've known Dan for a long time."

"Twenty years. I stayed with the Kristoffersons when I was first in the WHL and I'll tell you, I was one scared kid—"

"Not you!"

"Yeah, me, Lisa." He met her eyes, which were dark and intent. "I didn't know if I was doing the right thing, leaving school and going to a city in another province to play junior hockey. At sixteen? New high school, I never knew who my friends were, if the girls who seemed to like me only liked me because I played hockey—"

"I never thought of that," she said softly.

"Plus, look at me now...." It was a figure of speech, but he was amazed that she did just that— looked him over from socks to haircut—and doubly amazed at what it did to his pulse. "I'm thirty-five and basically finished. Back then, I didn't think about what would happen when I got too old for the game. Now I realize I need to carve out a second career. Maybe business of some kind. Or the media."

"You don't think you'll ever play again?" She sounded horrified.

"Maybe, maybe not." He shrugged a nonchalantly as he could. "But this season's over for me, and who knows about next season? Besides, it's time I made some decisions about my future. Lots of guys my age retire.''

Boxer had discovered the garbage can where he'd dumped the steak bones and appeared with one, festooned with a leaf of romaine Patrick had discarded when he made the salad.

"Boxer!" Lisa got up but before she reached the dog, Patrick had removed the bone and taken it to the kitchen.

"That's no good, girl. Here—" He rummaged in a cupboard and came back with a couple of dog biscuits. "Sit, Boxer."

The dog promptly sat, tongue hanging out in anticipation, eyes shining with enthusiasm.

"My goodness!" Lisa seemed amazed. "She's very cooperative for you, isn't she?"

Patrick delivered the treats and returned to the sofa. "Come here and watch this." He patted the seat beside him and Lisa walked toward him and slowly sat down. "Okay. Boxer, *come.*"

The dog bounded toward him eagerly.

"Sit." Boxer sat.

"Lie down." Boxer flopped onto the floor.

"Boxer, *where's your tail?*" The dog got up and eagerly lunged at her stump of a tail, whirling in circles. Lisa began to giggle. Patrick fondled Boxer's ears again and grinned at the woman beside him. "Now, watch this—Boxer, *hide.*"

Boxer flopped down and put both front paws over her eyes.

"I don't believe it!"

"Boxer, *peek-a-boo*." The dog uncovered one eye and Lisa squealed with laughter.

"That's totally amazing!"

"Isn't it? That's Tim's trick, by the way."

"It is?"

"Yeah. He suggested it. Okay, Boxer—" He leaned back and dug in his pocket for another biscuit. "Good girl."

He turned to Lisa. Her eyes were huge. "How in the world did you *do* that?"

"Walks. Here and there, in the park, when the kids were out playing road hockey."

"You know, I've been—" She paused, but Patrick knew what she was going to say.

"You've been training her on your message machine."

"How did you know!"

"I heard you the first day I went over to pick up Boxer. Dan left me a key and instructions to walk her twice a day. You called and I wondered who belonged to that sexy voice and who would try to train her dog over an answering machine."

"And now you know," she said softly.

"Yeah." He couldn't drag his eyes from hers. "Now I know."

"So—so she wasn't getting better because it was working?" She sounded bewildered.

He shook his head. "I don't think so."

"How do you know so much about dogs?"

"I've had a few. I can give you some tips about training. It's pretty simple."

"How are we ever going to manage when you leave?" Patrick could see uncertainty brimming in her eyes.

"What do you mean?"

"Tim's going to miss you terribly. Boxer, too. They have so much fun with you...."

"And you?" He realized that he wanted her to say she'd miss him, too.

"Me?" She gave a shaky little laugh. "Nobody needs me. I feel a little useless right now. Tim adores you and I can't even train my own dog. I'm not doing very well—"

"Lisa. Look at me."

Rather reluctantly, she turned her head toward him but didn't meet his eyes. He tipped up her chin.

"You're doing a terrific job. Tim doesn't know how lucky he is to have a mother like you. Someone who loves him and has time for him. Who makes sure he gets to play a game he loves even if she hates it. Boxer? Well, hell, she's just a dumb dog but she sure is a happy dumb dog. She adores you. You rescued her from the pound. That's a big responsibility and not everyone would've taken it on."

She looked down again, her lashes fluttering, and Patrick took the opportunity to glance away for a few seconds and to swallow—hard. This woman was doing something incredible to him.

"Look at me," he whispered. "You're a warm, generous, loving person and I-I have a huge amount of respect for you—no, really!"

He tugged her chin around to face him again, when she pulled away, shaking her head in denial. "I admire you, Lisa. I like you. I like you *a lot.* And you know why I especially like you?" His gaze searched hers. "Besides the fact that you're beautiful and sensitive and honest and a damn good cook?"

She smiled tremulously. "Patrick, don't—"

"Because you're not the slightest bit impressed by me," he continued forcefully. "I like that. You don't give a damn that I play hockey in the NHL, right? In fact, you'd prefer it if I didn't. You'd like me better if I was a pipefitter or a truck driver or a pilot, at half, at *a quarter* the pay."

Patrick fought the urge to capture that soft mouth he'd dreamed of for the past week, ever since the night he'd visited her in the rainstorm.

"Well, maybe not a pilot," she said, barely audible.

"No?" He cocked his head to one side.

Her voice shook. "You'd be away too much...."

What was he fighting? Patrick stroked her lower lip with the side of his thumb, his eyes locked on hers, then leaned forward to brush her lips with his. Feather-soft. Testing.

When she moved toward him ever so slightly as he broke contact, her eyes half-closed, releasing her breath in one long, ragged sigh, his restraint cracked. He reached out and pulled her into his arms.

Where she belonged.

CHAPTER EIGHT

LISA WOKE TO THE SOUND of her dog whining at the side of the bed. Her dog but not her bed.

She stared at the ceiling. Omigod, she'd just spent the night with a professional hockey player! A one-night stand, just like any sports groupie. She looked carefully over at Patrick, who lay on his back, still asleep.

His jaw was heavily shadowed—there were places on her own body where she'd felt that rough-ness—his hair was mussed, his chest bare to the waist. *His beautiful body.* A tough, rock-hard ath-lete's body in the absolute peak of physical condi-tioning. It was like waking to find herself in bed with one of those perfectly built models in a Calvin Klein underwear ad, only Patrick's body carried the scars—one across his shoulder, another on his jaw—that were a legacy of the violence of his sport.

Incredibly strong, incredibly tender...

She had to get out of here before he woke up!

She was shocked at her behavior. Shocked, dis-mayed, astonished—but not sorry.

He hadn't talked her into anything. She hadn't had too much wine, although she'd had four glasses, two before dinner and two during, which was certainly her limit.

She'd wanted him. As desperately as he'd seemed to want her. As passionately, as hungrily. It had been seven long, lonely years for her. Patrick McCarthy's knee injury might be keeping him off the ice, but it wasn't cramping his style in bed. But then, he'd obviously had quite a bit of practice....

Lisa inched over to the side of the bed as cautiously as she could, her entire body blushing, if that was possible. Where were her clothes? "Shh!" she whispered to the dog who whined, obviously in need of a pee.

As she was. She inched her way to a chair in the bedroom, where she spotted her slacks and sweater. She picked up everything she could find and went into the living room to dress. Her jacket was flung across the sofa and there was no sign of one earring and her panties. She wasn't stopping to look for them.

She let herself out the door into a morning of glorious blue sky and sunshine. It was only six o'clock on a late-winter Saturday morning. No one, thank heavens, was around. Boxer ran down into the parking lot where there was a strip of grass and relieved herself. Then she came bounding back up the steps, ready to play.

"Don't tell anyone, will you?" she muttered. "Not a soul!" Boxer looked up, one ear raised, the other down. Lisa wondered if that was another trick Patrick had taught her.

A shower, then bed for a few more hours. Later she'd call and see if Tim was ready to come home. There'd be grocery shopping and her usual Saturday afternoon activities—and then what? Dan wouldn't be back for several more days. At some point, she would see Patrick again, would have to meet his knowing eyes, would have to talk to him.

Nothing was going to be the same for her after this. *How in the world would she pretend that it was?*

SHE MIGHT HAVE KNOWN she wouldn't sleep. At eight, Lisa got up again, cinched the pink robe around her waist and went out to the kitchen to make coffee.

At quarter past eight, her doorbell rang. Tim? But he had a key—

"Patrick!"

"You ran."

"I what?" He looked big, handsome and...fully dressed. He also looked angry.

"You heard me. You woke up in my bed, you panicked and you sneaked out, leaving these behind." He held a lacy item of clothing and the missing earring in one hand. "What I want to know is *why?*"

"Oh!" She grabbed her panties and earring and stuffed them in the pocket of her robe. Then she met his gaze, desperately searching his expression for some kind of sympathy. There was none. Only a wariness. *Hurt?* Not Patrick McCarthy, star Canuck forward, tough guy. Not The Enforcer. Not Mr. Valentine, beloved of women.

"I-I thought it was best."

"In what way?" He frowned. "Is that the sort of thing you usually do—sneak out of a man's bed before he has a chance to say good morning?"

Lisa glanced around, afraid they'd be overheard. Patrick wasn't exactly keeping his voice down. "I don't know—I've never done it before," she whispered fiercely.

Abruptly he stepped inside. "Is that coffee I smell?"

She nodded.

"I think a cup of coffee is the least you can offer me, don't you?" He closed the door and Lisa stared up at him. He looked as determined as she felt shaken. "Since it seems I'm not getting an apology."

She walked back to her small kitchen and poured him a mug of coffee.

"Lisa?"

She wouldn't meet his eyes. She added cream and sugar to her own coffee and stirred violently. This was not part of her plan! He wasn't supposed to come storming over here like this!

"No, you haven't done it before, meaning you haven't bolted from a man's bed like this, or no, you haven't been with a man before? Other than your husband, of course.''

"Yes," she said in a small voice. "I've never slept with anyone but my husband and you."

Patrick swore under his breath. She glanced at him, then took her coffee to the living room. She didn't care if he followed her or if he went right back out the door he'd just barged his way through.

A moment later, she felt him behind her and stiffened as he rested his hand on her back, at the nape of her neck. "Hell, I'm sorry, Lisa. I'm sorry I talked to you like that just now." His voice was rough, apologetic. She felt tears prickle. "I had no idea…"

"I'd appreciate it if you didn't apologize for anything," she returned icily, resolutely clamping down on her feelings. "It happened, I'm glad in a way that it did, and now it's behind us, okay? Just another one-night stand for you and a long-overdue experiment for me, I suppose you could say."

"Is that how you think I see this—a one-night stand?" His voice was deadly.

"Of course I do. Your life must be full of women who're only too happy to hop into your bed until you get tired of them or leave town on a road trip."

Patrick swore again. "You have a hell of an idea of hockey players! You have a hell of an idea of *me*—"

"It's true, isn't it?" She turned, daring to meet

his eyes. "Do you have any idea how many women you've slept with during your career?"

"Listen, that's neither here nor there and—"

"Admit it, you can't remember! I've slept with two men. I suppose that's way below average for a woman of twenty-eight. I know it's not some kind of badge or anything to be proud of and, frankly, I'm grateful I had the opportunity to find out I'm not as cold and...and dried-up as I thought I was...."

"Lisa!" He stepped forward and put his arms around her. She refused to respond. "Oh, baby," he muttered into her hair. "There's nothing cold about you. You're warm and passionate and loving—"

He held her away from him, searching her eyes. She lowered her gaze. "Look at me, Lisa. Forget what you've heard about professional athletes. I'm not interested in one-night stands. I told you last night that you were different, that you weren't anything like the women I usually meet."

"Much less experienced, that's for sure," she said, hating the bitterness she heard in her own voice. "Not that I ever pretended to be anything else."

"Lisa, Lisa—that's not an issue, is it? I just wish I'd realized you hadn't...you know, been with anyone in the past seven years. I'm afraid I rushed you, pushed you into—"

"You didn't. Deep down, I must have wanted last night to happen somehow." She shook her head, bewildered. *Had she?* "I accept that. I have no regrets." She pushed away from him so she could look directly into his eyes. "Now I want to move on."

"Let me take you out, spend time with you. Get to know you better...."

"You're leaving, Patrick, in a few days. Back to Vancouver, the team, your career. I think it's best that we just leave things the way they are."

"You don't want to see me?" He sounded incredulous.

"I'm committed to my life here. My son. My dog. My job. I—" Her voice faltered. "We're too— too different. You're a professional hockey player, temporarily injured or not. You live in another world. Travel, excitement, no commitments. I'm an accountant. A mother. Boring. Predictable. This is just something that happened, okay?"

"Predictable! Who are you kidding?" He backed away from her, picked up his mug and poured the coffee remaining in it down the drain. Methodically, he rinsed the cup and put it on her drainboard. *A bachelor's habits.* She watched him in a daze. Where had she found the courage to say those things? More important—were they true?

"So this is goodbye?" he asked, standing by the door, his face unreadable. "You want nothing more to do with me."

"Yes," she said weakly. "I guess it is."

Patrick left, closing the door quietly behind him,

and Lisa sagged against the kitchen counter. She thought she'd heard a door earlier, but she must've been dreaming. Where was Boxer?

Ten minutes later, while Lisa was scrambling some eggs, Tim walked into the living room.

"Tim! When did you get back, honey?" Had he heard her exchange with Patrick? Maybe he'd been in his room the whole time!

"Trev's dad brought me home early 'cause they had to go somewhere." Tim looked subdued, pale. He didn't meet her eyes. "I thought you were still asleep, Mom, so I went to my room." Boxer had appeared with him, which made her think he'd come in while she was arguing with Patrick in the living room. Maybe he was pale because he hadn't had enough sleep last night....

"Have some breakfast. How was the party?" She had to play this straight. Cheerfully. Hope he hadn't overheard her and Patrick.

That's all she could do.

OF COURSE, she had to take Tim to his regular Sunday league game, which was in the town of Ladner, twenty minutes away. Of course she had to listen to the buzz in the stands when the Ladner parents realized that The Enforcer was helping to coach the opposing team. *The man she'd spent the night with, made love to…*

And, of course, she had to suffer agony of an extremely personal kind as she watched him with the boys—talking to one, patting the shoulder of another as he went out onto the ice, leaning forward, cheering his boys on. The team, with Ernie Milfort coaching and Grandpa Dan helping, would never be the same.

Lisa couldn't stop her traitorous memory from seeing that broad-shouldered figure in the jeans and windbreaker down in the players' box the way she'd seen him last night—naked, eager, passionate. In one sense, what she'd told him was right: it *was* an experiment on her part. But in another, she was wrong: she didn't think she'd feel the way she had with Patrick with another man. It wasn't just making love; it was making love with *this* man.

Nor did it help to hear his name on her son's lips constantly on the drive home. The Ravens had won and the team was ecstatic. Of course, Tim believed Patrick had made all the difference.

"Remember what he said, Tim," she reminded him. "It's the players that win the game, not the coach. And don't forget, Grandpa Dan will be back soon."

"Yeah," Tim said with a big sigh. "I miss Grandpa Dan but I'm sure going to miss Patrick, if he goes. Maybe he'll stay in White Rock. Maybe he'll move in with Grandpa Dan. He's got a spare room."

He shot a sideways glance at her. *If* he goes, Lisa thought, not *when* he goes. Her son's imagination was back to working overtime. And, yes, she thought guiltily—she knew all about that spare room.

Tuesday she returned from work just before six o'clock to find Patrick up on a ladder leaning against the roof of her small porch, banging away with hammer and nails.

"What do you think you're doing?" She shifted the satchel of work papers she'd brought home, from one hip to the other, staring up at him.

"Fixing your roof, ma'am, what does it look like?" He hammered in a couple more nails and Lisa could see now that he had half a box of asphalt shingles on the roof.

"Did I ask you to fix it?" she demanded.

"Nope." He kept hammering, a little louder, Lisa thought, than necessary.

"I didn't think so," she finished lamely, not sure what else she could say.

"I'm doing this because you're too proud to ask for help or to accept it if it's offered," he said, looking down at her. "Also because I'm leaving tomorrow and your damn roof leaks. Are those good enough reasons for you, Mrs. Hudson?"

He was infuriating! "I appreciate your fixing my roof," she said, contradicting him coldly. "Thank you very much." She marched toward her condo door and inserted the key. "And—oh, never mind!"

"And what?" He held his hammer in one hand. He was directly overhead, his face deeply shadowed by the setting sun behind him.

"And for everything else you've done for Tim," she continued stiffly. "And me."

"Everything?"

She knew exactly what he meant. She'd told him that sleeping with him had been an experiment for her, a chance to find out if she was still capable of having a physical relationship with a man.... "Yes, *everything!*"

"You're welcome, ma'am." He raised the hammer in a cynical salute. "Always happy to be of *service.*"

She slammed the door behind her. So that was what he thought—that she'd used him! Well, so what if she had? Fair was fair! It had probably been a shock to Patrick's enormous ego to find the tables turned for once.

"Is Patrick mad at you, Mom?" Tim was making himself a peanut butter sandwich at the kitchen counter when she stormed in. He was frowning, his freckles standing out on his pale skin.

"Oh, no, honey! We were just, you know, having a disagreement about something, the way adults do sometimes. How was school?" She ruffled her son's hair lovingly, changing the subject, but he pulled away from her, retreating to the living room where he turned on the television to some channel that featured a lot of car racing and police sirens.

So...Grandpa Dan was coming back tomorrow and that meant Patrick was leaving.

Good riddance. But she knew she didn't mean it.

What *did* she mean? Lisa felt like bursting into tears.

Everything in her life was suddenly all wrong and she had no idea why.

GRANDPA DAN CAME BACK the following day and Patrick was gone. When Lisa got home from work, her gray-haired neighbor was playing goalie for the road hockey gang in the parking lot. Her neighbor laughed uproariously when she told him about the mix-up with the note. Tim seemed thrilled to have Trevor's grandfather back again and didn't even mention Patrick's departure.

That was a relief. The Enforcer had upset their lives for two weeks. Now life could return to normal in the neighborhood. At least, that was what she told herself. At night, when she couldn't sleep for thinking of what had happened that last night they'd spent together, she knew life—for her—would never be normal again.

Then, on Valentine's Day, just when things seemed to be getting back on track, her worst nightmare came true. Her son disappeared.

CHAPTER NINE

IT WAS RAINING lightly when Lisa came home on Thursday night, exhausted after a long day spent on year-end details. Grandpa Dan, bless his heart, had offered to give the boys supper and take them to their seven o'clock practice. She glanced at her watch—nearly half past six already.

That was strange. There wasn't one light on in the house, and when she opened the door, Boxer shot out like a bullet, nearly knocking Lisa down with her greetings.

"Boxer, *down!*" The dog didn't listen to either her or Tim the way she'd listened to Patrick, but Lisa had never really expected that she would. "Where's Tim, Boxer? Where's Tim? Hey, you hungry, girl?"

She flicked on the lights as she walked in, stopping in the kitchen to pour some kibble into Boxer's dish. Usually Tim fed her around half past three or four, when he got home from school. It was one of his daily chores. Strange that he'd forgot to feed her. He must've really had his head in the clouds....

She jumped at a loud knock at her door. Grandpa Dan stood outside, smiling. "You're home, are ya?'' He indicated her roof with his thumb. "I see you got that fixed, finally."

"Your house-sitter fixed it for me. Dan, where's Tim?"

"Where's Tim?" Dan Kristofferson repeated, looking thunderstruck. "Why he's here, isn't he? Him and Trevor? They told me to pick 'em up here for practice because they wanted to watch some show on your TV."

Alarm bells ricocheted through Lisa's brain. "Didn't they eat at *your* place?"

"No, they said to get the pizza delivered here so they could watch their show. I gave Trevor twenty bucks to pay for it—you mean they *aren't* here?"

Lisa grabbed the coat she'd just taken off and quickly put it back on. There'd been no sign of any pizza eaten in the apartment. "They must be outside somewhere. Maybe they're playing road hockey on the other side of the parking lot. You go around and check, and I'll knock on a few doors." Her heart sank. They weren't playing road hockey—it was too dark and they wouldn't forget their practice like this.

There was no one in the parking lot, and most of the kids who played with Tim and Trevor were either indoors eating their supper or watching television or they weren't home. Jason Everett's mother, or whoever answered the door, said he wasn't home, either, but she didn't seem concerned as to his whereabouts. Mind you, Lisa told herself, Jason was twelve, not just turned eight.

"Dan! What are we going to do? The boys aren't anywhere around here." Lisa tried to maintain some semblance of calm. "Shall we call 911?"

All she wanted was Patrick McCarthy. He'd find the boys. There was something so large and comforting and solid about him. He'd know where to look. She knew he would....

"Don't worry, Lisa. They probably just walked around the corner to buy some candy with the change from the pizza. You know boys!" Dan actually chuckled. Then he went into his place to call his son, Trevor's dad, to see if they'd heard anything.

Gone for candy? Without leaving a note or telling someone? Tim would *never* do that! He also would've left half the lights on, as he always did, no matter how many times she told him to shut them off to save electricity.

"They're not there," Dan reported, coming back to the door of his condo, his face ashen. "I don't want to alarm you, Lisa, but maybe we should call somebody."

The police. She knew he meant the police.

"That's my phone!" Lisa jumped at the sound. She wasn't cold, but she was shaking so much her teeth chattered. *Her baby!* Maybe it was Tim....

"Lisa?"

Patrick! "Oh, my goodness, you have no idea how happy I am to hear you—" Her voice broke.

"What's wrong?"

Her knuckles hurt from clenching the receiver so hard. She started to cry. "It's Tim, Patrick. He's gone, we can't find him anywhere, Dan and I have looked all over—"

"That's why I'm calling, Lisa. Tim's here. Trevor, too. Also two other kids, Jason somebody and another boy. Don't worry, they're okay."

"*Here?* Where?"

"GM Place."

"In *Vancouver?*" Impossible! She waved frantically at Dan, who'd stuck his head around the corner of the foyer and held the receiver away from her face. "It's Patrick! The boys are in Vancouver at a hockey game. I don't know how or why they—"

"A hockey game?" Dan looked surprised, then pleased. "Well, the little dickenses! Son-of-a-gun!"

"Oh, sorry, Patrick," she rushed on, into the receiver. "I had to tell Dan. We've been frantic— well, I have. Oh, Patrick, I've been so stupid about—about everything. How can I ever thank you for finding the boys? You have no idea how much—"

"Well, you could let me squeeze in a word or two," he said dryly.

"Oh! I'm sorry. Listen, don't let them out of your sight. Do you hear me? Not for a second. I'll be down there right away to get them—we will, Dan and I. As fast as I can—as fast as *we* can. Oh! I'll have to call Trevor's parents first and tell them he's okay and—"

"Lisa, honey—"

"Yes?" She was still stunned. Stunned and re-lieved and overjoyed and—

"Listen to me—are you listening to me?"

"Yes." She could hardly catch her breath. He'd called her *honey*. He must still like her, a tiny bit at least. Maybe he'd forgiven her for being so stupid and stubborn about the night they'd spent together. "I'm listening."

"Good. Give the phone to Dan."

PATRICK WAS ALMOST AFRAID to hope.

He put his cell phone back in his pocket and glanced at the extremely happy boy beside him. Four boys—Tim, Trevor, their older friend, Jason and another boy, a friend of Jason's apparently. When he'd spotted them in the premier seats he'd expected to see them in—but without Lisa—he'd brought them down to the player's box so he could keep an eye on them while he found out what the hell was going on. They were ecstatic as they rec-ognized all their favorite players up close. Rob Dal-loway, the backup goalie, reached over and cuffed Trevor lightly on the shoulder and the grins got even wider, if that was possible.

Patrick's plan had been to get Lisa into GM Place for the Valentine's game, but he had no idea that he'd be getting her here like this, chasing down her truant son. She was on her way now, in Dan's car.

He'd told Dan not to let her drive under any circumstances, no matter how much she argued.

Now, when she got here… He took a deep breath. He'd never felt this nervous before a game.

His feelings for Lisa Hudson were no game. He'd lasted about a day and a half in Vancouver, telling himself he was better off without her, that she was right—their worlds were too different. Hell, what *was* another one-night stand—as she'd put it?

But why, he'd asked himself then, had she even mentioned that their worlds were too different? Too different for what? If they were just dating, just sleeping together, how could it matter? But if there was more, if she'd thought, even for a second, that there was a possibility of a future with him, then, yes, the differences in their worlds mattered. Because, somehow, they'd have to come to a consensus, an agreement about bringing those two worlds together. Now, with him out for the rest of the season, they had a chance to work on those problems.

If he was right. *If* she really cared for him the way he wanted her to care.

"We're going to have to move, guys," he said to the boys, who'd taken an express bus from White Rock all the way to GM Place, at least a forty-minute ride. There was going to be hell to pay when Lisa got here, but he had to admire the kids for their initiative. None of which excused what they'd done.

It was all his fault, which was how he'd have to explain it to Lisa. He'd given Tim and Trevor four tickets to the game before he'd left White Rock, telling them to bring Dan and Tim's mom as a Valentine's surprise. Instead, they'd shown up with their two road hockey friends and no sign of Lisa. The whole ploy had been designed to see her again, maybe get her to change her mind about him.

It had backfired, big-time. But at least she was coming to the stadium. And she was in an incredibly grateful mood, he could tell. Which had to be a factor on his side.

He shepherded the boys to the VIP box on the first level, where he'd told Dan to meet them. The second period had just started. The Canucks were down one-nothing to the LA Kings, but how he'd keep his mind on the game for the next half hour or so, he didn't know.

"TIM!"

Patrick stood as Lisa and Dan came into the private box. She ran to her son after a quick glance that set Patrick's heart pounding, and flung her arms around the boy. She looked gorgeous. Blue skirt, white blouse, beige raincoat.

"Oh, Tim, how could you have done this? You should've left a note!"

"I didn't even have to spend my allowance, Mom. I saved it. Patrick gave us the tickets." She looked up and Patrick shrugged. Explanations were going to have to come later.

She took a few steps to stand in front of him, her

expression as uncertain as he felt. "Patrick. Oh, Patrick!" She threw herself into his arms and he closed them tight around her. He buried his face in her hair, inhaling its glorious scent. He remembered that first time—was it only two weeks ago?—that he'd sneaked a brief whiff of her hair, her skin. She'd been wearing that pink bathrobe. He'd fallen for her, right then and there.

"Oh, Lisa!"

"Hey! Mom and Patrick, you're standing in the way, I can't see—look, Steve Smith nearly scored!"

Patrick glanced down and caught the boy's eye. He winked. Tim grinned. The kid was definitely in his glory, with his buddies, his hockey hero and at a real game.

Tim stuck out his hand, thumb up, a question in his blue eyes. Patrick returned the gesture behind Lisa's back and Tim's freckled face broke into a thousand smiles. All of which made Patrick think, fleetingly, that maybe there'd been some method to the kid's madness in taking the bus to Vancouver with his pals....

Dan was sitting at the other end of the row, beside the boys. Dan winked and threw him a quick thumbs-up, too.

"Here, Lisa. Sit down." She took the seat beside him. Her cheeks were red and her eyes were brilliant. Patrick put his arm around her and leaned toward her. He couldn't wait a second longer to kiss the woman he loved. Lisa kissed him back, slipping her arms around his neck.

"Hey, Mom! Patrick! They're announcing the new Mr. Valentine winner."

The crowd roared.

"You're my Mr. Valentine," Lisa said softly.

He bent to kiss her again. Somehow he'd managed, awkward as it was, to keep his arms around her. "And you'll *always* be mine, Valentine."

HER SECRET VALENTINE

Helen Brooks

CHAPTER ONE

'Who was the bright spark that suggested Jim's retirement presentation should be followed by drinks and food all afternoon? Whoever it was has a lot to answer for if you ask me.'

Jeanie glanced up from her littered desk and smiled at the tall dark figure standing in the doorway of her private office. 'Do I take it you aren't enjoying yourself out there?' she asked mildly, her warm amber-brown eyes focusing on Ward Ryan's handsome and distinctly irritated face.

He grimaced, stepping inside and shutting the door, and as ever the steady thud-thud of her heart went crazy for a few moments before settling into the regular even beat one would expect of an experienced and highly respected junior partner in a large thriving solicitors' practice in the heart of London.

'What makes normally reserved and sensible people suddenly go crazy when someone mentions the words ''office party'' anyway?' Ward walked across to Jeanie's desk and perched easily on the edge of it, raking back a lock of black hair as he did so and frowning darkly. 'It was the same at Christmas...

Jenny and Stephanie were practically paralytic then and the other two secretaries weren't much better which doesn't set much of an example to their juniors. Did you know Bob's been ensconced in the stationery cupboard with Catherine for the last twenty minutes, and John and Michael are taking bets on who gets to take Kim home?'

Jeanie shrugged. She had been with Eddleston, Breedon and Partners for five years now and the two senior partners—Joseph Eddleston and Dan Breedon—looked after all their employees handsomely, *too* handsomely at times. It was right that Jim Hatton's long years of service should be acknowledged and celebrated, but some individuals just weren't too good on handling free drink.

She glanced more closely at Ward and then said drily, 'You might want to wipe the lipstick off your cheek but I don't think you can do much about the pink shade on your shirt collar.'

'Damn women!' It was a low growl, and as Ward extracted a crisp white linen handkerchief from his pocket and scrubbed at the chiselled cheekbone Jeanie had indicated, she had to bite back a bittersweet smile.

All the women in the practice—from the nineteen-year-old office junior, Kim, with her fluffy blonde hair and come-to-bed blue eyes to Mildred Robinson, the two senior partners' sergeant-major type personal assistant—had a crush on Ward Ryan to varying degrees. And Ward's cool, distant manner at the office, his unwritten law about keeping work and play totally separate, seemed to make some of the more predatory females desperate to be noticed when office protocol was relaxed a little, like today.

'That looks like Jenny's colour?' Jeanie was determined to keep things light but ridiculously, after all the years of loving him from afar, it still hurt to think Jenny had actually done what she would give her eye teeth to do and kissed Ward. But then that would ruin the closeness between them that her self-control and reticence had been rewarded with, she reminded herself.

She knew he regarded her as his buddy, his close friend, probably the only woman friend he had because he never continued seeing the women he dated after he finished with them. The Ice-Man. That was his nickname among the female staff but it didn't stop them all fancying him like mad, she thought ruefully.

But he wasn't an ice man, not really. You only had to see him with his six-year-old daughter to know that, but then apart from herself she doubted if anyone at Eddleston and Breedon had had that privilege.

'Jenny!' Ward made an exclamation of extreme irritation. 'I was hoping to finish off the Bakerson report before we closed tonight but she seemed to think I'd asked her to come into my office for quite another purpose.'

'You're just an old meanie.' Jeanie had long since decided what tack she was going to take when some female or other threw herself at Ward—she'd had to, it wasn't an uncommon occurrence. 'Jenny just likes to flirt a little, that's all.'

The piercingly blue eyes surveyed her for a moment and then the hard handsome face relaxed in a smile that always had the power to make Jeanie go weak at the knees. 'Jenny's attractive enough,' he admitted easily, 'but she's my *secretary* for crying out loud.' That, in Ward's opinion, said it all.

Jeanie nodded briskly. She always found, with these sort of conversations, that her limit of endurance was reached fairly quickly and now she changed the subject as she said quietly, 'All ready for Bobbie's birthday party? It's this weekend, isn't it?'

'Uh-huh. The twentieth of January,' Ward agreed.

She loved his voice; it was part of his overall attraction and of a deep smoky quality that was pure dynamite on the hormones. And now, as he stretched his neck and shoulders and powerful muscles flexed and bunched Jeanie found she had to take a deep hidden breath and let it out steadily before she could trust herself to speak.

'I suppose Bobbie is excited?' she said with as much casual warmth as she could manage considering she wanted to leap over the desk and devour him. She should never have had those couple of glasses of wine earlier, she thought grimly. It was vital to have one hundred per cent control around Ward at all times.

'Off the wall,' he agreed with another 24 carat smile. 'Going from six to seven is an event of supreme importance apparently, and I don't think there's a kid in the neighbourhood who hasn't been invited. Add to that the repeated pleas for a hamster for her birthday and she's worked herself up to fever pitch.'

'And is Daddy going to deliver said hamster?' It was a purely rhetorical question. If Bobbie had asked for the moon it would have undoubtedly been parcelled up and placed with Bobbie's cards and gifts on her birthday morning this Sunday.

Ward's wife had died six and a half years ago when the car the beautiful redhead had been driving had been hit by a falling tree in the middle of a freak storm and ended up in a ditch. Bobbie had been strapped in a baby seat on the back seat of the vehicle which had undoubtedly saved the infant's life, but the nine-hour operation which had followed to save the tiny child's crushed legs had left the little girl with the slightest of limps.

'It's been living in Monica's bathroom for the last two days,' Ward admitted with a mocking twist to his firm mouth. He was well aware his tiny daughter was able to wind him round her little finger. 'Which is an act of extreme heroism on Monica's part considering she is antirodents of any description.'

Jeanie nodded. She wasn't at all surprised.

Ward's stout housekeeper worshipped the ground Bobbie walked on, and as Monica had never married and was now well over sixty, Ward and Bobbie were her family and she filled the role of indulgent grandmother perfectly.

'And you?' Ward drawled comfortably, leaning across the desk slightly and pouring himself a glass of wine from the bottle Jeanie's secretary, Stephanie, had brought in earlier when she'd given up trying to persuade her workaholic boss to come and join the 'fun,' as Stephanie termed it. 'What are you doing this weekend?'

It took a moment—well, more than one, Jeanie conceded crossly—for her to pull herself together sufficiently to think coherent thoughts. She always felt a terrible fascination grip her in Ward's presence, but today, with the warmth and scent of him filling her air space and his hard powerful thighs outlined under his trousers which had stretched taut as he balanced nonchalantly on the end of her desk, she felt positively liquid.

She had hoped, over four years ago now when she'd finally admitted the awful truth to herself and acknowledged that she was crazily, madly, *irrevocably* in love with one of her fellow partners, that she'd get a handle on coping with this thing that had hit her like a ton of bricks the first time she'd set eyes on Ward Ryan. She was still hoping.

The truth was she should have left the practice then, or in one of the four years which had followed.

It would have been the sensible thing to do, something she would have told someone else in her position was the only sensible course of action.

Ward never discussed his late wife, but it was common knowledge he had been like a living, breathing robot for months and months after her untimely death, and even when he had seemed to return to the human race it was with an air of rigid autonomy where members of the opposite sex were concerned.

He had started dating occasionally a couple of years after Patricia, his wife, had died, but any woman who got involved with him had to accept the relationship would only be semi-permanent and with no strings or commitment on either side. The only female who had a place in his heart was his daughter and he had no intention of changing the status quo.

'What am I doing this weekend?' she said after a moment or two. 'Meeting a friend for lunch tomorrow and then driving up to York afterwards to see my family. I haven't seen them since Christmas and that was hectic with all my nieces and nephews gathered en masse.'

She wished he'd remove those lean hips from her eyeline. The fact that Ward was totally unaware of the impact of his sex appeal didn't make it any the less difficult to deal with.

He nodded thoughtfully. 'I sometimes think it's a pity Bobbie hasn't got any cousins or family other than my parents in Oxford,' he said slowly, leaning forward again and offering her a sip from the glass in his hand. 'What do you think?'

She *thought* that his aftershave ought to be banned as being downright dangerous to a woman's state of mind, Jeanie told herself, as she squeaked a refusal to the wine and wondered how that tanned hard male chin with its faint stubble would feel beneath her lips. 'I... I think Bobbie's fine,' she managed eventually when she realised he was waiting for an answer to his question. And then she nerved herself and broke the silent code which underpinned her friendship with Ward as she added, 'Hadn't your wife any brothers or sisters, then?'

It was the first time she had mentioned Patricia—no one but *no one* ever did unless they wanted a granite stare and a frosty put down—but apart from stiffening slightly he showed no reaction as he said quietly, 'No, she was born to a single mother and brought up in a succession of foster homes.'

And then he shrugged himself off her desk, his impossibly blue eyes narrowed and remote and the hard angles and planes of his face closed against her as he walked across to the window and finished the glass of wine in one swallow. 'It looks like it's going to snow,' he said evenly as he stood with his back to her looking down into the busy London street beneath.

She was just opening her mouth to reply when a gust of high riotous laughter mingled with raised voices and the sound of a champagne cork popping reached them.

Ward swung round, his face and voice dry as he said, 'I think I'll disappear to my office and work on that report after all. I've already toasted Jim when Joseph and Dan presented him with his gold watch and his secretary got all emotional. I can't stand any more discussions about how he and his wife are going to spend their retirement. See you later, Jeanie.'

Jeanie nodded but didn't say anything as Ward left her office. He hadn't liked her mentioning his wife. It was the one thought which kept returning all through the darkening afternoon as Jeanie worked on, long after the others had begun to dwindle off home in their ones and twos. Obviously his pain was still as fresh, as raw as it had ever been. What must it have been like to have been loved like that by Ward?

It wasn't the first time she had brooded along these lines, and she let her imagination have free rein for some time which was stupid, she told herself sternly, miserable minutes later. She knew full well such rumination always left her feeling rotten. She had given up dreaming that one day Ward would glance at her across the desks and filing cabinets and Cupid's arrow would hit ages ago. It was time to count her blessings again!

She was thirty-two years of age, hugely successful in her own particular field of family law as her position at Eddleston, Breedon and Partners, and her nice fat pay cheque each month confirmed.

She owned her own little mews property, a small car; she had no financial worries and heaps of good friends. Her social life wasn't the stuff the tabloids liked, but it was full and active and she didn't have to spend one evening alone unless she wanted to. She was lucky. She *was*. She was very, very lucky, she reiterated grimly, springing up and walking over to the window in a flurry of irritated frustration and dissatisfaction.

It was quite dark outside, the lights from the offices and shops below her office on the third floor of the building, vying with the headlights of the busy, rush hour traffic snaking along the road. Well, it was the weekend again, something most people anticipated with some delight. For her, however, it just meant two days when there was no possibility of seeing Ward.

Oh, she was pathetic! A really sad case. She glared at the reflection in the glass, and dark eyes set in an oval face with delicate, elegant bone structure stared back at her. She smoothed her thick, sleek hair in its tight coil at the back of her head absently, suddenly aware she had a headache. It was probably more due to the amount of wine she had slowly consumed during the afternoon than the army of hairpins holding her hair in place, but suddenly she rebelled against the severe hairstyle she always wore for work and attacked the pins deter-

minedly, combing her hair through with her fingers
once it was hanging in a heavy shining blue-black
curtain to below her shoulder blades.

That was better. She lowered her chin as she shut
her eyes, rotating her head round and round as she
massaged bunched muscles at the base of her neck.
It had been a long day and in spite of remaining
glued to her desk she hadn't done half of what she
wanted to do, and no doubt she was the last one
here as usual.

And then she caught at the self-pity, hating it and
herself and this whole situation with Ward that had
no hope of ever turning out as she would like. She
groaned softly, biting her lip hard.

And then she nearly jumped out of her skin as an
urgent, concerned voice behind her said, 'Jeanie?
Are you feeling unwell? What's the matter?'

And she was turned round by a large pair of
strong hands and found herself an inch or so away
from Ward's broad chest staring up into the never
ending blue of his eyes.

Whether it was her previous thoughts, or the
wine, or the fact that she'd assumed he'd already
left and she wouldn't be seeing him for a lifetime,
or just the fact that his unexpected appearance
brought home just how much she loved him, Jeanie
wasn't sure, but the next moment she had horrified
them both by bursting into tears. And not ladylike,
controlled, solicitor-type tears either, but great loud

wails complete with streaming eyes and a runny nose and the whole package.

Neither was the flood stemmed at all when she found herself enfolded tenderly into the haven of his arms, her wet cheeks resting against the magnificent male chest she had dreamt about so often, and his voice warm and smoky above her head as he murmured soothing nothings.

It was torture. Exquisite, heavenly, worth dying for torture admittedly, but torture nevertheless.

Jeanie went for gold and cried until there were no more tears left, and to be truthful she was amazed where they had come from in the first place. She hadn't been aware she'd been so low or so despondent, but perhaps five years *was* a long time without one hug or loving caress from the man you loved, she comforted herself weakly.

Whatever, she had made a mammoth fool of herself. As the knowledge dawned she felt more bereft. Whatever was she going to say to him? she asked herself dazedly as the sobs faded to soft hiccups and he still continued to hold her against him.

She couldn't tell him the truth and Ward being Ward would detect a lie a mile off. What had she done? Oh, what had she done?

CHAPTER TWO

JEANIE would have been happy to stay in his arms for ever. For all eternity. Locked against him so closely she could hear the steady slam of his heart, and feel surrounded by his male warmth and smell which was partly expensive aftershave on clean tanned skin and something else which was purely Ward. Even if he *was* holding her as a friend if this wasn't heaven it wasn't far off.

She sniffed carefully and then, as she felt herself moved away from her nesting place and felt a handkerchief dabbing at her wet eyelids, she almost whimpered with disappointment.

She opened her tear-drenched eyes and saw Ward was looking down at her with speculative concern, and for the life of her Jeanie couldn't think of a single thing to say to ease the excruciating awkwardness of the moment.

Not that Ward seemed to find it so. His sexy cynical mouth was twisted wrily and his blue eyes narrowed and intent on her hot face as he said, with a soft huskiness that produced a riot of sensation in her stomach she could have well done without in the present circumstances, 'Want to tell me what that was all about?'

No, she didn't. She stared up at him helplessly as she tried to brace herself for more questions. Because they would come. Oh yes, they would come all right. Ward was a brilliant lawyer with an almost scientifically rational and probing mind. He had a formidable reputation among his colleagues, not least for his tenacity and strength of will, and she had heard the other partners refer to him more than once as a genius. And now every cell of that frighteningly intelligent brain was homed in on her. It was a daunting thought.

'Why didn't you tell me something was wrong before?' he probed softly. 'We're friends, aren't we?'

Oh, God, please don't let me humiliate myself any further, she prayed frantically, as the last words hit home. Please let me extract myself from this with a little bit of dignity at least. I promise you I'll never ask for anything else in the rest of my life if you do!

She reached out and took the handkerchief from him, utterly unable to meet his eyes as she turned away and walked over to the seat she had vacated earlier, sinking down into the soft leather as her legs gave out completely. 'I… I'm sorry,' she managed at last, and then froze in horror as he walked across to crouch in front of her, taking both of her hands in his.

'Don't be sorry,' he said gently, 'and don't be embarrassed either. We've been friends too long for that. And all the others have gone so don't worry about them.'

The others? She hadn't given them a thought!

And then her heart turned right over as his voice gentled still more, like warm velvet, as he murmured, 'It can't be the job. Dan Breedon was singing your praises only the other day and saying he is constantly amazed by the amount of work you get through in any one week. And you said you had a great time with your parents and your sisters and all their kids at Christmas, and you're seeing them this weekend again. So, call me old-fashioned or just plain presumptuous, but could this unJeanie-like despondency have anything to do with a man?'

She had been fighting the hot prickles of sexual awareness that had flushed her cheeks and were threatening to make her tremble, but now she jerked her hands free, a mixture of surprise and—amazingly for her where Ward was concerned—anger sending adrenalin pumping fiercely round her bloodstream.

Surprise firstly at his intuition, and anger because it had suddenly dawned on her with his last words that for years Ward had only seen what he wanted to see regarding her. How did he know whether despondency was one of her natural traits anyway? He'd always demanded the same old steady, uncomplaining, reliable, friendly Jeanie be there for him.

No complications, no messy emotions, no hysterics; he probably didn't view her as a *woman* at all. Just a dependable, predictable pal who happened to wear skirts and speak in a falsetto range!

Well she *was* a woman, a woman whose biological clock was ticking and who wanted a proper family home, babies, a husband. No, not just a husband—him; she wanted *him*. 'Yes, it is about a man.' She heard herself speak the words with a feeling of acute amazement and regretted them immediately, but it was too late. They were out and there was no going back.

She forced herself to meet the clear, darkly lashed blue eyes and saw they were soft with sympathy. Sympathy but nothing more. And it was only in that second that she realised she'd been hoping for something—*anything*— else. A spark of disquiet. The faintest trace of jealousy. Just a smidgen of disturbance in that cool, controlled, orderly freezer he called a brain box, where he thought he'd got everything wrapped neatly in little parcels.

And then she felt horribly, wretchedly guilty as he stretched out a tender hand and stroked one cheek gently, his voice warm with sincerity as he murmured, 'I don't know anything about it of course but I can say without any doubt that he's not worthy of you, you or your tears.'

Probably not but that didn't exactly help right now! And she had no right to expect anything at all of Ward, she reminded herself miserably. He couldn't help how he viewed her any more than she could help loving him.

She watched him crouch back on his heels again for a moment before rising slowly to his feet, and as she raised her eyes to his face she saw the sympathy was still there but threaded through with what she could only describe as faint surprise. 'Do you know I've just realised I don't know anything at all about you with regard to your relationships with the opposite sex,' he said thoughtfully. 'You've never talked about that area of your personal life with me, have you?' His eyes wandered over the shining, blue-black curtain of her hair as he spoke as though that was another thing she'd kept from him.

Jeanie shrugged carefully. She suspected there was the faintest touch of pique in this somewhere, but it wasn't quite the moment to remind him that he'd never had the interest to ask. That razor-sharp mind that made him a force to be reckoned with was already busy compiling data, and she had certainly said far too much as it was. She would die, shrivel away to nothing if he even so much as remotely suspected how she really felt about him. 'I could say the same about you,' she said quietly.

He nodded. 'True.' He seemed to digest that for a few moments and then said tentatively, 'Have you known him long?'

'A while.' She shifted uncomfortably in the chair.

'And you've had a row or something?'

She hadn't had so much as a something but she

couldn't very well say so! Aware she had to be very wary indeed she said cautiously, 'Not exactly a row. It's just that he doesn't want to settle down and I do.' That much at least was true, she comforted herself guiltily finding it was much harder than she'd thought to lie to Ward. Although if she considered what she *had* said she really hadn't lied at all, more…misled him?

'He'll change his mind, Jeanie. Give him time. Men need to work into responsibility sometimes.''

'No, he won't change his mind,' she said very steadily. 'He doesn't feel the same way about me as I feel about him, you see. His feelings aren't the forever kind.'

'He's *told* you that?' He sounded so shocked she almost could have smiled. Ward had run his love life on that theme for the last six years but apparently heartily disapproved of this man doing the same!

'Oh yes.' Well, he had in a way.

'Hell!'

That was it in a nutshell, she thought soberly. Sheer hell, especially when he was looking at her as though he wanted to take this other man and strangle him. 'It doesn't matter.' She forced a smile which considering she must look like she'd been pulled through a hedge backwards probably made her appear more pathetic, she thought on reflection.

And this seemed to be borne out when he said urgently, 'Dump him, Jeanie, if you haven't done so already. If it can't go anywhere and you're eating your heart out, it's better to cut and run.'

'I can't do that.' She spoke from her eaten-out heart and with an intensity that caused him to stiffen. 'He might not want to marry me and can't love me like I love him, but he's my world until he chooses to step out of it.'

He was staring at her as though he had never seen her before, his eyes narrowed and almost navy-blue with a dark emotion that made him seem more handsome than ever.

He shook his head, raking back his hair in a gesture she knew meant irritation or worse. She knew lots of little things like that about him; she'd had five years to absorb them into her being. 'As big a fool as he is, you're a worse one to waste your life on such an ungrateful swine,' he ground out harshly, making her eyes widen with surprise at his fierceness. 'You're not getting any younger, Jeanie.'

The adrenalin pumped harder, and her voice carried an acidic note that wasn't lost on the big tall man watching her so closely, when she said, 'Oh thank you, Ward. I really needed you to point that out. That makes me feel a whole lot better.'

He had the grace to look discomfited. 'I didn't mean... Hell, you know you're a beautiful woman, Jeanie, in the prime of life. It's just that—' He stopped abruptly, aware he was making it worse. 'I just don't like to think of you being used like this, that's all,' he said finally, his voice soft.

If this wasn't the height of irony she didn't know what was! Jeanie managed a fairly offhand shrug, and her voice carried a cool note that indicated the conversation was at an end when she said, 'I'm not being used, Ward. He never made me any promises and I went into it with my eyes wide open. It takes two to tango after all. Normally I can handle it just fine but you caught me at a low ebb tonight. Perhaps it's because this has been a particularly strenuous week and I'm tired, or the wine I've consumed on an empty stomach, I don't know. But I'm fine. Really.'

He didn't look at all convinced, surveying her thoughtfully from eyes which had taken on a steely hue. And she knew what that meant too, Jeanie thought ruefully. He had had a situation presented to him, had decided upon a logical and straightforward solution and the other party wasn't seeing it his way. She'd seen this look before in business when a client was being difficult or obtuse. That undeniably brilliant mind was now considering what other tack to take.

'Right.'

He'd clearly come to some decision, she noted with dark hidden amusement which was tinged, as always, by overwhelming sexual attraction. Both his tone and the enigmatic quality of his smile proclaimed it.

'You've just said your stomach is empty and all I've had today is a few nibbles from the buffet out there, so I'm taking you home for one of Monica's excellent lasagnes,' he said in a tone that brooked no argument. 'And then afterwards, once Bobbie's in bed and we've got the sitting room to ourselves, we're going to have a good chat, you and me.'

His expression was understanding but for once Jeanie felt—quite irrationally she admitted silently to herself—like kicking him. This was Ward in supremacy mode; manipulation by the iron hand in the velvet glove. He meant well, she knew he *meant* well, but she really didn't feel like discussing her bruised heart any further with the shredded tatters of her dignity pulled tightly round her. It was also far too dangerous an undertaking in the circumstances.

'I'm sorry, Ward, I can't, but thanks for the offer,' she said politely.

'Why not?' The piercing gaze fastened on her face. 'Are you seeing him tonight?'

Like a terrier with a bone, as always! 'No,' she managed fairly calmly, 'but I've heaps to do before I go to York tomorrow.' She dropped her eyes to her desk as she spoke, more to shut out his disturbing presence than because she needed to tidy it before she left.

Ward's charcoal-grey suit jacket was unbuttoned revealing a blue shirt tucked into the flat waistband of his trousers, and at some time during the afternoon he had loosened his tie and undone the first two or three buttons of his shirt. He looked less than his normal impeccable self and twice as sexy, and she really couldn't take it.

'Sorry, but that won't do.' Her head shot up at his words and whether it was because he'd seen her jaw set and her mouth tighten she wasn't sure, but his voice took on a distinctly soothing tone as he said, 'I'll be worrying about you all weekend if we leave it like this. At least come and have a hot meal and relax for a couple of hours, and we won't discuss it at all if you don't want to. And Bobbie would love to see you again. She still talks about the lady from my office who played snap with her all evening even though it was a few weeks ago.'

'She's a sweetheart.' Ward had been ill with the flu and had called her to bring some urgent papers round to him after work, and once there Monica had insisted on feeding her and Bobbie had pounced on a playmate. Jeanie hadn't minded; Bobbie was a naturally funny and truly lovable little girl, but seeing Ward in a home setting with his daughter had upset her equilibrium for the next twenty-four hours... For days... Well, ever since then really.

They had often had business lunches together or popped in the local wine bar after a stressful day for a drink to unwind, and on those occasions she knew Ward relaxed and emerged from the mask he normally wore, but that evening at his home she had seen him as a father and it had blown her mind.

In spite of feeling like death he had been gentle and patient and so tender with the small child it had been a revelation, and Bobbie herself had tugged at Jeanie's heartstrings. She'd gone home and cried all night. A repeat of that was the last thing she needed. She opened her mouth to refuse again but got no further than, 'Ward—'

'Please, Jeanie, if not for yourself then for friendship's sake?' he asked silkily with a winsome smile. 'It will put my mind at rest.'

He had turned on the charm and although she knew it—had watched him use every trick in the book and charm the birds out of the trees in various situations in the past when it had suited him to do so—it was different when the full force of that magnetic personality was coming her way. Jeanie floundered 'I... I really don't want to talk about...him if I come.'

'Fine. No problem,' he gentled.

'And I shan't be able to stay long. I need to catch up on some chores at home and tonight is the only chance I'll have this weekend,' she said nervously, wondering how on earth she had managed to put herself in this ridiculous position.

'I understand perfectly. Finish off in here and we'll leave in...what? Ten minutes?' he asked cheerfully.

Jeanie nodded a touch bewilderedly, feeling as though she had just been run over by a steamroller.

Ward slanted a look at her troubled face from under half-closed lids and clicked his tongue with genuine irritation. 'No more brooding about this worthless idiot, not tonight,' he said briskly. 'Okay? You won't be able to give Bobbie's birthday your full and undivided attention if your mind's elsewhere,' he added with an obvious attempt to lighten the charged atmosphere. 'What's in the parcel you gave me for her anyway?'

'A doll,' Jeanie said shortly. She didn't add that it was a bride doll in full wedding regalia because she had the nasty feeling it was something of a revealing gesture, and was regretting her choice of present bitterly. But she knew Ward's daughter would adore the sweet-faced doll, and since the day she had met Bobbie she had thought about her often and felt terribly sorry for the small scrap of humanity who had been forced to grow up without a mother's love. 'Right, ten minutes you said?'

Ward took the hint and left, but Jeanie sat for another two minutes in a state of blind panic, her mind racing back and forth, before she took hold of herself. Enough, she told herself silently. Everything's okay. He doesn't know it's him and he's not going to know unless you tell him. So, calm. Calm, girl.

By the time Ward poked his head round her door Jeanie's desk was clear, her private filing cabinets locked and everything was spick and span.

'Ready?' he smiled from the doorway. He had pulled on his big black overcoat which accentuated his particular brand of dark maleness, and the blue of his eyes was riveting as he glanced over at her, quite unaware of his air of arrogant sophistication.

The man who had everything. Even as she smiled and nodded her mind was working quite independently. Everything except the one thing he really wanted, his dead wife. What had she looked like, Patricia? What had she *been* like, as a person, to capture his heart so completely?

Office gossip had related that she had been a tall, slim redhead and stunningly beautiful, but when Jeanie had visited his home that time there had been no photographs of Bobbie's mother as she had expected. Bobbie herself was tiny for her age, with delicate pixie features and dark brown hair and eyes, but, adorable as the little girl was, she couldn't be termed beautiful or even particularly pretty, which was surprising with her parentage...

'Jeanie?'

She gave a guilty start, suddenly aware she had been miles away, and then flushed hotly at the expression on his face. 'Sorry,' she apologised weakly. 'I'm not myself today.'

'Quite.' It was terse, and she realised—with a little dart of painful amusement—that Ward wasn't used to women day-dreaming about another man in his presence, which was what he'd obviously assumed.

She had already slipped into her coat before he'd arrived and now she flicked her hair back over her shoulders where it shimmered like raw blue-black silk against the cream material.

The movement caught his eye, and again the faint surprise she'd read earlier on his face was there, along with something else she couldn't place, when he said quietly, 'Why don't you usually wear your hair like that? It's a crime to hide such beauty.'

'I don't think it's formal enough for the office.' The compliment—the first one she had received from Ward on a personal level and unconnected with her work—had totally thrown her, and she was concentrating on appearing matter-of-fact but it was hard.

He was still staring at her for one thing, and although he was leaning nonchalantly against the open door and appeared perfectly relaxed and cool—his normal self in fact—something had changed. There was electricity in the air.

And then she admonished herself silently for being so ridiculous. Pure imagination, she told herself sharply. Just because he had given her a compliment! The thing was, sexual provocativeness had never been part of her nature and she wasn't the sort of woman who blatantly invited flattery or even dealt with the occasional compliment very well.

She was the youngest of five sisters, and had always felt very much the odd one out. The others all had a couple of years separating them, but there was a six-year age gap between herself and Charlotte, her mother's fourth child, although that wasn't the only reason she'd always felt like the cuckoo in the nest. Lizzie, Susan, Miranda and Charlotte were all small and fair-haired—the colour ranging from blonde to golden brown—and on the voluptuous side.

She was tall and slender and had felt like a stick insect beside them through her teenage years, and her different colouring had been striking enough to emphasise the contrast even more and was invariably commented on when relatives and friends called by. She loved her sisters, every one of them, but had never really felt she *belonged* somehow, and the fact that they had all married fairly young and settled down to have large families within the same little community hadn't helped.

She moved quickly now, switching off her desk lamp and walking across the room as she said, 'I hope my turning up unexpectedly won't put Monica out.'

'Of course not, she'll love to see you again.' The expression of thoughtful gravity was gone and the blue eyes were smiling at her now, and as they walked out of the office and towards the lift at the end of the shadowed corridor, Ward's hand was in the small of her back in the normal friendly protective manner he always adopted with her. And as always his faintest touch was sending heat waves into every nerve and sinew.

Jeanie had long since given up feeling guilt and embarrassment and a hundred and one other similar emotions at her body's secret reaction to him, but tonight was different somehow, and she was glad of the sleek curtain of hair swinging forward to hide her flushed cheeks.

It was the unequivocally tough maleness of his body that always set the juices flowing, she thought silently as the lift doors opened in answer to Ward's finger on the control button on the wall. He exuded masculinity from the top of his head to the bottom of his feet; it was in every look, every gesture, the deep smoky sexy voice, even the way he walked with an easy, loping, almost animal-like grace.

She stepped quickly into the lift, glad his hand was gone from her back and yet at the same time regretting its loss. But then she was always like that around this man, she thought ruefully. Like a cat on a hot tin roof. It was a miracle he didn't know, although the years of hiding her feelings and pretending everything was all right through her childhood and youth had stood her in good stead for Ward Ryan.

Once she had met him she'd understood why she'd never felt overly tempted to fall into bed with previous boyfriends; she'd been waiting for Ward without knowing it. If only she'd met him before Patricia had come into his life, but then he would never have looked twice at her anyway. She only had to look into the mirror to be told quite frankly that she was averagely attractive, no more, and the women Ward dated were stunners from all accounts.

'I didn't bring the car, knowing I'd have a drink today,' Ward said easily as the lift doors closed. 'But there'll be plenty of taxis about at this time of night.'

Jeanie nodded, trying to match her tone to his as she said, 'I had the same thought.'

'There's the odd flake of snow in the wind and it's bitterly cold, so you wait in the foyer till I stop one.'

Jeanie was just opening her mouth to reply that she was more than capable of standing on the pavement beside him for a few minutes, cold or no cold, when the lift jerked violently to a halt between floors. One moment she was standing on her feet, the next she had been catapulted straight into Ward's arms which had opened automatically to receive her as he himself stumbled back against the carpeted walls.

The shudder the lift had given along with the momentum of her body sent him on to his knees, his arms still cradling her against his chest, and now Jeanie lay across his lap, her face uplifted to his and the silk of her hair like a fan across his arms.

It had all happened in a split second, and along with the panic and fright she felt about being trapped in what suddenly had become a frighteningly fragile little metal box, Jeanie was aware she was in his arms for the second time that evening and it felt wonderful!

The lights had flickered and dimmed for a mo-

ment but then, as the lift recovered from its hiccup
and began to whirr downwards again, they were
shining composedly on the two figures beneath
them. Ward had made no attempt to move and neither had she; she couldn't. The blood was pounding
through her veins with excitement not fear now, and
she was breathless in his arms.

'It's all right, we're moving again.'

'I know.' She responded to Ward's soft husky
voice without taking her eyes off his face. His eyes
were very blue as they stared down into the wide
amber depths of hers, and although they were
breathing and talking it was as though they were
both frozen in time, she thought dazedly.

Heady hot sensation had pervaded every single
part of her and she knew, she just *knew* he was
going to kiss her. She began to tremble deep inside
as her eyes left his to focus on the hard, sensual lips
which were coming closer.

His mouth closed over hers, warm and stunningly
sweet, and now her heart was thudding wildly as
through the explosion of her senses a little voice
was saying, I told you, I told you it would be as
good as this.

A burning insistent flow of desire was taking hold
as the kiss deepened, his lips and tongue exploring
her mouth as she quivered against the hard, steady
beat of his heart. Her hands were still gripping
his shoulders where they had clutched as they had
both fallen, and she couldn't believe—she simply

couldn't *believe* how he could make her feel with just his mouth alone. And yet she had always known...since the beginning of time.

And then—almost before it had started she thought despairingly—the kiss had ended as the lift stopped again and Ward raised his head sharply, as though he had just realised what had happened between them. He rose to his feet a split second later, taking her with him, and she was aware of him reaching up and removing her fingers from his shoulders as the door glided open.

'I'm sorry, Jeanie.' His voice was grim and controlled. 'That shouldn't have happened. I don't normally take advantage of damsels in distress,' he added with an attempt at lightness, obviously because he had realised the extent of his withdrawal, she thought with excruciating mortification.

She had invited him to kiss her. No, she had all but *begged* him to, she admitted painfully. And after all she had said earlier. He would either be thinking this great love she had spoken of wasn't worth her breath, or—and please, *please* don't let him go down this avenue, she pleaded silently—he'd suspect that maybe the object of her affections wasn't a million miles away.

'I'm sorry too.' She forced the words out through stiff lips and was amazed how normal her voice sounded considering how she was feeling inside. 'I think we had better put it down to Dan and Joe's generosity with the wine, don't you? Perhaps we should have eaten and partied more instead of working and drinking?' She'd *thrown* herself at him, nothing more or less.

'Perhaps.' They had stepped into the deserted foyer, and now he turned her round with a careful hand at her shoulder as he said, 'But you were extremely vulnerable tonight and I knew that.'

He was taking all the blame and they both knew she had been there every inch of the way. What could she say, what could she do to remedy this horrific situation? 'I don't know about the vulnerable bit,' she said quietly, 'but it was good to know that life still goes on even when your heart's taken a bit of a bashing. I'll survive him, Ward, in time, so please don't worry about me. And the kiss—' she forced herself to go on in the same soft understanding voice '—was because one friend was feeling sorry for another. I know that.'

And it was true, she thought as humiliation made her stomach muscles clench. Five years and not so much as a peck on the cheek, but then after she had finished crying all over him and telling him her story of unrequited love, she had all but asked him to confirm she was still attractive to the opposite sex. What was the poor man to do but kiss her?

She saw Ward open his mouth but whatever he might have said was lost in the next moment when the night security guard opened the door to his cubby-hole off reception. In the following exchange of 'Have a good weekend and see you Monday', they exited into the bitterly cold London street which was already dusted with a light coating of snow, and then Ward was hailing a black cab in his normal authorative manner which guaranteed one drew up immediately.

Once they were tucked into the back of the vehicle Ward set the tone by engaging in small talk for their journey across the city to Harrow where his home was situated, but Jeanie was well aware of the care he was taking not to touch her and the feeling that he was keeping her mentally and physically at arm's length intensified as the journey progressed.

She had shocked him tonight. Disgusted him even. She could hear herself conversing quite naturally through the maelstrom of her thoughts and blessed the inner strength that was keeping her tears at bay. And if nothing else the whole wretched episode had brought one thing home with unmistakable clarity. After tonight, she was going to have to do what she should have done a long time ago, and resign her position at Eddleston, Breedon and Partners.

There really was no other way out of this agonising mess than to take Ward's own advice and cut and run.

CHAPTER THREE

IT WAS gratifying that once the taxi pulled up on the big sweep of drive outside Ward's large and secluded detached house in a very quiet part of Harrow, and the front door immediately swung open indicating the occupants inside had been watching for the car, it was Jeanie who was the focus of Bobbie's attention.

Jeanie was deeply touched by the little girl's open delight in seeing her again, and as she was led into the house by Bobbie's small hands pulling her along, the child was chattering nineteen to the dozen. 'Monica said you're going to stay for dinner tonight,' Bobbie finished happily, after she had informed Jeanie that it was only one more night after this one—*one*—and then she would be seven years old.

Jeanie assumed—rightly—that Ward had phoned his housekeeper from the office, and now she flashed Monica a quick rueful smile. 'Only if Monica has enough food to go round.'

'Enough to feed an army,' Monica said stoutly. 'Give me your coat and then go and sit by the fire, dear, and get warm. Enough to freeze you out there, isn't it.'

It was nice to be fussed over for a change, very nice, and as Jeanie allowed Bobbie to lead her into the large and luxuriously furnished sitting room she had seen on her previous visit, she saw an enormous log fire burning in the fireplace sending warm flickering shadows dancing about the room, and she remembered the time before—a couple of weeks before Christmas—there had been a huge Christmas tree in the corner of the room. She smiled to herself as she recalled her conversation she'd had with Bobbie.

'What a beautiful tree.' Jeanie had been truly entranced.

Bobbie's face had been bright with excitement as she'd dragged Jeanie across the room, saying, 'Look at the fairy on top of the tree. I made her all by myself.'

Jeanie had looked up at the paper fairy and it had stared back at her stolidly, its squint eyes lopsided and its matchstick arms sticking out of its stomach.

'Daddy says she's the best fairy he's ever seen,' Bobbie had said with earnest pride.

'Oh, I agree, absolutely the best,' Jeanie had agreed. 'What's her name?'

Bobbie had looked up at her steadily, her brown eyes enormous in her heart-shaped face. 'Jeanie,' she'd said expectantly, in the manner of one bestowing an enormous favour.

Jeanie had glanced up at the gargoyle face topped by tinsel hair and then back to the little girl. 'That's my name,' she'd said in tones of great delight and surprise, 'but I'm not as pretty as she is.'

'I think you are,' Bobbie had replied, and then, overcome by sudden shyness, had galloped across to her father and hidden her face in his legs.

Jeanie watched now as Ward lifted the tiny child up into his arms, planting a kiss on the tip of the little snub nose with a naturalness that brought an ache of tenderness to her sore heart. Thin little arms wound immediately round his neck in a fierce bear hug, before Bobbie drew back a fraction and said beguilingly, 'I ate all my tea, Daddy, so can I come down again after my bath?'

'Hmm.' Ward pretended to consider and then glanced across at Jeanie. 'What do you think?' he asked lightly.

'I think that would be great,' she responded just as lightly, wondering if he had any idea of how it made her feel to see the ruthless, cynical, hard lawyer of business hours manoeuvred so willingly by this tiny scrap of nothing.

Monica had appeared in the doorway as they had been speaking, and now she held out her hand to Bobbie as she said, 'Bathtime, young lady.'

'Off you go.' Ward placed his daughter on the floor before ruffling the little head of sleek brown hair. 'I promise Jeanie will still be here when you come down,' he added teasingly as Bobbie scampered out of the room, Monica shutting the door behind them both.

'She's a darling.' With the shutting of the door the atmosphere had changed, the new and disturbing unease that had been in the car on the drive home back with renewed force. She had been so stupid, so utterly *stupid* to invite that kiss, Jeanie chastised herself for the hundredth time, regretting more than she could bear the loss of Ward's past comfortable and relaxed manner with her.

'Yes, she is,' Ward agreed quietly. 'The first couple of years of her life were spent going back and forwards to hospital, and right up until a few months ago the doctors weren't sure how her legs would develop with the injuries she suffered being so severe. But all is well, so they say, so that's good. Some kids would have either become terribly precocious or whiny, or just plain fearful, but she's quite amazingly well-adjusted.'

It was the most he had ever said about what had happened and Jeanie endeavoured to hide her surprise. 'She's had a solid base here with people who love her and a devoted father,' she managed after just the slightest pause. 'That's made a difference I'm sure.'

'Thank you.' He smiled at her but she was aware of a reserve, a distance in the riveting blue eyes that hadn't been there before and again sick self-reproach clawed at her stomach. His friendship had been the most precious thing in her life and now she had lost it through her own foolishness. And yet... Her thoughts raced on as Ward suggested a sherry before dinner and she smiled her acceptance. And yet maybe this was what had been needed to force her to take stock of her life and move on? But how *could* she move on if it meant a life in which she wouldn't see Ward, be able to watch him, hear him, even share a little in his triumphs, and occasionally, the odd case that didn't go quite the way he would have liked it to?

And then she raised her chin a fraction in defiance to the defeatist thoughts. The decision had effectively been taken out of her hands, she reminded herself harshly. Something precious had been lost during those heady moments in the lift when all the longing of five years had come together and she had been in his arms, his mouth on hers. They couldn't go back to how it had been but there was no going forward either. The writing was on the wall. She needed to leave Eddleston and Breedon, and *soon*.

Bobbie had what must have been the fastest bath in history, and was back downstairs in record time looking adorable in matching puppy-dog pyjamas and dressing gown, her tiny feet bare. The limp was more noticeable as she ran across to the sofa where Jeanie was sitting—Ward having seated himself in a chair some feet away—whether due to tiredness or the fact that the child was wearing no footwear, Jeanie wasn't sure.

Whatever, Jeanie found she was more than a little

relieved when the small girl appeared; the last few minutes had verged on the painful, and the child's physical vulnerability took away any diffidence and made her open her arms wide as Bobbie wriggled up beside her on the sofa and onto her lap.

Bobbie smelt of talc and baby shampoo, and the overall sweetness of the little girl brought a lump to Jeanie's throat as she cuddled her before saying, 'That was a quick bath, wasn't it?'

'I know,' Bobbie agreed solemnly. 'Monica said Daddy will have to bring you home every day if it makes me so quick.'

Oh yes please.

'An' guess what I've got in my pocket?' Bobbie continued, bringing her packet of cards out of her dressing gown with the air of a conjuror performing a trick.

'Bobbie.' Ward's voice was cautionary. 'Jeanie's worked hard all day and she is tired. She doesn't want to play snap.'

'I don't mind.' Jeanie smiled down into the hopeful little face. 'But if it's anything like last time I shan't win, shall I. You are very good at this game.'

'It's only 'cos I practise,' Bobbie explained earnestly. 'You'd be as good as me if you practised too. You can come and play with me lots more if you want can't she, Daddy?'

The disturbing blue eyes rested lightly on Jeanie and then smiled at the little figure snuggled on her lap. 'Jeanie is a very busy lady,' he said easily.

Yeah right. Well that had told her all too plainly she was as likely to get another invitation to Ward's home as a snowball in hell. Jeanie smiled brightly, refusing to dwell on the hurt as she said to Bobbie, 'Come on then. You deal and we'll see how I get on.'

They played until Monica called them through to the dining room for dinner, Bobbie immediately pleading to be allowed to sit at the table rather than be sent upstairs to bed, her brown eyes beseeching. Jeanie added her own entreaties to that of the child's, and they both received a mock stern glance from Ward as he said, 'Ganging up on me, eh? Okay, if you're good, young lady, because I, for one, don't want indigestion.'

This was too cosy, too intimate, too altogether painfully wonderful to be bearable, Jeanie told herself silently as they walked through to the dining room; Ward carrying Bobbie on his shoulders and making her giggle with delight as he had to bend almost double to fit through the doorways.

Since she had met Ward she had come to heartily despise the person who coined the phrase 'It's better to have loved and lost than never to have loved at all.' This—tonight, seeing him in his home with his family—was bad enough, but if she'd actually been *loved* by him and then he had walked away or been taken from her, she wouldn't have been able to go on. Perhaps the person in question had never really loved someone with every fibre of their being? Or perhaps it was simply that they'd never come into contact with Ward Ryan? she reflected with dark, self-derisory humour.

By the dessert stage Bobbie was sitting on Ward's lap, settled comfortably in the crook of one arm as he ate his food with a practised ease that told Jeanie Bobbie being allowed to stay up while he ate wasn't an unknown occurrence.

The little girl was fast asleep by the time he finished his last mouthful and Monica came and picked Bobbie up in her arms. 'I'll settle her down and then put the coffee on,' she murmured softly to Ward. 'Why don't you and Jeanie go through to the sitting room and I'll bring you yours in there before I clear up in here?'

'Thanks, Monica.' Ward's voice was relaxed and even, and Jeanie glanced at him with a thread of resentment.

She had been dreading this moment all through Monica's delicious meal, especially in view of the earlier atmosphere when they were alone, but he clearly didn't give a fig. He might have found the incident in the lift briefly embarrassing, and he perhaps was faintly annoyed that the result of it meant he'd lost his staunch ally and dependable, no-nonsense—and most important of all—completely platonic co-worker and friend, but *he* hadn't got his insides turning cartwheels. If she didn't love him so much she'd hate him!

Jeanie drew herself up straight and stared steadily

across the table as Monica bustled out with her precious bundle, drawing in a deep breath and letting it out silently before she said calmly, 'That was a wonderful dinner, Ward, and I appreciate your kindness tonight but I really do need to get off home as soon as possible. Perhaps I could borrow your phone and call a taxi?'

He had been in the act of rising from the table and apart from a slight pause continued, walking round to her and drawing back her chair as she stood to her feet, before he said quietly, 'I want to talk to you first, Jeanie.'

Jeanie was taken aback for a moment. She'd expected him to be only too pleased to get rid of her as soon as possible. Her observations through the years, heightened by her love for him, had told her that once something was over for Ward it was over. Be it a personal relationship, a client, a case or whatever, he never indulged in sentiment or futile regrets but finished the matter swiftly and incisively, like the surgeon's scapel. Messy entanglements or complications were not an option with this man; certainly not for himself and where others were concerned she knew it brought irritation at best and scathing condemnation at worst.

The incident in the lift apart, he would be considering her attitude regarding this other man to be the height of folly and her emotional weakness would appal him. She should never, *never* have started this ball rolling. She still could hardly believe she'd been so incredibly stupid.

'I thought you said back at the office that we didn't have to discuss anything further if I didn't want to?' she reminded him carefully, keeping a check on the tone of her voice. There had been enough emotion flying about for one night and he wouldn't appreciate any more.

'I lied.' It was so unrepentant that for a moment all she could do was to gape at him.

Then her mouth shut with a little snap before opening to say, 'You don't mean...' She took another hidden breath before continuing, 'You aren't saying you got me here under false pretences, are you? That you always intended to question me whether I wanted it or not?'

If she was hoping her terminology would shame him—it didn't. 'That's exactly what I'm saying, Jeanie,' he agreed pleasantly. And he had the audacity to try one of his charming smiles. But she had noticed the hard twist to his mouth and the way the blue eyes were unblinking and as piercing as a razor-sharp blade and she wasn't fooled.

And it was only in that moment that she realised she didn't know Ward as well as she had thought.

CHAPTER FOUR

JEANIE kept a very dignified and cool silence until they were seated in front of the roaring fire. She had found this form of self-protection early on in life when she'd felt out of things and hurt and vulnerable, so it wasn't hard to retreat into the shell now.

The shell cracked a little when, instead of Ward reseating himself in the chair he had vacated before dinner, he chose to sit by her on the sofa. But almost immediately the edges closed again and she presented a calm and neutral face to Ward when he said, his voice carrying what in anyone else but him she would have considered a petulant note, 'All these years we have been friends and I've just realised I don't know you as well as I thought I did.'

It was on the tip of her tongue to tell him she'd just had the same thought about him, but then she bit it back quickly. She knew better than most that Ward was a dangerous adversary and somehow, over the last hours, that was what he had turned into. She had to remember that or suffer the consequences.

Secretly stiffening her spine she forced a cool, faintly surprised smile as she said, 'I'm sure that's not so, Ward.' This was the manner to adopt, she assured herself. The Jeanie he was used to was businesslike and competent; a confident, organised and practical career woman who knew where she was going and how she was going to get there.

The other Jeanie, the one who cried herself to sleep every time she knew he had a date and who was a shivering lovelorn mess inside with passions and desires of such an erotic nature that they even shocked her, had to be kept hidden from him.

'I'm sure it is. Take this boyfriend of yours for instance.'

He was frowning, she noticed, as she risked a quick glance at the hard handsome face before returning her focus on the red and gold flames licking at the partially burnt logs on the fire. Pine logs if the smell was anything to go by. They, added to the warm dancing shadows which gave the room an unbearably intimate, cosy feel, and emphasised hearth and home and everything enduring, didn't help her hammering heart an iota. Neither did she trust her voice to sound anything but weak and trembling.

'Can I ask if this relationship has been going on for a matter of months or longer?' he asked after the seconds had stretched into a minute and neither of them had broken the screaming silence.

'Longer,' she admitted, her voice a study in control.

'Longer?' His explosive expression confirmed it was not the answer he had been expecting. 'And

you say I know you? Hell, Jeanie, why haven't you mentioned him before, especially if you're so unhappy? And you are unhappy, aren't you,' he added more softly.

'Sometimes.' He was half turned towards her in the semi-darkness, one arm resting on the top of the sofa at the back of her shoulders. He had discarded his suit jacket and tie before they'd gone in to eat and his shirt was unbuttoned at the collar, showing a smidgen of body hair at the base of his throat. The blue silky material cloaked the powerful male shoulders in a way that brought his aura of brooding masculinity frighteningly to the fore, emphasising the tough, sensual quality to his attractiveness in a way that told Jeanie she didn't dare to look at him again. She just didn't trust herself not to demand a repeat performance of the kiss in the lift.

'Sometimes.' It was caustic and her skin shivered at the tone. 'Most of the time more like. Are the few hours you spend with him in the average week really worth all the pain you suffer the rest of the time?'

'Yes.' It was one simple word but he couldn't doubt the sincerity, and his mouth tightened, his eyes glittering angrily in the flickering firelight.

'He's *using* you, Jeanie. Can't you see that?' he snapped furiously, before breathing deeply and patently taking a hold of himself. 'Look—' his voice was almost insultingly patient '—just try and step back a pace and look at it reasonably. Bring logic to bear.'

It was so utterly Wardish she could have laughed. Or cried. Or both. 'Logic has no place in this,' she said with total honesty. 'And before you say anything more, I know you're right. He cares about me in his way, but he'll never marry me, I know that. He doesn't want commitment or promises of undying love, and he's not the sort of man to send me a Valentine card or buy me chocolates or flowers. In fact in all the time I've known him he's never even remembered St. Valentine's Day.'

'Valentine's Day?' He stared at her as though she was mad. 'We are not talking about Valentine's Day for crying out loud. We're discussing you wasting your life on some—' He stopped abruptly, dragging in a hard pull of air. 'On a man who isn't worthy to lick your boots,' he finished grimly.

'How can you say that when you don't know him?' she shot back quickly. 'Surely you know me well enough to realise he must be pretty special if I love him?'

'Jeanie, I don't know you at all,' he ground out angrily. 'You seem to have made up your mind that this man is the be all and end all. You're a young woman, you'll fall in love again if you get rid of him now and give yourself a chance. I hate to talk in clichés but there really are plenty more fish in the sea.'

'There haven't been for you.' It was out before

she realised what she had said and she froze immediately, knowing even before she looked at his face that she had gone too far.

He had stiffened, the blue of his eyes arctic, and his lips had a white line of rage round them when he said, 'What exactly does that mean?'

She could have backtracked, made some sort of faltering excuse and played for the sympathy vote, but in the last few moments a spirit of recklessness had taken her over. She was going to go out of his life soon, she had to, she'd made up her mind about that, but suddenly she rebelled against the years of always putting Ward and his feelings first. Of hoping she would become indispensable in some way.

Okay, so soon her time at Eddleston and Breedon would be history, along with her friendship with him, but she was darned if she was creeping out of the picture like a small whipped puppy. If she had to go it was going to be with a bang, not a whimper! She'd had enough of watching what she said and treading on eggshells: he'd asked for the truth and he was going to get it!

'Your…your wife,' she said tremblingly, her voice shaking in spite of all her noble thoughts. 'Since she died it's been like part of you died too.'

'Rubbish,' he grated tightly.

'It's not rubbish.' She knew she should stop but somehow she couldn't.

'I've dated since Patricia died.' It was the first

time she had ever heard him say his wife's name and, ridiculously, it hurt hearing it on his lips.

'You might have dated but always strictly on your terms,' she said, hearing the starkness of her words with something like disbelief at her own temerity. 'And you've always chosen a certain type of woman, ones that are on your emotional wavelength and just want a good time for a while with no strings attached.'

'I can't believe I'm hearing this.' She had never seen him so angry and although she longed to stand up and put some distance between them she didn't dare move an inch. 'What gives you the right to think you know anything about me?' he bit out with such fury she actually winced.

'The same right you had when you talked to me about the man I love,' she said bitterly, his words piercing her through like tiny, poison-tipped arrows. 'You think he just wants sex from me with no commitment or responsibility, but you're just the same with your women friends so don't play holier than thou, Ward.'

'Why, you—' His hands tightened on her shoulders as he ran out of words, his blue eyes threatening to burn through her head with the force of his blazing anger. What would have happened then Jeanie didn't like to think, but in the next second there was the unmistakable sound of crockery rattling and then a thump on the sitting room door a second before it swung open.

'Here we are then, a nice pot of coffee,' Monica enthused happily as she trotted in with a trolley. 'And I've put out a plate of those brandy snaps I made today, and some shortbread.'

It took a moment more but then Ward's voice was amazingly composed when he said, 'Thank you, Monica. We'll serve ourselves in a minute or two.'

'Right you are. I'll see about clearing the dining room and tidying up in the kitchen, and then I'm to bed if that's all right. I'm a wee bit tired. Bobbie was up at the crack of dawn this morning and I was worried she might come into my room and see the hamster, so we were downstairs having breakfast at six o'clock!'

She beamed at them, completely oblivious to the electric atmosphere, and from somewhere Jeanie found the strength to say fairly normally, 'Before you go I must say thank you again for that wonderful dinner. The ready meal I was going to pop into the microwave tonight can't even begin to compare with it.'

'Go on with you!' But Monica was plainly pleased by the compliment, bustling off with a cheery, 'Goodnight then.'

Jeanie waited until the door had closed again and then she said quietly, 'Do you want me to go, Ward?'

A muscle knotted in his cheek. 'Not until we've got a few things straight,' he growled.

In Ward language that meant the other party capitulating and seeing things his way. Five years in close proximity to this man had left her with few illusions, Jeanie reflected wrily, as she poured them both a coffee, handing Ward's to him black and adding sugar and cream to her own before she took a reviving sip. If ever she had needed a shot of caffeine it was now!

'You seem to have a pretty low opinion of me on the whole,' Ward said grimly after a moment or two. 'Could it be that this man is souring you towards the male sex in general?'

The male ego in all its arrogant glory! It couldn't possibly be that there was anything wrong with him or his actions, oh no. 'Not at all,' Jeanie said evenly, holding on to her temper with some effort. 'And I haven't got a low opinion of you, merely a realistic one.'

He glared at her, draining half the cup in one angry swallow without taking his eyes off her pale face. 'How come you haven't given me a list of my failings before super lover came on the scene?' he asked acidly.

'Perhaps because you didn't ask?' she returned succinctly.

'I resent being compared to this low life and found wanting.'

For a moment, a crazy moment, she almost thought there was a thread of what sounded suspiciously like jealousy in his voice before she told herself that was impossible. It was pride she was hearing, injured male ego, a powerfully destructive force all on its own.

'Look, Ward, we seem to have wandered off the beaten track,' she began tightly, only to be interrupted with a startlingness that was as dramatic as it was chilling. There was the sound of a high, drawn-out scream from outside the room followed by the unmistakable bump of a body falling down the stairs amid what sounded like crashing crockery.

Ward was across the room and out of the door before Jeanie had found her feet, and by the time she joined him in the hall it was to see him kneeling by a distraught Monica, who was surrounded by the wreckage of what had obviously been her supper tray which she was taking up to bed. Fragments of china were everywhere, along with thick splashes of what looked like cocoa and bits of shortbread, and a crumpled book with a somewhat lurid cover.

'Where have you hurt yourself?' Ward had one arm under the elderly housekeeper's shoulders, and Jeanie noticed with some concern that Monica's face was as white as a sheet.

'Everywhere.' Monica tried to smile but her lips were quivering too much. 'Oh, Ward, I'm so sorry. I was almost to the top and the wretched book began to slip off the tray and I tried to save it, and the next thing I knew my foot had slipped and I was falling.'

'I've always told you love and romance are more trouble than they're worth.' Ward stroked a strand of grey hair off Monica's brow. 'Just lie still and Jeanie's going to call an ambulance.'

'Oh no, no, please.'

Jeanie ignored Monica's protests and did as Ward had directed, and once the ambulance was on its way hurried upstairs to the airing cupboard on the wide landing and fetched a blanket which she tucked round Monica, blessing the fact that Bobbie seemed to be sleeping through all the trauma.

Monica was crying in earnest now, as much with worry about the proposed birthday party on Sunday as with the pain in her legs, one of which was obviously broken by the look of its twisted position. 'He…he doesn't know how to boil an egg,' Monica sniffed, clutching at Jeanie's hand once she had finished folding the blanket in place, 'let alone sort out food for twenty children and organise a party.'

Ward was trying not to look put out at his house-keeper's marked lack of faith in his prowess as a domestic, but the more he tried to assure Monica all would be well, the more upset the old woman got. 'I've ruined Bobbie's birthday,' she said tearfully. 'That's what I've done.'

'Of course you haven't.' Jeanie added her assurances to those of Ward. 'And please don't worry about Ward and Bobbie any more. If you tell me some of the things you still need to do I can delay leaving London tomorrow until I've helped out here.'

'I thought you had a lunch date,' Ward said softly

at the side of her, and it was only then, as she looked into the challenging blue eyes, that she realised he'd assumed her date was with her supposed lover.

'I do but I can cancel it,' she said shortly, some perverse emotion stopping her from disillusioning him. And then she turned to Monica, adding, 'I'll come to the hospital with you while Ward stays here with Bobbie, and you can fill me in on everything I need to know. And it might be that you'll be home again before the night's out anyway,' she said encouragingly, although she didn't think there was any chance of that.

'Bless you, dear.' Monica was white-lipped with pain, but as they heard the ambulance draw up outside Jeanie saw the small plump housekeeper had relaxed slightly, now she knew things were a little more under control again. 'You're heaven sent.'

Jeanie didn't know what made her glance at Ward at that precise point but in the seconds before he rose to go and open the door she saw the narrowed sapphire gaze was very clear and very cold. And she got the impression—probably understandably so in view of their earlier conversation—that 'heaven sent' was not the way Ward would have described her tonight.

But then it never would be. On the ride to the hospital Jeanie found Ward's words to Monica about love and romance being more trouble than they were worth, along with the cavalier way he had dismissed Valentine's Day, burning in her mind.

Okay, so perhaps the card industry and the rest of the commercial world made a killing out of Valentine's Day, but that didn't mean it still wasn't great for one to be told how much they were loved on that special day once a year, did it?

She'd had the odd card or bunch of flowers from an admirer in the past of course, and that had created a nice warm feeling, but for the man you adored, the man who meant more than life to send you a card or present, that would be... She ran out of words in her head to express what it would mean if Ward did just that.

But he wouldn't. He didn't even lust over her for a start, let alone love her, and without the first the second had no chance.

Oh why was she thinking like this now of all times? She came out of her musing with a very real flash of guilt, glancing across at Monica lying on the other side of the ambulance with a paramedic crouched at her side.

There was a time and a place for everything, and right now this was *not* the time to be thinking about Valentine's Day!

CHAPTER FIVE

X-RAYS confirmed the worst. Monica's right leg was broken in two places but the main problem, the consultant in charge of Accident & Emergency explained, was that the breaks were such that Monica would need an operation. It would certainly be a day or two before she was able to go home.

Jeanie telephoned Ward several times to keep him up-to-date with progress, and by the time the long night was over and Monica had been wheeled away to theatre from the little room off the women's surgical ward where she and Jeanie had spent the night, a pale sun was well and truly up in a white, wintery January sky.

Somehow—and Jeanie still wasn't quite sure at what point this had occurred—she had found herself promising an emotional and pathetically vulnerable Monica that she'd step into the breach regarding both the preparations for the birthday party and the organising and running of the actual event. She could see her family the following weekend, she assured the housekeeper.

'I'm going home to crash out for a couple of

hours,' she told Ward as she telephoned him for the last time, 'but I'll be back later to do some cooking and ice Bobbie's birthday cake, and I'll come again Sunday and stay to help with the party.' He might not love her, or even be aware of her as a member of the opposite sex, but she was going to take this weekend and savour every moment of it for the rest of her life.

'We'll come and pick you up.' He hadn't made a murmur to the effect of, 'I can't possibly let you do this,' or 'You mustn't alter your arrangements for me,' but—selfish and undeserving ingrate that he was—she didn't care. Somehow, by some miracle, she was going to share part of a special weekend with him, and just the thought of it was intoxicating.

However, once Ward's sleek and very presentable Mercedes drew up on the cobbles outside her little mews house later in the day—after Ward had popped into the hospital and ascertained the operation had been a complete success and the patient was sleeping off the effects of the anaesthetic—Jeanie discovered it wasn't just part of the weekend she was going to share, but all of it.

'It's ridiculous you travelling backwards and forwards when there's a perfectly good guest room,' he said determinedly, Bobbie dancing round them excitedly, utterly beside herself at the prospect of Jeanie coming to stay. 'You must be worn out as it is after last night, I know I am.'

He didn't look worn out, Jeanie reflected silently. He *looked* fantastic. Apart from the time he had had the flu, she'd never seen him dressed casually before, and even then he'd been ensconced on the sofa wrapped in a huge blanket with papers strewn about him, refusing to give in to the virus and go to bed like any normal sensible person would have done.

Today the smart formal suits had given way to black jeans and a dove-grey turtleneck sweater, a heavy black leather jacket completing the picture of good-enough-to-eat masculinity. Even his hair looked different, the odd curl or two falling across his forehead and softening the severe everyday office formality.

The ruffled hair style was probably due to the weather though, Jeanie reflected, glancing out at the whirling snowflakes before shutting the front door and following Ward and Bobbie into her small open-plan living room cum dining room.

'This is very nice.' Ward was standing in the middle of the light maple wooden floor, and Jeanie had to swallow hard before she could respond. How many times had she imagined the pair of them in here, wrapped in each other's arms on her sofa or lying in front of the fire on her luxuriously soft rug making wild passionate love until the dawn broke? Hundreds. *Thousands.*

'Thank you.' It *was* nice. Tiny, but nice. Because of the smallness of her compact one-bedroomed dwelling place she had kept the colour scheme light and bright, the maple flooring which ran throughout the house being perfectly complemented by the pinky terra-cotta and poppy red shades in her living room and the cream of her small kitchen off the minute hall. The charming bay window and exposed beams in the living room gave a real cottagey feel to the property, and Jeanie had been happy here from day one.

'I wish *I* lived here.' Bobbie was clearly enchanted by the little house which was more her size than Ward's large, five-bedroomed detached house. 'And I like that picture.' The little girl pointed to the framed print over the small fireplace of a polar bear cradling its infant in the warmth of its fur. Little of the mother bear could be seen but the way she had curled round her tiny baby, who was picked out with exquisite detail, had captured Jeanie's heart from the moment she had seen the picture in a frighteningly expensive art gallery a couple of years before.

It had somehow encapsulated all her dreams for the future, of cherishing and being cherished, and in spite of the price tag she had bought it that minute.

She saw Ward staring at it now, and after a few seconds he turned to face her, penetrating blue eyes looking into her soul—or that's what it felt like. And it was extremely uncomfortable.

To cover her confusion Jeanie wrenched her gaze

from his and directed it at Bobbie instead, lifting the little girl into her arms as she said smilingly, 'How about you help me decorate your birthday cake when we get home? First we'll ice it, and then you'll have to tell me what you want on the top of it. Your name and your age for sure, but what else?'

Bobbie considered for a moment. 'A hamster.'

'A hamster?' It wasn't what she had expected and she wasn't at all sure she could do rodents!

'Uh-huh, a hamster.' And then Bobbie hugged her tightly. The small, slight body felt terribly fragile and vulnerable in her arms, and as a fierce flood of maternal protectiveness swept over her with shocking suddenness it was all she could do not to close her eyes and groan.

She didn't want to fall in love with this delightful little scrap; she had enough heartache coping with her feelings for Bobbie's father!

By the time Jeanie's small suitcase and overnight bag had been loaded into the car she had regained her composure. This Good-Samaritan thing probably wasn't the cleverest decision she'd made in her life, but she'd really had little option, she comforted herself silently, as Ward's Mercedes nosed its way through heavy London traffic towards Harrow.

Monica had been so distraught and in such pain she would have promised the elderly woman anything to make her feel better, but besides that she wanted to make sure Bobbie had a good birthday.

And Ward? the honest probing voice of her conscience challenged. He didn't have anything to do
with this act of self-sacrifice then?

Well yes, she admitted weakly, and then, in a rush
of emotion, he was *everything* to do with it. Her
eyes were fixed on the fat swirling feathery flakes
of snow falling on the windscreen which the wipers
were labouring to sweep away, and which were
sending Bobbie—strapped in the back seat—mad
with delight, but Jeanie was acutely aware of the
big muscled body at the side of her.

The broad shoulders, lean hips and long legs were
on the perimeter of her vision but crystal clear on
the screen of her mind, every plane and angle of the
powerful male anatomy forcing her to acknowledge
her overwhelming sexual desire where Ward was
concerned.

It was inconvenient and unwelcome as well as
downright dangerous, but it was there and she
couldn't do a darn thing about it.

'I hope your parents weren't too upset that you
had to postpone until next weekend?' Ward said
quietly at the side of her.

Jeanie flashed a quick glance at the hard handsome profile before she said, 'No, they understood
you needed a hand when I explained the circumstances.'

He nodded slowly. 'And your dinner date?' he

asked silkily. 'I trust they weren't too disappointed?'

She didn't answer immediately and his eyes narrowed, but she was contemplating whether to tell him the truth or continue to let Nicki be a man. She decided on the latter. Ward had jumped to conclusions but it was better to let him continue to think what he liked rather than get an inkling of the truth—that *he* was the man she was in love with. 'Not too disappointed, no,' she said finally, her voice dismissive.

He gave her a hard look. 'Good.' The word belied the tone.

'Me an' Daddy made your bed this morning,' Bobbie piped up from the back seat into the awkward silence which followed. 'Daddy let me choose which duvet cover an' I picked the one with poppies on. Do you like poppies?' the little voice asked anxiously.

'Love them,' Jeanie answered warmly. 'They're my favourite flowers along with freesias because freesias smell nice.' She was pleased her voice was so natural because the thought of Ward making her bed had sent a shiver straight into the core of her.

'An' Daddy put the 'lectric blanket on to make the bed nice and warm,' Bobbie added earnestly.

'Thank you.' The car had just pulled up at red traffic lights and she glanced at him as burdened shoppers staggered across the crossing in front of them.

'You're welcome.' The devastating blue gaze had been waiting for her. 'Please feel free to call on any personal services you'd like me to perform during your stay,' he said smoothly, his mouth curving slightly as blue eyes witnessed the startled widening of brown.

He was *flirting* with her? Jeanie's brain suddenly scrambled and she couldn't think of a single thing to say in reply. No, she must have been mistaken. Or did he think—now she had told him about this other man and then responded to him like she had in the lift—that she was in the market for a little sexual comforting? A cosy weekend in every sense of the word? Poor Jeanie, I'll do her a favour type thinking?

And then she immediately felt mortified. Ward wasn't like that; he would no more take advantage of someone in her situation to satisfy his own needs and desires than fly to the moon. He might date women who knew the score and were as tough as he was in the no commitment regard, but he wasn't cruel or self-obsessed.

Over the years she had watched him choose women who would leave him with a smile and maybe just a smidgen of brief regret when the affair ended. And from what she had revealed about this 'other man' he knew she was a woman who desired much more than that.

He was merely being gallant, she decided at last as they neared the outskirts of Harrow. And after the caustic conversation of the night before she ought to be glad he had resorted to teasing friendliness. It was her wicked mind that had taken his attitude a step further; the longings and desires of her subconscious taking over. She'd have to watch that over the next few days.

Nevertheless, she couldn't quite quell the faint uneasy excitement that had started deep inside however much she reproached herself for her carnality. Just being within three feet of Ward had always had the power to turn her into a fluttering sixteen-year-old schoolgirl inside, but with wants and needs that were very grown-up!

Their relationship had always been one of calm and friendly courtesy but over the last twenty-four hours that had been blown to smithereens. He had seen a side to her that obviously annoyed and appalled him, and she had seen her normally smooth, controlled and rather cold work colleague so angry she'd thought he was going to strike her in those moments before Monica had brought the coffee last night. Not that he would have, she was sure.

As they drew into the driveway of Ward's home Jeanie realised she had been lost in thought for miles and that Bobbie was fast asleep in the back seat. 'Poor little mite.' She drew round from glancing at the sleeping child with a tender smile still softening her lips. 'She's already worn out with excitement. Oh to be that age again when a birthday has the power to thrill so much.'

'Thanks for doing this, Jeanie.' His voice was deep and sincere, and as her eyes met his he turned off the engine and twisted in his seat to face her. 'You've made Bobbie's day—in fact her weekend—in coming to stay. 'You know that, don't you.'

Bobbie's, but not his. Jeanie smiled brightly. 'What else are friends for?' she said steadily.

Why did he have to look so gorgeous? Why was she such a mess inside? *Why did she love him so much?* It wasn't fair, none of this was fair. Why couldn't she have been born a beauty, the sort of woman who would send him crazy with desire? Like Patricia, his dead wife, who still had claim to his heart and his life, and whom he had loved so utterly that it had spoilt him for anyone else.

'This is beyond the call of friendship but I do appreciate it.'

She stared at him, her eyes dark as she struggled to hide what his closeness was doing to her, and then, like that time before in the lift, they were in another world.

'Your eyes are like warm honey. Why haven't I noticed that before?' he murmured softly, his hand lifting to take a lock of her hair before letting the blue black strands slip through his fingers like shimmering silk. 'And your hair, it's the most beautiful thing I've ever seen. Any other woman would flaunt such an asset every day, but you hide it away. Why, Jeanie?'

'I... I told you.' It was too breathless but she couldn't help it. Her stomach was going over and over and her heart was thudding so hard she felt faint. 'It's not suitable for the office loose.'

'Do you wear it loose for him?'

'What?' To her mortification she felt herself blushing furiously.

'Him. The rat. The damn fool who doesn't know what he's got,' he said huskily. 'Do you wear it loose for him? But of course you do,' he answered himself softly. 'It must make him feel like a sultan, a god, to see what other men are not allowed to see.'

'You're seeing it,' she managed faintly.

'Yes I am, aren't I.' His smile was crooked. 'Would he mind?' His voice dropped an octave as his eyes narrowed still more. 'And did you tell him that we kissed when you said you couldn't see him today, Jeanie? And that you'll be living in my house—with me—this weekend?' he asked with silky intent.

Jeanie felt utterly trapped, and she shielded her panic by lowering her thick black lashes as she realised, too late, that she should have ended this conversation firmly and politely aeons ago. 'He knows exactly what happened.'

'And he still let you come here with me?'

'Of course,' she said, nervousness making her voice stiff. 'He knows we're friends, nothing more.'

'He either trusts you to the point of stupidity or his ego is jumbo size,' Ward pronounced flatly. 'Either way he doesn't deserve you. And you know that, you must know it deep, deep inside even if you won't admit it to me. I've seen you with Bobbie; you'd make a wonderful mother and if you hang around for this guy you're going to lose any chance of having a marriage and a husband who really loves you.'

She swallowed hard. If he didn't stop she was going to cry, she thought brokenly.

'You accused me of being like him yesterday and of acting holier than thou,' Ward went on as the snowflakes settled like a thick white blanket over the windscreen and windows and locked them into a silent silvery world. 'But you forgot one important thing, Jeanie.'

'What?' From somewhere inside she didn't know existed she found the strength to raise a composed face to his.

'The women I date know the score,' he said roughly, 'from day one. I make sure of that. I also make sure that if there's the slightest indication their feelings are changing, that they're getting attached to me, I finish it immediately. This guy isn't playing fair, Jeanie, whatever you say in his defence. If he can't love you like you want and deserve he should let you go for someone who can. *Make* you accept it. Sometimes you have to be cruel to be kind.'

She couldn't take any more of this. 'It's me who wants to keep things the way they are,' she said flatly. 'Not him. I'm the one who won't let go.'

'Then I'll have to make you see that however good he is in bed and however much you think life after rat doesn't exist, you're wrong,' he rasped suddenly. 'If you can kiss me like you did yesterday, I know you can learn to love someone else. Oh, okay, you might have been tipsy and emotionally exhausted with every defence down, but hell, I was there, Jeanie, and I've got enough experience to know what I'm talking about.'

She knew that. She knew *that* all right.

She was still reflecting on his last words when his mouth came down on hers, and in a second it was too late to even think of resisting. She was taking in the scent of him, the feel of his lips as he stroked hers open and then plunged into the territory beyond and it was heady, thrilling, absolutely mind blowing. And crazy and stupid and dangerous...

The need inside her was so sharp, so hungry that it was part pain, part pleasure but totally unstoppable. He was holding her closely and securely but not so tightly she couldn't have jerked away if she'd a mind to, but her mind was his. It always had been.

His tongue was probing her mouth and sending flickers of fire radiating into every nerve and sinew, melting her limbs and causing her to become fluid in his arms. She could feel the warmth of him through the rough wool of his sweater, the sensation of leather as her hands moved up and over his shoulders to tangle in his hair as she hungrily searched his mouth for more.

And then they heard Bobbie stir behind them and his mouth rose slowly, regretfully from hers, before he dropped one last lingering kiss on the tip of her nose and settled back in his seat.

'See?' he said very softly, his gaze holding her wide dazed one in the second before he turned to his daughter. 'You underestimate your power of survival after rat, Jeanie.'

CHAPTER SIX

CONSIDERING the state of her emotions Jeanie thought she did very well throughout the rest of the day.

It had been just after three when they had arrived back at Ward's house, and after her brief nap Bobbie was twice as excited and virtually on springs.

The snow had settled well and was coming down even thicker and Bobbie was desperate to build a snowman in the garden, so while Jeanie fixed a quick mid-afternoon snack of hot chocolate and muffins before the three of them went out, Ward telephoned the hospital again for news of Monica.

The sister on the housekeeper's ward informed him Monica was still sleeping and wouldn't really rouse until later that evening, but Ward was more than welcome to pop in for just a few minutes then if he liked? Ward did like and said so. 'And tell her not to worry when she's compos mentis, would you,' he added quietly. 'And that we love her and miss her of course.'

'I think she'll realise that when she wakes up, Mr. Ryan,' the sister said drily. 'We can barely find the patient for the amount of flowers surrounding her bed.'

Ward was grinning as he put down the receiver and when Jeanie asked why and he repeated the conversation, she smiled too. But inside she found she was envying Monica, poorly as she was, with all her heart. Ward obviously cared deeply for the elderly woman and looked on her as part of his family, a second mother in effect, and when she said as much Ward nodded slowly.

He glanced at Bobbie who was eating her muffin perched on a stool by the kitchen window as she looked out at the snow, and seeing his daughter was oblivious to them he said quietly, 'Monica has been more of a mother to me, and more of a grandmother to Bobbie, than my own mother has even been. She and my father never wanted children... I was the proverbial 'mistake,' and although they were never unkind and very supportive in their own way, there was no natural parental warmth there.'

She stared at him, sensing the well of hurt beneath the brief explanation. 'I'm sorry, Ward,' she said softly. 'I didn't mean to pry.'

'I know that.' He shrugged slowly. 'And it doesn't matter now. I make the odd duty call two or three times a year to show them their granddaughter, and they are very patient and polite until we're gone. There's no animosity on either side.'

So he had always had to rely on himself from a small child. This explained so much about him,

Jeanie thought, not least the total devotion and love he had given his dead wife.

'What do they do? Does your mother work?' she asked carefully, struggling not to show what the thought of Ward as a lonely, isolated bewildered child and self-sufficient, independent teenager did to her.

'Very much so,' he said cynically. 'My mother is a quite brilliant chemist involved in food science research, and my father is an ophthalmic medical practitioner with his own private practice.'

Two highly intelligent and gifted individuals who obviously hadn't had the first clue about bringing up their equally intelligent and gifted son. How tragic. Jeanie could have cried.

'*Daddy.*' The childish treble was irate. 'You haven't even *started* on your muffin and it will be dark soon. *Hurry up.*'

They both turned to look at the diminutive figure perched by the window and Jeanie saw Ward's expression change as he surveyed the little face frowning back at him. How he loved Bobbie, Jeanie thought with a big lump in her throat. And what a blessing the child must have been to him when his wife was killed so tragically. The little girl must be a precious reflection of the brief year or two of happiness he had with her beautiful mother, a pocket-sized reminder of the seemingly perfect union that he'd enjoyed with Patricia. How could she—how could *anyone*—begin to compete with a relationship that memories would have enhanced with an even rosier glow?

And then she shook off the dark cloud that was threatening to settle with a determination that was an integral part of her character. This was a special weekend and even the elements had conspired to make it magical; the white scene outside the window unbearably lovely. She was not going to mope for one minute throughout what was left of it, but take every precious moment as a gift. She'd cope with the aftermath—when she walked out of heaven—when she had to.

They had great fun building a snowman, partly because the snow wasn't really deep enough for the job and Ward made Bobbie shriek with feverish excitement as he made a great play of scraping up every morsel; shaking the branches of the trees so a cloud of white descended on them all and sent Bobbie wild with glee.

At one point, as the tiny child rolled in the snow like a small puppy, they both stood looking at her convulsed with laughter. When Jeanie felt Ward's arm slip casually round her shoulders she steeled herself to show no reaction and treat it as the natural, friendly gesture he meant it to be, but immediately the moment heightened with painful poignancy.

The winter wonderland of the garden, the hundreds and thousands of big fat feathery flakes descending from the laden sky, the small snowman with his borrowed hat and scarf and the excited child, and Ward—*Ward*—became bitter-sweet.

They could be any old married couple standing here like this, she couldn't help torturing herself by thinking. Standing close together and linked by the tenderness of the moment as they watched their child playing so happily in the snow. But Bobbie *wasn't* her child and Ward—what was Ward exactly?

Not just a work colleague—they had gone beyond that some time ago, but friend? She couldn't think of him in that light, she never had. She wanted more, much more than mere friendship from this man, and she could never go back to the months and years before that breathtaking moment in the lift. So what was he?

Everything she had to leave behind.

'I think we've done our stint out here, don't you?' He grinned down at her, stunningly handsome with his hair wet and daring to curl slightly and as far removed from the Ward of office hours as the man in the moon. 'Hopefully that's worked off some of her excess energy,' he added wrily, nodding at Bobbie, who had stood to her feet and was now brushing the snow off the frozen bird bath with one encrusted mitten.

Jeanie smiled back but she didn't trust herself to speak. Not with his arm still round her. And then he bent and deposited a swift kiss on her surprised lips. 'Sorry but you look like a small abandoned

Rudolph with your red nose,' he said lightly as she stepped back a pace in instinctive retreat.

'It's…it's cold,' she said breathlessly.

He nodded, the somewhat disparaging content to his words negated by the look in his eyes as they wandered over her flushed face and bright eyes beneath the scarlet woollen cap she'd pulled over her ears. And then he reached out and drew her against him again, tucking her hands inside the warmth of his jacket as he said softly, 'Let me warm you.'

She could feel the hard steady beat of his heart beneath the wool under her nerveless fingers, the faintly delicious smell of him surrounding her intoxicatingly. 'My gloves are wet,' she protested weakly.

'I don't care.'

His face was quite unreadable but then it mostly was. 'We ought to get Bobbie in for a hot bath,' she managed at last, knowing if she stayed for one more second in this position with his arms round her waist and her hands against the wall of his chest, all her resolve would melt and she'd be virtually begging him to kiss her again.

'It's all right, Jeanie, you're quite safe,' he said mockingly. 'I'm not about to drag you into the undergrowth and have my wicked way with you. Bobbie is a small but very adequate chaperone.'

More's the pity. 'I didn't think for a moment anything like that had entered your mind,' she said with an indignance which carried the unmistakable ring of truth. Now the possibility of it being the other way round...

'No? Why?' He was suddenly put out and she was astonished.

'Because you're not like that,' she said innocently.

'Like what? Red-blooded, virile?'

'I didn't mean—'

'Is *he* like that, Jeanie? Macho man? A vigorous Ramboesque type whose brains are situated considerably lower than his head?' he snapped tightly, his eyes taking on an arctic silveriness which made the blue all the more amazing.

She stared at him, utterly astounded. Why was he taking this tack and was it—could it possibly be—*jealousy* in his voice? she asked herself faintly. But no, that was ridiculous and she knew it. She had known Ward for five years and in all that time he had invariably treated her as a friend, a pal, a buddy. He liked her, cared for her even in his way and he didn't want to see her hurt by this other man, but jealousy? Jealousy was a whole different ball game. And the emotional undercurrents of such imaginings were far too dangerous to risk even putting a toe in.

She took a deep hidden breath and tried to answer him as calmly as she could considering he was still holding her, and his touch always had the power to make her melt. Even sharing a coffee break at work had been fraught with danger due to it resulting in her being a quivering wreck for minutes afterwards.

'*He* is a very intelligent and articulate human being,' she said reprovingly. 'And I only meant that we're friends, Ward, and I trust you implicitly,' she added, fully expecting that to do the trick.

Instead his frown deepened to a scowl. 'You're still locked into this guy like a nuclear missile, aren't you,' he ground out irritably, 'unable to see the wood for the trees.'

Yes, yes, yes. Always had been, always would be. 'Not at all,' she lied decorously, and then felt bereft when he unceremoniously moved her away from him, swearing softly under his breath as he turned away and began to walk towards Bobbie who was now busy wiping every little single flake of snow off the remnants of the muffins Jeanie had put on the bird table.

She stood where he had left her, a great heaviness on her heart. Control. That's what all that had been about. And there was more than a touch of the machiavellian to Ward at times. The more she got to know him away from the office the less she knew him it seemed. And now he was in a filthy fit and the evening would be ruined—

'Come on, dreamer.' He was standing in front of her again, Bobbie in his arms and the crystal eyes as clear as a blue sky, his mouth smiling. 'This one needs a bath, and while I'm seeing to the little Snow Queen you're going to put your feet up in front of the fire with a nice glass of wine, and relax.'

She stared back into the enigmatic face in surprise, aware however much he was smiling there was more going on behind that lethal blue gaze than Ward was prepared to let on. He was inscrutable, she decided with a touch of anger. Inscrutable and perplexing and unfathomable, and if she didn't love him so much he was just the sort of man she would loathe!

'I need to do some things for the party,' she said flatly. 'And then organise dinner for tonight. And there's the cake—'

'We'll sort out the cake and stuff later, but Bobbie and I have been talking, haven't we, sweetheart?' Ward added to the little girl in his arms who nodded, her face bright as she giggled. 'And we have decided it's baked potatoes in their jackets with sour cream and cold meats for tonight, all of which we are quite capable of dealing with. So, go and relax for a while, Jeanie. Okay? I'll bring you a glass of wine before we go up.'

Why did he have to do this? Why did this big, definitely ruthless and often aggressive male have to stroke and soothe her frayed nerves with that sexy, smoky voice? It made her forget to be annoyed and want to purr like a kitten instead. 'I don't think—'

He slanted an amazingly sensual look at her from under half-closed lids, that she was sure he was unaware of but made her toes curl into tight little pads. 'It's an order, not a suggestion,' he said silkily.

'But—'

'Bobbie and I are aware of how you've had to alter your plans at a moment's notice to look after us, and we intend to do our share, okay? You can be the general and we'll obey orders.' He turned his glance from her to Bobbie. 'Right cupcake?'

Bobbie nodded vigorously, her arms tight round her daddy's neck. Jeanie gave up. She knew when she was defeated and actually the thought of a few minutes relaxation after the turmoil and pace of the last twenty-four hours was incredibly tempting. She had tried to catch a few hours sleep after leaving the hospital earlier that morning, but her mind had been a seething mass that just wouldn't turn off and she had only managed an hour or two of light dozing that had left her feeling more tired than before she'd gone to bed.

Once seated in front of the roaring log fire on one of the beautifully deep and soft sofas in Ward's gorgeous sitting room, a glass of deep red wine at her elbow and her head resting on plump cushions, Jeanie stretched luxuriously. Ward had switched on the TV before he'd taken Bobbie for her bath, and now the low drone of some quiz show or other provided a backdrop to her thoughts.

She had never dreamt, not even in her wildest imaginings, that something like this weekend would ever happen. But it had, it had. She was here, in Ward's home, sharing his daughter's birthday and that was a miracle for a start. Why couldn't another miracle happen, that of Ward falling in love with her?

It wouldn't happen, it could never happen given Ward's slant on the female of the species since Patricia's death, but she could pray for a miracle nevertheless, couldn't she? Nothing else had worked! 'Please, God,' she whispered softly into the gently flickering shadows of the darkened room, lit only by the fire and the light from the TV screen, 'please *please* make him love me. I don't care how long it takes—' She stopped abruptly. 'Well, yes I do, God, I can't help it. Please let it be soon.'

She took several sips of the blackcurranty wine that smelt richly of spices and oak, and surveyed the tiny orange flames licking round the pine log which Ward had helped Bobbie place on the fire with due ceremony before they had disappeared.

She loved him, unequivocally and absolutely, and for the moment she was too tired to think beyond that. The future, with its looming goodbyes and black hole of desolation was far away and tonight there was just warmth and colour and a numbing lassitude. Jeanie closed her eyes, her lids too heavy to fight the exhaustion a second longer, and within moments she was fast asleep.

The kiss was coaxing and persuasive, teasing her lips open with a lazy eroticism that spoke of experience and finesse before moving to her eyelids and then her throat in burning hot, feathery kisses that sent her blood racing through her veins in a flood of hot sensation.

She had been dreaming, she knew she had been dreaming but she also realised that the kiss was not part of the dream. It was real. And if she opened her eyes it would finish. So...she didn't open her eyes. She just kissed Ward back with a hunger and a passion she could never show normally.

She heard him make a sound of pleasure low in his throat and her body echoed the sound, responding to the age-old mating call with a desire that would have shocked her if she'd been thinking rationally. But she wasn't thinking rationally; that had stopped the moment his hard firm lips had met her mouth.

He could arouse her so easily without touching her; one look, one glance often bringing her senses to fever pitch at the office where she was supposed to be prim, respectable Miss Potter, and it hadn't helped her feeling of humiliation that he'd been completely unaware of her body's traitorous response to his sensual attraction.

His mouth was covering hers again and she knew she couldn't hope to make the moment last any longer; it would be taking credibility a mite too far and Ward was no fool. She stirred, shifting on the sofa and moving her hands and the lips lifted from hers. She opened her eyes.

'Sleeping Beauty.' His face was just an inch or so away from hers and he was making no effort to

pretend he hadn't kissed her. 'I could never understand why the prince would bother to fight his way
through all the snares and perils just for a kiss, but
I think I understand now. Years ago when I was a
boy, before life and the ugliness of the real world
got in the way, I used to think what it'd be like to
kiss this girl or that, and in those innocent days the
imaginings never went beyond that first kiss.'

'And then?' she asked softly.

'Then I grew up,' he said quietly. 'I learnt all
about the games lovers play, about how there is always a winner and a loser, and that gentleness and
consideration and love can be seen as weakness and
used as weapons.'

So he had been hurt by a woman in the days
before he had met his wife. Which would have made
him love Patricia and their child even more. Jeanie
couldn't speak at all. She was afraid that if she even
breathed he would withdraw again. She was seeing
a side to Ward she had always suspected was there
and it was as fascinating as it was disturbing.

And then light running footsteps sounded outside
and Ward straightened just as Bobbie came bursting
into the room calling, 'I'm in my 'jamas, Daddy!
And I was *really* quick. I'm a good girl, aren't I?'

'Pretty good,' Ward confirmed lazily with a teasing smile.

'Good enough for a hamster?' Bobbie asked fer-
vently. 'A golden one with little hands and everything, like Gemma Prichards at school?'

'Ah, now that's for you to find out tomorrow.'
Ward ruffled Bobbie's hair before adding, 'But now
we need to serve dinner, yes? Let's go and see how
the baked potatoes are getting on, shall we, because
you can't be too late to bed tonight. It's going to be
a busy day tomorrow, and you know why, don't
you?'

'My birthday party!'

Jeanie managed to catch Ward's eye as Bobbie
danced out into the hall in front of him, and to her
mouthed 'Golden?' he replied with a nod and a
pursing of his lips which denoted extreme relief.

How would she be able to bear all the weekends
which followed this one? Jeanie asked herself when
she was alone again. She sipped at her wine, looking
deep into the fire.

But perhaps, just maybe, this new relationship
with Ward might lead to something else? Especially
when she left Eddleston and Breedon and they
weren't work colleagues anymore? Ward was scathing about office romances, but if she had left...

Pipe dreams. She sat up straighter as the words
hammered home. Born of the circumstances, the
wine, and not least her low defences. Just because
he'd kissed her as though he enjoyed it she couldn't
forget what he was like. Commitment or a long-term
relationship was not on Ward's agenda, and she
would have no excuse if she tried to convince herself otherwise on the strength of a couple of kisses.

Earlier today in the car when they had been sitting talking outside the house, he had made it as clear as ever how he saw things. 'The women I date know the score from day one.' The words had burnt into her subconscious and were now crystal clear without any mind searching.

'I also make sure if there's the slightest indication their feelings are changing and they're getting attached to me, I finish it immediately.' That was what he had said just hours ago and she forgot it at her peril.

And he'd also said something about making her see that life would go on if she finished with this man. His kisses, the way he'd looked at her once or twice, were just to prove she could be sexually attracted to someone other than her lover and therefore back in the market for a new relationship in the future which would possibly provide her with the degree of commitment she needed.

Such reasoning would be perfectly logical and acceptable to Ward, Jeanie thought bitterly. A successful solution to a problem which had been presented to him. But she wasn't one of his cases waiting to be stamped, concluded and locked away in his filing cabinet.

She narrowed her eyes at the dancing flames and finished the last of her wine with one big gulp. She was flesh and blood with a mind of her own, that's what she was, and if she thought about it it was downright insulting of Ward to assume she could fall out of love so easily, even if he was acting—as he thought—in her best interests.

Oh, she was sick of thinking about the whole thing! She frowned ferociously into the inoffensive fire, sighing irritably. And she was not going to do it any more. Once the meal was over and Bobbie was tucked up in bed, she would sort out a few things regarding the party but make sure she was upstairs in her own room before Ward returned from visiting Monica at the hospital. Her mind didn't feel as though it belonged to her today, and she needed some solid uninterrupted hours of rest to steady her shaky equilibrium.

She loved Ward, she would always love him, but he had to be the most annoying, arrogant, *unshakable* man in the whole wide world!

CHAPTER SEVEN

ALMOST eight hours of deep dreamless sleep
worked wonders, and when Jeanie awoke early the
next morning to the sound of excited shrieks from
Bobbie's room next door to the luxurious guest
room she was occupying, she found herself smiling
at the sound. The next moment the door to her room
was flung open and a small, brown-haired and wide-
eyed human missile launched itself onto the bed,
Bobbie's whole body wriggling in ecstasy as she
cried, 'Come and see! Come and see my hamster.
Oh I love her, I just love her.'

'She's the colour you wanted then?' Jeanie sat up
against the pillows, brushing the hair out of her eyes
as Bobbie bounced on the bed at the side of her
with enough energy for ten children. The question
was rhetorical; once Bobbie had been fast asleep the
night before and just before Ward left to see Monica, they had crept into Bobbie's room, positioning
the cage and its precious occupant on the small
chest of drawers in a corner of the room. But Jeanie
didn't want to spoil Bobbie's pleasure in showing
her the new pet by letting the child think she had
already seen it.

Bobbie had looked impossibly angelic the night before, curled under the covers and fast asleep with one arm round her teddy bear. Jeanie had stood with Ward and gazed at the sleeping child for a moment or two, and when she'd thought of all the little girl had gone through in her short life—not least losing her mother before she had ever known her—she'd found she'd had tears in her eyes once she and Ward were outside on the landing again, and the door to Bobbie's room was shut.

She had struggled not to show her emotion, gulping once or twice and breathing deeply as she'd endeavoured to keep the tears at bay, but the sight of the small child cuddled up to the frayed, somewhat shabby and obviously well-loved bear was heart-wrenching.

'What is it?' Ward had lifted her chin in the subdued light as he had caught the glitter of tears in her eyes.

Jeanie had almost shivered as his flesh had made contact with hers but had controlled the instinctive response of her body to his just in time. The little heart-to-heart she'd had with herself before dinner was still with her and strengthened her resolve, and now she spoke quietly as she stepped back a pace away from his body warmth. 'I was just thinking how vulnerable she is and how brave she's been. You must be very proud of your daughter, Ward.'

'Yes, I am,' he said softly, watching her with that penetrating gaze that was so much a part of him, and which was more than a little unnerving at times. 'Bobbie is one in a million.'

Like her mother had been. The thought brought Jeanie's chin up and stiffened her spine, and her voice was even and flat when she said, 'Thank you for letting me share such a special moment in there. Now I mustn't keep you. You must be wanting to get off and see Monica.'

'Must I?' he asked slowly, a quirk to his mouth.

'And I've got masses to do for the party,' Jeanie said briskly, taking another step backwards and then turning for the stairs. She spoke over her shoulder as she said, 'There are all the party bags for the children to take home to make up for a start. Monica has bought little bead bracelets and sweets and party blowers and all sorts to put in them.'

'Clever Monica.' They were downstairs in the hall now, and he smiled in the slow, sexy way that always sent her hormones flying into confusion as she glanced at him. 'Never mind, there's always tomorrow night to look forward to.'

Jeanie's eyes jerked away from his. She was sure he hadn't meant his words the way her sinful heart had taken them, but suddenly the wonderfully seductive image of the big plump sofa pulled close to the flickering fire and two naked bodies entwined on the soft cushions had been so real it had turned her face scarlet. 'Yes. That's…that's all right then. I…' She made a huge effort and pulled herself together. 'I'll see you in the morning, Ward,' she managed fairly coherently.

Ward was surveying her thoughtfully when she met his eyes again but he had said nothing more, merely nodding, his crystal blue gaze silvery and unblinking and his uneven mouth curved in a way that made her wonder what he was thinking.

Jeanie had got ready for bed in just a couple of minutes, too tired for more than just a cursory wash, and immediately her head had touched the pillow she had been asleep. And if she had dreamt at all she couldn't remember it, she thought now, as Bobbie tested the springs of the bed with gusto, knocking off Jeanie's little travel alarm in the process.

'Hey, where are the herd of elephants that I can hear stampeding around?'

Jeanie was just throwing back the covers to reach for her robe on a chair nearby when the deep male voice from the doorway made her give a little squeak of surprise and drag them up to her chin.

Bobbie immediately threw herself off the bed and sprang over to her father, whereupon she was whisked up into his arms in a way Jeanie could only envy as she stared over the top of the duvet, letting her tousled hair fall about her face to hide the hot tide of sensation flushing her cheeks.

As Bobbie thanked Ward over and over again for the hamster, Jeanie drank him in, eternally grateful she didn't have to trust her legs to hold her up. Clothed Ward was pretty amazing but clad only in black cotton pyjama bottoms and an open matching robe, he was out of this world for pure, flagrant and uncompromising maleness.

He'd obviously just got out of bed, his black hair ruffled and the sexy stubble on his chin indicating he hadn't had a shave yet, but it was the acres—or that's what it seemed like to Jeanie's feverish mind—of bare flesh beneath his chin that was causing problems with her breathing.

The open robe showed his torso to be thickly muscled, the black body hair on his chest narrowing to a thin line as it disappeared into the pyjama bottoms, and he was lean and tanned and magnificently powerful. He looked tough and sensual, his body possessed of a lithe, hard masculinity that was a fascinating challenge in itself.

Jeanie swallowed hard. She hadn't bargained for this. Stupid maybe, but she'd expected—if she'd thought about it at all which she had to admit she hadn't really—that they would all leave their rooms dressed and groomed for the day. A nice, tidy, no one infringing on anyone else's privacy type of affair. She might have guessed Ward wouldn't play by the rules. What was she saying? The man wasn't even aware there *were* any rules!

'Good morning, Jeanie.' His voice was mortifyingly casual which made her lobster red face all the more embarrassing. 'Did you sleep well?' he asked over Bobbie's urging to come and see Suzy—as the small rodent was now named.

'Fine, thank you.' It had taken a moment or two but she was rather pleased how normal her voice sounded when she at last got her vocal cords in working order.

'Excellent.' He smiled, and she wondered if he knew how sexy the fullness of his bottom lip was.

'Can we open the rest of my presents and cards now, Daddy?' Bobbie clearly wasn't in the mood for social pleasantries. 'I can bring Suzy and we could sit on your bed.' The child turned to Jeanie with a bright innocent smile, holding out one little hand invitingly. 'Come on, there's room in Daddy's bed for you.'

Jeanie raised her drowning eyes to Ward and saw he was looking vastly amused. She thought she heard him murmur, 'Out of the mouths of babes,' as he bent down and placed the small child on her feet, but decided in the next moment she must have misheard when he sent Bobbie skipping off to her room with a promise that he'd be along directly, but they would be opening the presents and cards downstairs.

'I hope it isn't broken.'

'What?' She knew she was still staring at him mesmerised but she couldn't help it, and then, when he indicated the alarm clock on the carpet at the side of the bed she nodded weakly. 'Oh, I'm sure it's all right,' she said quickly, wishing he would just *go* so she could come out from under the covers and at least have the protection of her thick fleecy robe between those devastatingly experienced eyes and her gossamer-thin nightie.

And then her heart stopped beating, every muscle in her body tensing as he stepped inside the room and walked across the floor towards the bed, his stance easy and relaxed and his bare feet sure-footed. She watched him as he retrieved the small clock and placed it on the bedside cabinet, her eyes wide and the blood racing and roaring in her ears. And then she was conscious of the blue eyes surveying her, his voice husky as he said, 'You're a different woman to the one I've known for five years.'

She had dreamt of him saying something similar for all the years she'd been in love with him. She had pictured them at a small, discreetly elegant restaurant seated in a quiet alcove, and Ward looking at her and seeing her with new eyes. Or maybe at some function or other which all the junior partners were expected to attend now and again. Or— Oh, the list was endless, she admitted desperately, but never, not once in all her wildest imaginings, had she thought it would be when she was without a scrap of make-up and looking like something the cat had dragged in! No wonder he thought she looked different to the perfectly groomed, cool and very controlled Jeanie Potter of business hours!

'Different as in a mess?' she said with as much lightness as she could muster.

'No, different as in beautiful,' he corrected softly.

'A real fairy tale Sleeping Beauty.' He lifted up a lock of her silky hair, his eyes slumberous.

'I'm not beautiful,' she said flatly, forcing her voice to betray none of the panicky excitement and longing that was gripping her. This was just Ward being nice, that's all. He probably assumed that her ego had taken something of a beating in the last little while. 'And I'm wide awake.'

'Don't argue.' He bent and took her lips, and right from the moment his mouth touched hers this kiss was as different to the others as chalk to cheese. It was hot and heady and urgent, a fierce assault on her senses that took without asking permission and with a deep passion that spoke of arousal and need.

He had sat down on the bed, his hands firm and strong as he'd reached out and pulled her against his bare chest so she was half lying across him, and as the duvet fell away to expose the soft creamy swell of her breasts under their flimsy covering of pale jade silk, the kiss deepened abruptly.

She could feel his heart pounding like a sledge-hammer and in the position in which she was lying his body told her all too plainly he was aroused, the thin cotton of his pyjamas hiding nothing.

This wasn't pity. It might not be for everness or a passion that would last beyond the few months which was Ward's normal time span for involvement with a member of the opposite sex, but whatever, pity wouldn't have him breathing hard and his body tense and rigid against her softness. The knowledge swam in her mind, and as his hands moved over her slender shoulders, stroking the pure clean line of her throat before moving to the rounded globes beneath, she answered his desire with passion equal to his own.

'Now do you believe me when I say you're beautiful?' he said roughly a second after Bobbie's voice had called them again. 'Prim and proper at the office with not a hair out of place and looking as though butter wouldn't melt in your mouth, and now... Now...'

'What?' she asked shakily, knowing he would have to leave in a moment, that they would both have to share the morning with Bobbie.

'Now you're a black-haired siren who's threatening to send me mad,' he said huskily. 'I want you, Jeanie. I can't help it. It might not be what you want to hear right now but it's the truth, so help me.'

Want. Sexual need. An animal kind of hunger. All those but not a word of love. But of course there wouldn't be, she knew that—*she knew it*. This was Ward for crying out loud. And maybe, when she had first started loving him and she had been just another business colleague to him and then later a friend, maybe then if he had seen her as he was seeing her now, in a sexual way, she might have risked her heart and gone for the sort of affair Ward indulged in, hoping that her love would *make* him love her back in time.

But she couldn't do that now, she dare not. The

last long lonely years of loving him from afar had taught her one thing; she would love him until the day she died. And the last few days had taught her something else. If she let him into her body as well as her heart, got to know him intimately and became part of his life—and Bobbie's too—for the length of time the affair lasted, she would never survive the aftermath when Ward finished it.

It had only been a couple of days ago that he had spelled out how he saw the women in his life, had emphasised that at the first signs of an affair getting serious it was ruthlessly terminated.

She couldn't do this, couldn't be what he wanted, she thought feverishly. He thought she was in love with someone else and that physical attraction and yes, friendship, would be enough for her at this time. Perhaps he even thought to wean her away from the other man so she could go out into the big wide world again? She didn't know. How could anyone know what a man like Ward was thinking? All she did know was that *she couldn't do this*.

'You can't deny the chemistry between us?' he murmured. 'I want you and your body tells me you want me, too.'

She straightened in his arms, moving away from him and back against the pillows and then watching him as he rose slowly to his feet.

'Wanting isn't enough for me, Ward,' she said very softly. 'Can't you understand that? I could never live with myself if I had an affair or a relationship just on that level. I have to love too. I should never have responded to you like I have over the last day or two, I know that. It was just that...' She floundered. How could she explain the unexplainable? She couldn't tell him the truth but she couldn't think of a feasible lie. And then Ward did it for her.

'You were miserable and upset about this other guy,' he said evenly, the imperturbable mask telling her nothing.

She stared at him helplessly, not knowing what to do or say, the situation utterly beyond her.

'It's okay, Jeanie, I'm not about to throw a tantrum or scream and cry.' The dark voice was faintly mocking with what she felt was an amused quality, and that was all the confirmation she needed to know she had done the right thing. This would always be a dangerously unequal relationship with all the cards stacked on Ward's side, because his heart wasn't really involved.

If she was stupid enough to be tempted into some sort of an affair with him she would tear herself apart trying to be what he wanted, and she would never succeed. She had been playing with fire and she'd got burnt, but there was no one to blame but herself. Ward had always been very clear on how she fitted into his life and he had assumed she saw things the same way. Now, somehow, everything had got tangled and messy, and so she had to set it back on a level footing and be the calm and cool woman he thought he knew.

'I never thought for a moment you would throw a tantrum, Ward,' she said smoothly, 'and I'm flattered you're attracted to me of course, you know that. Maybe if things had been different...'

He surveyed her for a moment more, and then as they both heard little feet come skidding along the landing he nodded abruptly. 'Maybe,' he said laconically as he turned and walked towards the door, meeting Bobbie in the doorway.

He picked the child up before he turned to face Jeanie again, and then his voice was its normal self and the only expression on his face was one of warm indulgence when he said, 'We'll meet you downstairs in a minute, and I'll put the kettle on for a cup of coffee. I've got a feeling the day has well and truly started.'

CONTRARY to what Jeanie expected following the cataclysmic start to the morning, she actually enjoyed the rest of the day.

Once she had heard Ward and Bobbie go downstairs she had shot out of bed and into the en suite, having a quick sixty seconds under the shower with her body shampoo before towelling herself dry. She pulled on a well-washed pair of jeans and a thick baggy sweater she'd brought with her, bundling her hair into a pony-tail and hurrying downstairs just in time to meet Ward in the hall carrying a coffee tray.

The black brows rose at the sight of her, but beyond his mild, 'Why do I suddenly feel underdressed?' he'd made no comment on her appearance.

Ward—of course—had had no such scruples with regard to modesty, as the pyjama bottoms and robe proclaimed.

Bobbie had just a few presents and cards to open—most of her presents would be arriving with her friends later that afternoon—but she went into transports of delight over the bride doll, hugging Jeanie hard and then kissing her. She was a truly sweet little girl.

After breakfast preparations began in earnest for the birthday party that afternoon. Monica had already done a certain amount of cooking, but there were still some sausage rolls and other child-sized nibbles to do, and of course the finishing touches to the birthday cake which Bobbie had helped Jeanie ice the evening before.

The two of them had great fun piping out the shape of a hamster on the top of the cake, which Jeanie then filled in with honey-coloured icing, adding currants for the eyes and a large sultana for the nose. Jeanie wasn't sure if it looked more like a dog than a hamster, but Bobbie was thrilled and that was the only thing that mattered.

They were just transporting the very last remnants of the icing from the bowl into their mouths with the tips of their fingers, and giggling guiltily, when

Jeanie happened to glance over to the doorway. Ward was standing there, a very strange look on his face as he stood surveying them both.

'Daddy! Come and see what we've done.' Bobbie was off her stool and over to her father in a moment, and by the time Ward had reached her his face was so normal Jeanie told herself she had been seeing things. But that was what this man did to her, she told herself silently. Turned her inside out and back to front until she didn't know what day it was, let alone anything else.

'That's a terrific hamster.' Ward gave due homage which satisfied his small daughter, and once Bobbie had disappeared to the bathroom to wash her hands, Jeanie began to clear the sticky dishes away after placing the cake carefully to one side.

'Thank you so much for doing this, Jeanie.' Ward's voice was low and husky and brought her turning to look at him. Suddenly the easy companionship of the time spent with Bobbie was gone and the atmosphere took on an electric quality that caused her throat to dry up.

'You don't need to thank me, I've had a great time,' she managed fairly normally. 'Bobbie is a lovely little girl and fun to be with.' She smiled in what she hoped was a buddy-buddy type way, trying to disguise what the vivid blue eyes did to her. He was so gorgeous, she thought despairingly. That was the trouble. Too sexy, too handsome, too overwhelmingly male to ever be truly comfortable with, given their present circumstances. She just hoped he kept a fairly low profile when all the other children were here; she needed to be totally on the ball then with an army of small infants invading the house—distraction wasn't an option.

It wasn't as if he was even trying to look good today, but he really couldn't look anything else. The long lean legs were encased in old faded blue jeans, and the massive chunky cream sweater he was wearing might look perfectly ordinary on any other man but on Ward's powerful frame it turned into something dreams were made of. The hard tanned face, jet-black hair and vivid blue eyes were heart stoppers all right, but she couldn't dwell on them now. Not now.

With that thought firmly at the forefront of her mind she turned back to loading the dishwasher, saying quietly over her shoulder, 'If you want something to do there's a couple of loaves of bread to be buttered for sandwiches. Okay? And then we really need to decide what games we're having and when; I'll leave that to you.'

She had expected him to say something more, but when she next turned round he was tackling the mound of bread with single-minded determination. She stared at his bent back and rolled up sleeves with a feeling akin to despair. Why was it that the touch of domesticity increased his lethal appeal a thousandfold? This just wasn't *fair*.

The party went as smoothly and happily as one

could wish for with twenty plus little girls to control, and when the last child had gone Bobbie announced she wanted Jeanie to give her her bath. Once undressed, the tiny body bore evidence to the tragedy which had claimed the life of her mother although Bobbie seemed quite oblivious to the scars on her legs, giggling and splashing as they played a game with the child's wind up frog and blowing countless bubbles into the air from a bubble-making kit one of her friends had bought her.

Jeanie was glad of the little girl's happy disposition and ability to entertain herself without too much input from Aunty Jeanie as Bobbie had decided to call her. The afternoon had been bittersweet and she was more tired than she had thought she would be. It wasn't the party or the children which had exhausted her though; it was the strain of playing happy families with Ward. Seeing him playing games with the small tots and just generally being in Daddy mode had been a real killer on her already taut heartstrings, and she had had to come to terms with the fact that she cared far too much for Bobbie too.

Bobbie's bath finished, Jeanie began to towel the child dry, her thoughts racing on. She loved this little girl. The feeling she had been subconsciously fighting from the first time she'd been introduced to Ward's daughter, and which had grown over the last few days as she'd got to know Bobbie better couldn't be denied any longer.

The knowledge was not welcome; loving Bobbie was another complication in the already tangled mess her pseudo-friendship with Ward had become. But—and this was a hard one to face—she had no one to blame for this development but herself.

Once Bobbie was in her pyjamas they went downstairs, where the small mite ate her tea of crumpets and strawberry jam sitting on Jeanie's lap. She was already asleep on the last bite.

Jeanie felt as though her heart was being wrenched out by the root when Ward disappeared upstairs with his small offspring. This was the last full day she would ever have with Bobbie, and once she had left Eddleston and Breedon she probably would never even see Ward again, let alone his daughter. But for now all she could do was to cook them both dinner and continue the act. The last thing in the world she wanted was for Ward to guess the truth.

She had half expected—or was it hoped? she asked herself caustically as the evening progressed—that Ward would refer to what had happened between them that morning, but he seemed to all extent and purposes to have slotted their relationship back into its previous mould of mutual respect and friendship.

He sat and chatted to her at the breakfast bar in the kitchen while she prepared a stir-fry for them both, and Jeanie found she had consumed two large glasses of a particularly rich, fruity, mature Rioja before she had even served the food. They ate off trays in front of the log fire, and although Jeanie knew the meal was good it could have tasted like sawdust for all the impact it made on her senses. Because she suddenly realised what had happened in Ward's mind after the episode in her room that morning.

That cool, logical, relentlessly male brain had considered his brief lack of control, dissected all the data including the implications a relationship with her would involve, and had come to the conclusion after all she had said that an affair was definitely more trouble than it was worth. He was probably breathing a heartfelt sigh of relief at this very moment that she had reacted as she had, thus letting him off the hook that his uncharacteristic and temporary lack of control could have made if her response had been different.

'That was delicious.' He had eaten his food with every appearance of rapt enjoyment, which was a further nail in his coffin as far as Jeanie was concerned considering she'd had to force every mouthful past the dry leaden lump of misery in her throat.

'Good.' Her smile was brittle and bright. If there was any justice in the world it would have choked him.

'And now I'll make the coffee,' he said easily, stretching his long legs comfortably for a moment before rising to his feet. The action had lit an immediate fire in her as hard muscles had flexed and then relaxed, and she was furiously angry with herself that she couldn't deny what he could do to her. He didn't have to touch her, he didn't even have to *look at her to make her liquid with desire, and it just—was—not fair!*

'You haven't tried my coffee before, have you,' he drawled lazily, smiling down at her with those incredible blue eyes. 'I'm told it's slightly wicked but you'll have to judge for yourself. It includes malt whisky and whipped cream and one or two spices, so it has to be savoured slowly.'

Jeanie hadn't got past the 'I'm told' bit which meant—*of course,* she told herself sourly—his other women. 'None for me, thank you,' she said with a brilliant smile. 'It's work again tomorrow, and I think I have had quite enough alcohol for one night. In fact I'm dead beat, Ward, so I'll call it a night if you don't mind.'

'It's only nine o'clock!'

His amazed face told its own story, and if she'd had it in her she would have laughed. The great Ward Ryan, the epitome of the love 'em and leave 'em brigade and lover extraordinaire having a woman finish the evening at nine o'clock. If nothing else she would stick in his memory for this, she told herself with silent dark humour.

'Maybe, but the last few days have been pretty wearing on the whole,' she said with a firmness that was born of desperation. If she stayed with him she would make a fool of herself, she knew it. She had always faintly despised women who allowed themselves to be walk-overs with the opposite sex, but she was in danger of behaving far worse than that. She wanted to recant everything she had said to him that morning, to beg him to make love to her, to tell him that she would accept any criteria he wanted to lay down as long as he let her be close to him. She didn't want to leave him—couldn't he see that? Couldn't he *see* how much she loved him?

'I see.' They stared at each other for a second and Jeanie watched the warm, smoky look in his eyes freeze to the arctic crystal hardness he did so well. She had seen him intimidate people with that look many times before in the past, but until this moment it had never been directed at her.

Well, there was a first time for everything, she told herself with excruciating bravado as she forced herself to stand up and reach forward to kiss him coolly on the cheek. 'Goodnight, Ward.'

'Goodnight, Jeanie.'

He just stood there as she walked across the room to the door and she had opened it when his voice caused her to pause, still with her back to the room. 'Do you think he is thinking about *you* right now, Jeanie? Do you?' he snarled softly

And she could answer with absolute conviction before she walked out and closed the door behind her. 'Yes, Ward. Yes, I do.'

And it gave her no pleasure at all.

CHAPTER EIGHT

THE next few days were possibly the worst of Jeanie's life. Ward had been more than a little grim-faced the morning after Bobbie's birthday party, when Jeanie had insisted on calling a taxi rather than letting him drive her into work. She knew he had spoken to one of the partners over the weekend to explain the circumstances and they had urged him to take a day or two away from the office to organise things at home, so there was no need for him to go into the heart of London, she'd maintained with desperate firmness. She had hugged and kissed Bobbie, marched out to the waiting taxi with her overnight bag and case, and then fought back the tears all the way to the office.

She hadn't heard from Ward over the next couple of days but she hadn't really expected to. However, on Wednesday morning he dropped into her office with two cups of coffee mid-morning like he often did when he wanted a chat, and once she'd got her pounding heart under control she was able to ask quite naturally, 'How's Monica doing? Is she home yet?'

'Last night.' He smiled at her, and—quite irrationally on her part, Jeanie admitted—she wanted to slap him. It was just that he seemed so totally *normal,* and, her breaking heart asked, how *could* he be that way after the weekend when they had nearly... Nearly what? If she thought about it they hadn't nearly anything!

'That's good.' She forced a bright smile.

'Yes, it's all worked out very well,' he said cheerfully. 'Monica's sister was at the hospital when I called to see her on Monday along with her daughter who, it turned out, is a qualified nanny and has just recently left her last position when the family decided to move abroad. She's more than happy to fill in for the time being, and if she works out I might just offer her a job permanently. I've been thinking for some time that Monica needs help, and this girl has her own car and so on.'

'It sounds perfect,' Jeanie agreed, the mental image of a gorgeous, eager, exuberant young thing causing her stomach muscles to knot.

'We'll see. It would certainly cut out the sort of panic that occurred this weekend,' Ward said quietly.

And would mean his home life was as well planned and constructed as his working life, Jeanie thought. All possible complications anticipated in advance and intercepted. The man who didn't need anyone. Well, she could no more make him need her like she needed him than she could force him to love her. Patricia still held the key to his heart and she'd taken it to the grave.

He continued to talk a little more, leaning against the wall of the office and apparently relaxed and totally at ease. Jeanie, on the other hand, was a quivering mess inside. He stayed longer than usual that day, and on Thursday longer still until Jeanie—terrified she was going to betray herself in some way—made it clear she had some urgent correspondence to deal with.

The 'urgent correspondence' ploy didn't work so well on Friday morning, but knowing she was going to take off and flee the capital to the sanctuary of her parents who, it had transpired on the phone the previous night, had organised a big family dinner with all her sisters and their families for Friday night, enabled her to maintain the efficient Miss Jeanie Potter facade until he left. She hadn't expected to see Ward again that day, so on Friday afternoon when he opened the door of her office she stared at him in surprise.

'You're going to your parents this weekend, yes?' And at her nod, he added quietly, 'Give me a call when you get there.'

'A call?' she repeated faintly. 'Why?'

'Isn't it obvious?' he said a touch testily, raking back his hair as he spoke which always did the weirdest thing to her equilibrium. But then *everything* about him did the weirdest things to her equilibrium!

'Not to me, no,' she answered truthfully. Obvious was not a word that reared its head in Ward's presence. There were enigmatic men and there were enigmatic men, and then there was Ward Ryan.

'I want to make sure you have arrived safely,' he said shortly. 'The weather's foul again and high winds are forecast.'

It shook her. She hadn't expected him to be that bothered once she'd gone—out-of-sight, out-of-mind type reasoning she supposed, she admitted silently—and in spite of all the warnings she had drummed into herself over the last few days her heart turned over as a ridiculous little seed of hope sprouted. Was it remotely possible he was beginning to see her as something other than just another female? she asked herself.

They had been friends for a long time—something she knew was unique for Ward with regard to the opposite sex—and perhaps he had meditated over that in the last few days, along with the fact that he now found he could actually fancy her too?

And then hard reality hit. She had stayed in London to step into the breach and do him a favour; he was just feeling beholden to her, that was all. Added to the fact that the way his wife had died must always be there at the back of his mind, and it had been bad weather conditions which had caused Patricia's car to end up in a ditch.

She had to stop reading what she wanted to see into anything he said or did. He might like her and not want to see her hurt, but that didn't mean he was beginning to fall in love with her. She knew this man very well and she had faced facts a long time ago regarding the hopelessness of her feelings for him.

'I'll ring,' she said quietly.

'Good.' They looked at each other for a moment, and then he walked across the room to where she had risen from behind her desk when he had opened the door. 'Drive carefully.' He bent his head, brushing her smooth cheek with his lips, and the subtle scent of his aftershave sent the usual flickers of desire coursing through her bloodstream.

A hopeless case, that's what she was, Jeanie thought mordantly, watching the way his body moved as he turned and walked back to the half-open door. A totally hopeless case. She managed a fairly neutral smile as he turned and raised his hand before shutting the door behind him, and then stood for some seconds with her hands clenched and her head back as she willed herself to calm down.

She wished she'd never come to London; she wished she'd never trained to be a solicitor; she wished she'd never taken a position at Eddleston and Breedon, but most of all—*most of all*—she wished she had never set eyes on Ward Ryan.

Deep breath. Deep, deep breath. She relaxed her fingers one by one. At the end of the month she was going to give notice to the partners and from that point she could start taking control of her life and emotions again. This was not the end of the world. It might feel like it, but it was *not* the end of the world.

Right, she was leaving early for the drive to York so now was a good time to exit. All her things were in her car situated in the underground car park, so she could be on her way within minutes. She cleared her desk by the simple expedient of bundling everything into a drawer, slipped into her coat, picked up her briefcase and left the office, and she was halfway through the larger outer office when one of the secretaries called to her, waving what looked like a wad of tickets in one of her hands.

'Jeanie? Are you doing anything for Valentine's Day, only my husband's cricket club has got up a dinner/dance and we've managed to get a terrific band.'

Valentine's Day. If there was one thing she didn't need to be reminded of just at this precise moment it was that torturous event—or rather it had been torturous since she'd fallen in love with Ward—which occurred with grim monotony on February 14th each year.

Jeanie forced a smile to her lips. 'Sorry, no can do, I'm afraid. Perhaps another time?' And as Ann subsided back into her seat Jeanie made swiftly for the door.

ONCE in the car she purposely slid a CD of dance music into the car's CD player rather than one of the romantic ballads she usually favoured, determining to concentrate on the road and nothing else.

It was snowing again but not too thickly by the time she reached Lincoln, but it had been dark for over an hour and the weather was really setting in when she eventually drew up outside her parent's big sprawling semi in York. She could see from the cars parked on the drive that her sisters were already in residence, and after turning off the engine she stretched a little, easing aching neck muscles before she got out of the car.

She was just pulling her bags out of the boot when the front door opened and her sisters piled out into the drive, calling out as they came.

'Jeanie! At long last. Come and have a drink.'

'What happened last weekend then?'

'We've missed you, kiddo! Seems like ages since Christmas.'

'Who's the lame duck you've been ministering to anyway?'

This last was from Charlotte and as Jeanie opened her mouth to reply, she horrified them and herself by bursting into tears.

It was the warmth of their greetings that had done it, that and the genuine love and pleasure at her arrival that had been shining out of the four pairs of blue eyes that were now looking at her with such concern.

'Fledgling! What is it? Whatever has that brute done to you?' This was from Lizzie, her eldest sister, and Lizzie's use of her nickname for Jeanie only made Jeanie cry the harder. Four pairs of arms were patting and comforting her and for the first time it dawned on Jeanie that her four sisters loved her just as much as they loved each other, but differently— in a protective, maternal way rather than the provocative and often competitive feeling they displayed one to another. And right at this moment it felt wonderful.

She sniffed and snuffled for a bit, insisting she didn't want to go in the house until she was herself again and that their parents definitely mustn't have their weekend spoilt by her problems, and then she quickly told the four women the gist of the dilemma.

They were all sympathetic, fiercely indignant on her behalf and to a woman called Ward every name under the sun, and then they all gave different opinions as to what she should do from this point. The heart-to-heart finished with Jeanie laughing helplessly as the four of them vehemently took each other to task. And laughter was something she hadn't expected to indulge in at all this particular night, she reflected warmly, when her parent's arrival in the lighted doorway of the house cut the discussion short.

She was so glad she had come home. It might be pathetic, and it certainly wasn't in keeping with the successful, smart, quick-witted and bright career woman she now purported to be, but it felt indescribably good to be held so dear and loved so unconditionally. She would phone Ward now, a brief friendly call and nothing else, and then put him out of her mind! She *would*.

'Ward Ryan.'

The telephone was picked up immediately the other end barely before it had had time to ring, and in spite of all her good resolutions Jeanie's stomach lurched as the deep cool voice sounded down the wire. His hard handsome face with its piercing blue eyes was instantly on the screen of her mind, and she had to take a deep breath to prevent her voice from shaking before she said, 'Ward? It's Jeanie. I'm just phoning to say I've arrived safely as promised.'

There was a moment's pause before he spoke again, and then the husky quality to his voice was emphasised when he said softly, 'I was getting worried. I'd worked out you should have arrived some time ago.'

'I drive a Polo, Ward, not a Mercedes,' she said drily. She was rather pleased with that response, and added, 'How are things your end? Give Monica and Bobbie my love, won't you.'

'Bobbie's missing you.'

Jeanie held the receiver away from her ear for a moment and stared at it, her heart thudding. How was she supposed to take that? she asked herself silently. And that note in his voice... Had she imagined the deep throaty tenderness?

'Jeanie? Are you still there?'

She pulled herself together sufficiently to answer, 'Yes, I'm here. Look, I've only just got here so I need to say hallo to everyone. See you Monday, okay? Goodbye for now.'

'Take care, Sleeping Beauty.'

She was still standing holding the telephone moments after Ward had replaced the receiver the other end, and then she forced herself to logically examine everything which had been said.

He had been worried when she hadn't kept to the time-scale he had worked out. That was friendly concern, and she knew full well his past had probably made him more sensitive to journeys in bad weather conditions and so on; it was perfectly natural. He had said Bobbie was missing her—Bobbie, not him. That was hard cold fact.

And Sleeping Beauty? her ridiculous heart asked. What did that mean? In view of all the rest nothing, plain common sense answered. She couldn't keeping hoping, seizing on the odd word or inflexion in his voice and building it up to mean something quite different to what he meant. She had to stop this now, finish it in her mind once and for all. If she didn't she would go stark, staring mad.

That talk to herself set the tone for the rest of Jeanie's weekend in York.

She immersed herself in her family, saturating herself in being nothing more complicated than daughter and sister and aunty, and in spite of the deep well of regret and longing that enveloped her whenever her thoughts strayed to Ward and Bobbie, she discovered a strength in herself she hadn't suspected was there. It didn't stop the tears in the dead of the night when she was alone, but it did help her face each day with a smile and a bright and cheerful countenance as she determined she would *not* cast a shadow over everyone else's weekend and wear her heart on her sleeve.

Lizzie, Susan, Miranda and Charlotte vied for her company and she was always at one or other of their homes, causing her long-suffering mother to bemoan the fact that even when Jeanie was here, she wasn't *here*.

By the time Jeanie drove back to London very early on Monday morning, she was congratulating herself on how clear-headed and rational she was about Ward, and about what she had to do in the immediate future.

Her first mistake had been in remaining at Eddleston and Breedon for so long after she had realised the extent of her feeling for him.

Her second, in allowing and even encouraging a friendship that was all pain and no gain on her side.

And her third, and—she had to admit with hindsight—the one that knocked the others into a cocked hat, in listening to her heart and Monica's entreaties, and agreeing to stand in as temporary housekeeper-cum-cook-cum she wasn't quite sure what, last weekend.

But she was realisitic now. Calm, practical, even

dispassionate? She had come to her senses at last, and she accepted she had to remove herself completely from the pull of Ward's dark orbit which sucked all her reasoning and common sense and emotions into it like a great black hole.

She would tender her resignation this very day, and would begin looking for another job at once. She was tied to a three-month contract with Eddleston and Breedon, and even if she didn't find another position within that time she knew it was still the right thing to do.

Her bank account was very healthy, and if necessary she would consider a radical change of direction, even of career. Perhaps it was time to get out of the capital for pastures new? Miranda had mentioned an aid organisation her husband knew of which had recently advertised for a solicitor in the north of England, or she might even look for an opening abroad? The world was her oyster, that's how she had to look at this, and the little voice in the back of her mind that kept whispering a world without Ward in it would be a very grey and empty place would learn to die in time. It would have to.

There were a string of messages on her answering machine when she let herself into the house, but nothing from the one voice she wanted to hear. Not that she had expected it, she told herself firmly as she quelled the sick disappointment in the pit of her stomach, and she wasn't going to start going down that road either. She'd made a promise to herself on the way home that her days of crying were over, and she intended to keep to it even if it killed her!

Jeanie had left York long before the rest of the world was awake knowing she needed to give herself enough time to go home and shower and change, and still get to the office before anyone else arrived. She needed to look good today—it wasn't every day one tended their notice—and she also needed to feel in control of herself, her workload and the whole situation with Ward. The latter might be an illusion, but she still needed to feel it.

She had dressed with an eye to boosting her confidence, and the wildly expensive cream suit and equally expensive gold silk blouse was an outfit she had only worn once before, when an important function had necessitated lashing out with very little thought of cost. But the amount she had balked at then now seemed worth every penny. The cut of the suit and the pencil-slim skirt was smart but extremely feminine, and the soft gold blouse brought out the amber shade to her eyes and made them seem enormous.

She had put her hair up but not so severely as usual, leaving a few silky wispy tendrils curling about her neck to soften the style. She didn't want to look *too* obvious but she did need to look good, and as she was meeting Nicki for their postponed lunch date she could always use that as an excuse if anyone commented.

She felt better once she had typed out her resignation, printing it in duplicate and then putting the copies into envelopes. It had become fait accompli somehow, and seeing the physical evidence in black and white made her all the more determined to go through with it. She sealed the envelope addressed to the senior partners and put her own copy in her handbag, and then set about sorting out her priorities for the day.

Half an hour later, her mind given over to the intricacies of a particularly ugly custody battle, she felt her stomach jump and turn over when she heard her door open.

'Morning.' Stephanie grinned at her from the doorway and Jeanie had to stop herself sagging as a feeling of anticlimax made her spine fluid as she smiled at her secretary. And then Stephanie gave a little whistle of admiration before adding, 'And you look like you've had a great weekend if you don't mind me saying. Can't you twist his arm and come to the St. Valentine's dance?'

'What?' And then as understanding hit Jeanie blushed slightly. 'I've a lunch date,' she said, 'and it's still no to the dance.'

'Boy, he must be pretty special. You look sensational.'

Jeanie smiled that aside before saying, 'Shut the door, Steph. I've got something to tell you and I'd prefer to keep it private at least for the next couple of hours.' Stephanie had been her secretary since Jeanie had first started at the firm and had been a

great support to her, and Jeanie felt it was only right
to explain she was leaving before she popped along
to see Joseph and Dan.

Jeanie was gratified at how genuinely upset
Stephanie was at the news, and when she spoke to
the senior partners half an hour later they too ex-
pressed deep disappointment and regret at her decision, but after seeing how determined she was
they reluctantly accepted her resignation.

Once back in her office she worked for a couple
of hours in seclusion as she prepared the way forward for her client on the custody case, and when
Stephanie brought her coffee at eleven was able to
ask fairly casually, 'I don't think I've seen Mr. Ryan
today. Is he in?'

'It appears he's in court all morning.' Stephanie
now glanced behind her and shut the door before
she continued, her tone confiding, 'Jenny told me
his housekeeper had an accident recently and Mr.
Ryan's now taken on a nanny permanently for his
kid. Now that's a job I wouldn't mind; living with
Mr. Ryan!' She winked cheekily at Jeanie, who just
managed to bite back the comment that the nanny
wouldn't be living in before it left her lips. Office
gossip needed little fact at the base of it at the best
of times, and it was better to just play dumb and
nod than let on she knew more than Ward's secretary apparently did.

Obviously Monica's niece had worked out okay
then. Jeanie sat musing for a few minutes while she

drank her coffee, and then forced herself to put the image of a fresh-faced, modern and undoubtedly lovely—knowing her luck—girl out of her mind. It was no business of hers what Ward did or didn't do, or whom he did it with. And cradle snatching wasn't Ward's style anyway. It was just mortifying to know she would have given the world to be in that girl's position, and not just to be near Ward either. Bobbie had touched her heart in a way that was both permanent and painful.

She frowned irritably, annoyed at the way her rogue thoughts kept focusing on Ward in spite of herself. But it would be easier when she had left here, she reassured herself firmly, pulling a file out of the pile at the side of her and opening it. And now she was going to concentrate on this case and nothing else.

Just after half past twelve she heard her door open again. She had asked Stephanie to remind her of the time about twenty to one so she wasn't late for Nicki, and now, her eyes glued on the list of figures she was checking, she said absently, 'Thanks, Steph, I hadn't forgotten, but I just need to finish this first. I promise I won't keep him waiting though!' adding the last on a teasing note after Stephanie's earlier comment.

'Hallo, Jeanie.'

Her head shot up at the deep, cool voice, and as she saw Ward framed in the doorway her heart went haywire. 'Oh, I'm... I'm sorry,' she managed breathlessly. 'I thought you were Stephanie. She...she's just keeping a check on the time.' She swallowed hard. 'I've a lunch date,' she finished weakly.

His eyes narrowed slightly. 'I'd gathered that,' he said softly, his gaze taking in the cream suit and focusing on her hair. 'Anyone I know?'

'No.' She didn't know why but somehow she didn't like his tone of voice, or maybe it wasn't his voice but the way he was looking at her? She forced herself to show no reaction and said carefully, 'Successful morning? I understand you were in court for most of it.'

'Yes, I had a successful morning,' he ground out tightly.

She stared at him. If this was how a successful morning left him she would hate to see him when a case went wrong! 'Good.' She smiled dismissively, indicating her desk as she said, 'Well, I must finish this, so...'

He completely ignored the hint, pinning her to her chair with his lethal blue eyes as he kicked the door shut behind him.

He looked fantastic. She didn't want to think it and she tried not to dwell on how seeing him again was making her feel but it was hopeless. He was wearing a pale silver-grey shirt and matching tie and a deep grey suit, and for some obtuse reason the very formality of the clothes reminded her how he had looked half-naked, and she felt herself blushing a burning crimson.

'When did you get back?' he asked evenly. 'I called round last night to tell you Monica's niece has worked out great and she's now permanent.'

He'd called round? But only to tell her about Monica's niece, she reminded herself fiercely in the next instant. And—surprising though Ward might find it—she didn't want to know about Monica's apparently ideal relation! 'I came straight from York this morning,' she said coolly.

'Hence the lunch date?' he bit out grimly.

What on earth was the matter with him? Jeanie stared at the very masculine, cold face in surprise for a moment or two, before a healthy dart of anger made itself felt. Whatever it was she didn't have to put up with this. She hadn't expected him to fall on her neck but this was the other extreme. Someone had obviously upset him this morning, and it must have been something bad for Ward to show his feelings so blatantly, but there was absolutely no reason for him to take it out on her! She wouldn't be treated as though she'd done something wrong.

'Is something the matter, Ward?' she asked frostily.

'Yes, something's the matter,' he bit out savagely as he glared at her, his eyes like two chips of blue ice in a granite hard face. 'Don't you value yourself at all, Jeanie? Haven't you any self-respect?'

'What?' She stared at him in amazement.

'This bozo lets you come and stay with me—*in my house*—without so much as the whiff of a protest from what I can make out, and then you dress yourself up to look absolutely fantastic to go out to lunch with him, and don't bother to deny that it's him you are seeing because I know it is. I *know*.'

Jeanie's soft mouth tightened. 'Now look, Ward—'

'No! *You* look. Damn it all, Jeanie, I can't believe you're letting yourself be treated this way. Can't you see he wants you for one thing and one thing only? What are you going to do this lunch-time? Disappear into a hotel room somewhere for dessert? You're away for a weekend, and the minute you're back and he snaps his fingers, you jump.'

'How dare you!' Her voice rose and she checked it with an effort, reminding herself the thin partitioned walls only gave a limited amount of privacy. 'You have absolutely no right to talk to me like this.'

'Why the hell don't you tell him to take a running jump?' he rasped testily. 'What's this guy got that makes him so damn irresistible anyway?'

Black hair, blue eyes and a smile to die for, not that the smile was anywhere in evidence today. 'I'm not discussing this with you now, Ward. Not with you in this mood,' Jeanie snapped angrily. She rose to her feet, gathering her handbag and long cream lambswool coat before marching over to the door and exiting her office before he could say another word. She knew she had surprised him with her sudden departure; she'd seen the brief widening of the beautiful blue eyes a second before he had narrowed his gaze.

She stopped for a moment in the main office to tell Stephanie she was taking a long lunch, and then continued into the lift without a backwards glance, her cheeks fiery with righteous indignation. Maybe she should take Ward's advice and tell him to take a running jump? she thought furiously as the lift took her swiftly downwards. Maybe that's *exactly* what she should do!

She caught sight of her reflection in the mirrored walls, gazing at her flushed cheeks and flashing eyes for a moment before all the anger evaporated and she leant limply against the side of the lift. What a tangle. What a 24 carat mess. Even though she hadn't actually told Ward any lies she had twisted the truth to the point where they were at each other's throats, she thought miserably. And there was no easy solution to the web of prevarication and falsity either. She couldn't tell him the bald truth, so she had no option but to see the whole ghastly charade through to the bitter end.

He thought she was sleeping with a man who was using her for his own pleasure, who was unprepared to make any sort of commitment or show her any loyalty or devotion, and he despised her because she was letting herself be used in this way. It would be funny if it wasn't so tragic.

And she had nobody but herself to blame for all of this. She should have at least made it plain she was meeting Nicki for lunch and not her supposed lover, but he had made her so *mad*.

Irritating, blind, obstinate, intractable man that he was!

She sighed deeply and then straightened as the lift doors opened, emerging with her head held high and her back straight. She could hardly believe that a sensible, thirty-two-year-old woman who had been in charge of her destiny for years and knew her own mind to the point where she had used to drive her parents mad, had contrived to get herself locked into this present checkmate. But she had. What fools love can make of the most sane people.

And the last thing she felt like right now was meeting an old university friend and being bright and cheerful all through lunch!

THE lunch went far better than Jeanie had expected, mainly because it turned out Nicki was having man trouble of her own and they spent most of the time agreeing the world would be a far better place with just females in residence.

Jeanie arrived back at the office at just before three, and as she passed Stephanie's desk on the way to her office her secretary grabbed her arm, saying urgently, 'Mr. Ryan is in your office and he's in a real temper over something or other. I thought I ought to warn you. He's been waiting in there for the last half an hour although I said you were going to be late back.'

Great. The day was getting better and better, Jeanie thought derisively, but apart from a brisk, 'Thanks, Steph,' she didn't delay the dreaded moment.

As she opened the door Ward swung round from the window to face her, for all the world as though he hadn't budged since she had left two hours ago. He certainly looked just as mad. 'What's all this about you resigning?' Never one to beat about the bush he went straight for the jugular. 'And why the hell didn't you tell me you were thinking of leaving?'

She stared at him for a full ten seconds and then said crisply, 'From what I can recall of our conversation before lunch you didn't give me much chance to say anything.'

He didn't even have the grace to look slightly shamefaced. 'Is it to do with him? The rat?' he growled angrily. 'Don't tell me he's had a change of heart and asked you to marry him or something.'

Oh for goodness' sake! Jeanie glared at this man she loved with all her heart and soul and mind, and snapped, 'Yes, it is to do with him and no, he hasn't asked me to marry him or even suggested "something." I've decided to finish it once and for all if you must know, and make a completely fresh start in every area of my life, my job included.'

'Have you told him? Is that why you went to lunch with him today?' he asked suspiciously.

'I didn't say I was going to lunch with him, you assumed that,' she said tightly. 'I was actually having lunch with an old friend, a female friend.'

'You said you wouldn't keep *him* waiting, when you thought I was Stephanie.'

'It was a joke…something Steph had said earlier—' She stopped abruptly. 'Look, Ward, I don't have to justify myself to you. I had lunch with a big buxom blonde called Nicki, all right? Believe me or don't believe me, it's up to you. And yes, he does know, and while we're on the subject…' She took a deep breath, her eyes flashing, 'Why would I resign anyway if he *had* asked me to marry him? This isn't the Dark Ages you know. Modern, independent women do still work if they want to once they are married, and I am both modern and independent,' she finished with a flourish.

He walked over and perched himself on the side of her desk, never taking his eyes off her flushed defiant face. 'How did he take the news?' he asked softly.

She shrugged. 'I've made up my mind and that's it.'

'And how do you feel?' he asked even more softly.

'Determined, resolute, upset.' Desperately, desperately upset, you unfeeling swine.

He nodded. 'Have you got another job lined up?'

'No.' This was hard, it was so, so hard. She took a ragged pull of air and said abruptly, 'I might go abroad for a while actually, have a year or two working in the sun. A sort of legal sabbatical. I might even do waitressing or bar work, or maybe apply as a holiday rep. Something completely different.' The thought had only just occurred to her but it suddenly seemed right somehow. 'Financially I wouldn't struggle if I didn't find something straight away.'

He was pinning her with the steady, unrevealing stare she'd seen him adopt so often, so when he hitched off the desk and walked over to her, lifting her chin to gaze into the velvet amber depths of her eyes, she didn't know what he was going to say. 'You seem to have it all worked out.' He traced a path down one silky cheek with his finger. 'But I'm sorry you are upset, and just for the record never for a moment did I think you're anything other than modern and independent.'

She didn't trust herself to say anything, she was too emotionally shattered, and after gazing at her for a moment more he shook his head slightly, turning and walking to the door.

'But you aren't going to sit and brood for the next three months until you fly out to your Utopia,' he said silkily over his shoulder. 'I won't let you. So I'll pick you up for dinner tonight at eight, okay? And dress up. I'm taking you somewhere nice.'

And her mouth was still open in dazed surprise when he shut the door behind him.

CHAPTER NINE

IF JEANIE had had to describe the next two weeks, only one word would have done—unreal.

Ward wined and dined her, took her to the theatre, art galleries and the like, but the times she enjoyed the most were quiet meals at his home once Bobbie was in bed and Monica had gone to her quarters, because that was when he really talked. For the first time in the five years she had known him he had totally opened up to her, and she found it amazing. And perplexing. And incredibly frustrating. Because not once during all the evenings out and the heart-to-hearts at his home did he make any sort of move on her.

Oh, he'd sit with his arm round her; hold her hand when they were out together; kiss her lightly on the lips now and again and stroke her face with that tender, gentle way he had at times, but *never* did he try to take things any further. For two weeks she didn't have one evening to herself, and he didn't try to hide the fact he was taking her out at work either.

Jeanie had lost count of the number of people who had asked her when, exactly, she and Ward had started dating, and when she gave her stock response—that they weren't dating but just seeing each other as friends—she knew, however polite they were, no one believed her. And she couldn't blame them for being incredulous. She felt that way herself. And confused and bewildered and utterly at a loss.

They had some wonderful days out with Bobbie at the weekends, and Jeanie met Henrietta, Monica's niece, who was sweet and funny and resembled a little wise owl with her big black-rimmed spectacles and enormous brown eyes.

Jeanie was happier than she had ever been and more miserable than she could bear—sometimes in the same hour—and through it all Ward never once referred to her decision to leave Eddleston and Breedon, or asked her not to go.

The whole thing was surreal, Jeanie thought one night towards the middle of February. She and Ward had just finished a meal she had prepared and cooked—Monica still being unable to do much, and Henrietta having cooked for herself, Bobbie and her aunt earlier before Jeanie and Ward had got home—and were now taking their coffee through to the sitting room where a roaring fire greeted them.

'This is nice.' Jeanie sat down on the sofa which had been pulled close to the hearth and stretched out her toes to the red and orange flames. It had been raining and sleeting all day and now a fierce wind moaned about the house, sending the icy drops of rain lashing against the windows and splattering down the chimney now and again. 'There's something so *elemental* about a real fire on a night like this. You can imagine people sitting in their caves thousands of years ago and feeling exactly the same satisfaction. Do you know what I mean? It's like—'

She turned to glance at Ward sitting by the side of her and then stopped abruptly, the words dying on her tongue as she met the sapphire eyes trained on her face.

'I need to talk to you, Jeanie. *Really* talk to you,' he said very quietly, and the look on his face frightened her.

'I thought we *had* talked tonight, and all the other nights,' she managed fairly lightly. Whatever this was, whatever he was going to say, she didn't want to hear it. If he was going to tell her that he considered her time of nuturing and support over, or that he had met a new woman and would have to curtail seeing her, or *whatever,* she'd rather it be in the cold, clinical light of day at work, where she couldn't disgrace herself by throwing herself on his chest and refusing to let go.

'Yes, we have,' he agreed evenly. 'In fact I think I've told you more than I've ever revealed to another living soul, but there is something you need to know. Something…difficult for me to talk about because it feels like a betrayal of Bobbie.'

'Bobbie?' She stared at him, totally taken aback. Whatever she'd expected it wasn't this. 'I don't understand?'

He shifted sharply, his eyes leaving her bewildered face and turning to look into the flickering flames, and when he spoke it was in a flat, expressionless voice. 'Bobbie's mother was a very beautiful woman,' he said quietly, 'and she had charisma. She drew men to her like moths to a flame. I was fascinated by her, everyone who came into contact with her was, and when she told me she was pregnant with my child we married within the month. I felt like I'd captured an unbelievable prize.'

He rose from the sofa, but not before she had been shocked by the way his eyes had narrowed and hardened, his mouth setting in a grim, uncompromising line. 'Ward, you don't have to say anything more,' she said quickly, watching him as he strode across the room and drew back the heavy drapes at the window to stand looking out into the dark, storm tossed night. Her heart was thudding wildly but she wasn't exactly sure what was happening. He had loved his wife totally and utterly, everyone knew that, but how could that relate to a betrayal of Bobbie?

'I knew Patricia needed attention,' he continued steadily as though she hadn't spoken, 'and she was an outrageous flirt, but I thought it was just her way. It didn't mean anything. She had had a rotten childhood, pushed from pillar to post and never really settling in any of her foster homes. So, I put up with the sulks and tantrums her hatred of being pregnant caused, although I think I knew within the first week of marriage that the woman I thought I'd loved was a figment of my imagination.'

'But… But I thought—'

'That we were the perfect couple?' he said harshly, turning to glance at her for a moment. 'I'm not surprised you've heard that, we played our parts very well. Then Bobbie was born and Patricia found there was something she hated more than being pregnant and that was being a mother with a child to care for. Monica took over Bobbie lock, stock and barrel. By then I suspected there were other men but Patricia was clever and cunning.'

Jeanie had her hands to her mouth, her head whirling as she tried to grasp the reality of what he was revealing. She couldn't have spoken to save her life.

'The only time Patricia had contact with her daughter was in the afternoons when she would take Bobbie in the car and visit friends,' he went on bitterly. 'Or that was where she told Monica she went. And Monica encouraged her to take the child, feeling she needed to bond with the baby and that then things might be different. In reality Bobbie spent the time strapped in the car seat in hotel car parks while her mother was inside with her lovers. Patricia used her as a smokescreen, that was all. It was when my wife was on her way home from one such liaison that she crashed the car, and it was the subsequent police investigation which revealed the truth. They were very good,' he finished grimly. 'Very discreet.'

'Oh, Ward.' Jeanie wanted to put her head down on a cushion and cry her eyes out, but knowing how much he'd hate it she forced herself to say, through the tightness in her throat, 'I'm so very sorry. I don't know what to say.'

'Oh the best is yet to come,' he said with a crispness that spoke of rigid control. 'Patricia died instantly in the accident and it was touch and go with Bobbie. She needed blood transfusions galore and a whole load of stuff, and to cut what is a very unsavoury story short she has a rare blood group. A blood group which means I couldn't possibly have been her biological father. Note I said biological, Jeanie, because in every other sense Bobbie *is* mine.'

Through the stunned disbelief a separate part of Jeanie's brain had accepted the truth instantly. It explained so much. Ward's total withdrawal from the human race after his wife's death, his repudiation of further commitment with another woman, his cynicism and overall coldness regarding the opposite sex...

'No one knows,' he said tightly, 'not even Monica, and Bobbie will never know. She is mine. If you had seen the way she fought for life—' He stopped abruptly, and when she saw the tears in his eyes she would have gone to him but he waved her back down in the seat. 'No, let me finish. She is mine, Jeanie. I couldn't love a child of my flesh more. She has nothing of her mother in her and I don't care who the hell her father was. I know what *she* is and that is my daughter.'

'I know.' Why had he told her this? Could it be that he had fallen in love with her? She thought back to all the little tender moments over the last weeks and her hopes soared, and then plummeted when she reminded herself that not once had he asked her to stay, not once had he spoken of the future or *really* kissed her, like he had those couple of times before. Surely a man in love would try to stake his claim? He didn't love her. He would never love her. Patricia might not have his heart like she had thought, but his ex-wife had seen to it that it was buried along with her nevertheless.

'Ward, why have you told me all this?' she asked at last, knowing she had to put what she was feeling into words however he might answer.

His eyes were quite unreadable. 'Because it was time you knew,' he said simply.

'I see.' No, no, she didn't see, so why had she said she did? she asked herself silently. 'Well, thank you for trusting me.' She couldn't exactly cross-question him on his motives after all.

'That's all right,' he said softly. He had changed his clothes earlier whilst Jeanie had sat and chatted with Monica and Henrietta in the kitchen, Bobbie snuggled contentedly on her lap, and now in the shadowed room the black jeans and dark grey shirt he was wearing made him seem all the more darkly masculine and alien.

She thought back to what he'd told her about his parents and what a lonely, unhappy little boy he must have been. Patricia's betrayal must have been his worst nightmare coming true. *Oh, Ward.* Her love brought her to her feet and she had crossed the room to him before she even thought about it, reaching up and touching his face like he had done with her several times in the last weeks, as she said very softly, her eyes wide and liquid with the tears she dare not let fall, 'I think Patricia was mad not to realise what she had got in you and Bobbie.'

He smiled, a twisting of his mouth, taking her hand and holding it to his lips for a brief moment before he said quietly, 'Don't pity me, Jeanie. Whatever else, don't do that. I know you've been in love with this other man for years and being the sort of person you are it'll take time to get over him, but even if you do still love him you can't deny there's something between us.'

He was talking physical attraction again…wasn't he? She stared at him, unsure and uncertain of where he was coming from.

'And why have you told people we aren't dating?' he asked very evenly.

'What?' She felt she was in danger of losing her grasp on reality here.

'People at work,' he said quietly. 'You've told

them we aren't dating according to the office grape-vine.'

'Well we aren't, are we?' she asked confusedly.

'The hell we aren't.'

She was startled by his vehemence, her eyes opening wide as she saw the blue eyes spark.

'Obviously this idiot you've been involved with has confused you as to how a real man goes about courting,' he said tightly, 'but there is a right way, believe it or not. And that's what we're doing. Got it?'

The old-fashioned word had delighted Jeanie more than he would ever know, but she forced herself to keep control of her wayward emotions which were threatening to go haywire. He still hadn't said a word about commitment or love or anything that really mattered, she warned herself fiercely, and after all he had said in the past—*emphasised* in the past—she couldn't assume anything, not feeling about him the way she did. She'd never survive further disappointment.

'Joe and Dan wouldn't like the complication of two of their junior partners dating,' she said weakly.

'Ah, but you aren't going to be an employee of Eddleston and Breedon much longer,' he said triumphantly, 'so in my opinion that negates that one. Added to which I don't give a damn what Joe and Dan like. Come and drink your coffee.'

'What?' She was saying that far too much but she just couldn't keep track of this evening.

'Come and drink your coffee,' he repeated with a coolness that deflated Jeanie utterly.

Surely, if he was serious about having anything more than one of his temporary affairs he would at least say *something?* she thought dazedly. Not necessarily a vow of undying love or eternal devotion—that wasn't Ward's style any more than Valentine cards and chocolate hearts—but he'd been more controlled and correct since the moment he found out she had finished with her supposed lover than before, at least on a sexual level.

She didn't understand this. She didn't understand *him.* And he hadn't even asked her not to disappear out of his life to pastures new. She had said she was planning to go abroad once she had worked out her notice. Didn't he *care* about that? Obviously not.

Jeanie was very quiet on the drive home and Ward seemed disinclined to break the silence in the car which couldn't possibly have been described as comfortable.

Once in the mews he saw her to the door as always, and if she was hoping for a sign to let her know what he was thinking it didn't come. 'Good night, Jeanie.' He bent and kissed her briefly on the lips, his mouth warm and firm but constrained. 'See you in the morning.'

She nodded, too flat and miserable with an overwhelming sense of anticlimax to speak.

'And don't worry,' he said huskily, holding her for a second longer before stepping back a pace and looking at her with glittering blue eyes, his black hair ruffled by the wind and damp with the rain. 'All men aren't blind morons although experience might have led you to think so. Some of us have our eyes opened in spite of ourselves.'

He had turned and walked back to the car in the next moment, leaving her—as always where Ward was concerned—with a sense of things left unsaid and unfinished business. And she was fed up with it, she told herself as she stepped in the house and closed the door without waving him off as usual. Sick and tired and fed up.

All that about his wife had upset her more than she could have believed, considering the final line meant he hadn't loved Patricia like she had thought he had. But his pain and desolation, and not least the fact that Patricia had robbed him of his biological parentage of Bobbie, had cut deep enough for Jeanie to realise she'd have gladly spared him all that heartache at the cost of him loving Patricia to the day he died.

What was she going to do? *What was she going to do?* She prowled about the house for a good hour as her mind continued to whirl.

Hang around and hope that he would learn to care for her, even if it wouldn't be the grand, for everness she felt for him? Hope that she could become part of his life and Bobbie's to the point where he couldn't do without her? Or would it be better for everyone concerned if she did what she'd said she was going to do—what he might be expecting her to do for all she knew—and disappear abroad for a few years?

Why had he so determinedly swept her into his orbit the last few weeks anyway? And he had, he had. He had done all the chasing, all the insisting on seeing her every night and drawing her into his and Bobbie's lives.

And she had been so *clear* about what she'd got to do when she had arrived home from York, she wailed silently to herself as she stood under the shower some time later. And then somehow, as soon as she had seen Ward again, it had all snowballed into a bigger tangle than ever.

She was still debating the issue when she lay down in bed and closed her eyes, weary in mind and body. She couldn't take much more of this hot and cold from Ward, that was for sure, she told herself just before she drifted into a restless, troubled sleep. She'd start seriously making plans to go abroad tomorrow and let him know what she was doing. And then, if he still didn't at least ask her to stay, she would know.

But she didn't want it to be like this— her forcing him to say something if he didn't really mean it...

FOR the first time in years Jeanie overslept the next morning, and it was only when she was sitting eating a hasty breakfast of toast and coffee that the disc jockey on the radio reminded her it was St. Valentine's Day.

St. Valentine's Day. She shut her eyes as one solitary tear slipped through the defence barrier she thought she had erected in the last weeks. For years this day had been a subtle torture with the one person in all the world she cared about not even knowing she existed as a woman, let alone sending her a card. Not that all that romance stuff was Ward's forte, she knew that, and a piece of folded card with a few fancy words on it meant nothing in the overall plan of things, she knew that too. But nevertheless...

She sniffed disconsolately, feeling very young and very small as she sat at her tiny breakfast bar and glanced miserably at the electricity bill the post had brought. Just one bill. Nothing else.

After that she couldn't hurry to get ready somehow, and it was well past nine o'clock and verging on the half past dot on her dainty gold wristwatch when she passed through the doors of the building which housed Eddleston and Breedon and entered the lift for the third floor.

She had to pass through the main office to her own office, and as she opened the door and stepped into the room an immediate hush fell over the place. Jeanie glanced round at the faces dotted about in surprise, feeling her face flush in spite of herself. She wasn't *that* late, she told herself uncomfortably, besides which the junior partners worked very much on a flexi-time basis owing to the amount of extra hours they were expected to fit in to the average week. Everyone knew that.

She pitter-pattered down the centre aisle towards Stephanie's desk at the far end which was situated just outside her office, trying to ignore how loud her high heels sounded in the sudden quiet, and when she reached her secretary's desk she paused for a moment. 'Everything okay, Steph?' she asked quietly.

'Fine.' Stephanie was looking at her strangely, almost excitedly but definitely oddly, and now Jeanie felt a slight sense of alarm grip her which she struggled not to betray.

'Nice card,' she said lightly, nodding at the big satin number propped on Stephanie's desk. Every year the desks in the outer office were full of them, but it had never grated quite so much as this year.

'Thanks.'

Stephanie wasn't usually monosyllabic; something was definitely wrong but she couldn't for the life of her imagine what it was.

She looked at Stephanie for a moment more and Stephanie stared back at her, not at all her normal chatty self, before saying, 'Coffee?'

'Great, thanks.' She nodded brightly and walked on, opening the door to her office and then finding herself rooted to the spot. She was conscious of the immense quiet behind her in which you could hear a pin drop, and she knew she ought to step inside

and close the door, but that was only on the perimeter of her consciousness. Her whole being was
taken up with the sight in front of her.

Her desk, her windowsill, the filing cabinets, the
floor—every single bit of available space was filled
with flowers leaving just a pathway for her to walk
through. The scent and colour was heady, the main
source of the perfume emanating from the hundreds
upon hundreds of freesias that dominated the display, and on her desk in the middle of a circle of
freesias and poppies in little wicker baskets was the
most enormous bouquet of red roses.

Her heart was thudding so hard it was a physical
pain but she was too dazed to actually think as she
closed the door behind her and walked to the desk
purely on automatic.

Delicately tinted orchids and lilies of every hue,
violets, Michaelmas daisies, ostrich plume asters,
vibrantly coloured chrysanthemums, cornflowers,
dahlias, baby's breath, various kinds and colours of
poppies; the list was endless as her unbelieving gaze
struggled to take it in, and intermingled throughout
were the freesias.

She bent over and lifted up the bouquet of red
roses—at least fifty or more enclosed in a cloud of
fern—but then she found she had to sit down suddenly before she could take the little card attached
to the cellophane.

When the door opened in the next moment and
Ward stepped into her office, his handsome face ex-

pressionless and his piercing blue eyes fixed on her face, she knew Stephanie had told him she was in. 'Happy Valentine's Day,' he said softly, his voice holding a note she hadn't heard before.

'This…' She couldn't speak through the strange emotion in her throat, and had to swallow hard before she could try again. 'All this; is it you?' she said faintly.

'Haven't you read the card?' He nodded at the flowers in her arms and when she shook her head dazedly, walked across to her, taking the little card off the bouquet as he said, 'Then let me tell you what it says.'

He opened the small envelope but looked at her rather than the little card. 'You said he never sent you flowers but I want to fill your life with them. He doesn't want commitment or to hear promises of undying love, but there is nothing I want more. I love you, Jeanie. With all my heart, for ever, and if it takes the rest of my life to make you love me then so be it because I'm not going to give up. Do you hear me? I'm not going back to the way it was and I'm not going to let you leave my life. And even if you love him still, you're beginning to love me too. I know you are.'

'That's…that's an awful lot for such a small card,' she whispered.

'I don't understand why I didn't see it before but that weekend it was like a light turning on in my understanding,' he said softly. 'But you loved someone else. And then when you said you'd made the break I knew I had to be patient, to give you time to get used to the idea of being with me. I had to show you that whoever he is, I'm far better for you than he is. And so I've been patient,' he said with touching arrogance.

'But…but it's only been a few weeks,' she protested faintly, terrified of letting herself believe for a moment this was real.

'We've known each other for years and we've been friends first; there's hardly anything we don't know about each other, Jeanie.'

He pulled her to her feet and into his arms, capturing her mouth with urgent, burning lips and kissing her until she was dizzy and fluid in his arms. 'You see?' He raised his head to look down into her flushed face. 'You couldn't respond to me like you do unless you are halfway to loving me. You need me, Jeanie, I know you do. I don't care whether you understand that yet, you'll just have to trust me on it.'

It was so Ward at his most arrogant and imperious that Jeanie shut her eyes at the flood of love that swept into her heart. The hot tide of emotion melted the frozen disbelief that had taken her over and she knew, instantly, she believed what he was saying. She might be being terribly naïve here, credulous and trusting, but for the sort of man Ward was to do what he had done this morning…

'Don't shut your eyes against me,' he said huskily, 'and don't start thinking you are responding to me on the rebound. This is real, I promise you it's real.'

She opened her eyes then; her love intuitively telling her that the rebound comment was a secret fear of his. She had to tell him the truth and then do exactly what he had urged her to do and trust him. If he loved her, really loved her, knowing there was no other man lurking in the background to tempt her away from him would be a joy and a relief but it wouldn't make any difference to the urgency of his feeling.

If his desire was a composite of sexual attraction and the challenge this other man presented, then she would know from his reaction.

'Ward, I have to tell you something,' she said shakily, straining back a little in his arms and looking straight into his dear beloved face. '*You're* the man I've loved for years, and there isn't anyone else. I... I would never have told you because I knew you didn't feel that way about me, but then that day at the office I said too much and the whole thing just seemed to snowball. I resigned because after being with you for that weekend I knew I couldn't take any more.'

He stared at her, and she had the unique privilege of seeing Ward Ryan utterly stunned and silent.

'There...there has never been anyone else,' she said softly, wishing he would say something—*any-*

thing. 'I knew as soon as I met you I'd been waiting for you all my life.'

'Me?' he whispered dopily, the brilliant, instinctual, frighteningly intelligent lawyer. *'Me?'*

'You.'

And she saw his face light up and become radiant. *'Me?'* he shouted at the top of his voice, picking her up off her feet and swinging her round as baskets of flowers and posies were knocked everywhere. 'All this time, when I've been tearing myself apart you loved *me?*' he said huskily when she was on her feet again, giddy and trembling.

'I had five years of torment, remember?' She reached up and cradled his face in her hands, loving him so much it was a physical pain.

'Then you'll marry me straight away? As soon as I can get a special licence? Or do you want a white wedding with all the trimmings?' he added quickly, uncertain again.

It was a revelation to Jeanie that Ward could be unsure about anything, and as she looked up into his hard handsome face that was quite literally shining with the love he had kept hidden for the last agonising, excruciatingly precious weeks, she knew if she lived to be a hundred she would never forget the intensity of this moment. The heady smell and colour of the flowers, being held in Ward's arms, the look on his face and most of all—*most of all*—the miracle of his proposal.

'I'd marry you today if I could,' she said very

softly, 'but a couple of days will give me time to buy a white dress for myself and a bridesmaid's dress for Bobbie.'

'I love you, Jeanie. With all my heart. You believe that, don't you?' he said passionately, gathering her to him with a sensuousness that made her weak at the knees. 'By the end of the week you'll be Mrs. Ryan whatever strings I have to pull to make it happen quickly.'

She stared back at him, her heart too full to say anything but her shining eyes speaking volumes to the tall dark man looking down at her so lovingly.

And when Ward kissed her she responded with such unbrindled desire and deep unashamed hunger that it was some time before he could bring himself to stop, and only then because of where they were.

'I think you'd better look for those dresses this afternoon,' he said unevenly as he adjusted her rumpled clothing with hands that weren't quite steady. 'If tomorrow night isn't your wedding night it won't be for the lack of me trying.'

'I can't believe this is happening.' She smiled tremulously, overwhelmed with the swiftness with which her life had changed.

'It's happening all right,' he said with the fierce intensity she recognised, kissing her once more before reluctantly drawing away. 'And now, my love, we had better go and put all those people out there out of their misery, and announce we're getting married.'

'Oh, Ward.' She clutched hold of him, suddenly shy.

'Come on,' he said softly, drawing her into the side of him where she fitted as though she'd always belonged there. 'I want the world to know I've found my perfect valentine, and you are, my love, you are. I'm going to spend the rest of my life telling you so.'

And Ward Ryan was a man of his word.

We're delighted to announce that

is taking place in

This month, in THE BELLINI BRIDE by Michelle Reid, #2224

Marco Bellini has to choose a suitable wife.
Will he make an honest woman of his
beautiful mistress, Antonia?

In March you are invited to the wedding of
Rio Lombardi and Holly Samson
in THE ITALIAN'S WIFE by Lynne Graham, #2235

When Holly, a homeless young woman, collapses in front of
Rio Lombardi's limousine, he feels compelled to take her and
her baby son home with him. Holly can't believe it when Rio
lavishes her with food, clothes…and a wedding ring….

Harlequin Presents®
The world's bestselling romance series.
Seduction and passion guaranteed!

Available wherever Harlequin books are sold.

Visit us at www.eHarlequin.com

HPJANMM

HARLEQUIN *Super*ROMANCE®

Old friends, best friends...

Girlfriends

Your friends are an important part of your life. You confide in them, laugh with them, cry with them....

Girlfriends

Three new novels by Judith Bowen

Zoey Phillips. Charlotte Moore. Lydia Lane. They've been best friends for ten years, ever since the summer they all worked together at a lodge. At their last reunion, they all accepted a challenge: *look up your first love.* Find out what happened to him, how he turned out....

Join Zoey, Charlotte and Lydia as they rediscover old loves and find new ones.

Read all the *Girlfriends* books! Watch for *Zoey Phillips* in November, *Charlotte Moore* in December and *Lydia Lane* in January.